THE KILLING CUP

THE KILLING CUP

A NOVEL

by

PETER VAN GREENAWAY

LONDON
VICTOR GOLLANCZ LTD
1987

First published in Great Britain 1987
by Victor Gollancz Ltd,
14 Henrietta Street, London WC2E 8QJ

British Library Cataloguing in Publication Data
Van Greenaway, Peter
  The killing cup.
  I. Title
  823'.914[F]   PR6072.A65

  ISBN 0-575-04062-9

Typeset by Centracet
and printed in Great Britain by
St Edmundsbury Press Ltd, Bury St Edmunds, Suffolk

Author's Note

It may appear, the centrepiece of this story stretches fiction beyond credible limits. In fact, such a cup has been known for nine centuries. The "sacro cantina" is venerated in Genoa—an emerald cup brought from Caesarea in 1101 by a crusader. It also, apparently, has a connection with Solomon and Sheba . . .

The blue plastic gun, invented and produced in Virginia, is also a reality.

PART I

ITALY

One

"THE MARCHESA IS undoubtedly mad."

Delivered of indictment the little priest paused, to rest and reflect, on a mossy bridge straddling the icy waters of the Orno, or was it some fugitive tributary from the not so distant Alps in the Gran Paradiso region? The bridge marked the boundary between his parish and the *latifondi* of the Marchesa Vittoria del Deodati—Madame la Marquise as she was much known.

Padre Gaspare Carrema sleeved his perspiring brow, removed his round black hat, not in salutation to the illustrious name fresh in his mind, but as tribute to the Piedmont sun bouncing and rolling off the mountains to bring swelter to the scores of Elysian valleys aspersing the province.

Comfortably warm; the stones of the parapet to his touch; cool to the mind that swirl of streamwater below; but the sun above seemed more than usually pitiless, fit, verily, for pagans to worship.

Piano! Don't let yourself be upset by godless unmentionables since she is one. With such an errand to perform you must be calm, collected and—and most circumspect.

Well pleased by the *mot juste* he fanned his heated face all the more vigorously.

"Indeed, the Marchesa is mad," he repeated, before taking a step that brought him entirely out of his world and into hers.

Not a bad world at that, Carrema seemed to convey by his predatory survey. The blossom of a great cherry orchard to his left spread like a linger of snow, mocking the far white of the alpine peaks. To the right an ancient grove of chestnuts bordering the stream's bank followed the turn of the road for half a mile, very nearly to the eastern slopes of the foot-hills on which stood the Castello Deodati itself. Cherries and chestnuts. They talked of a good harvest this year and no doubt her vines, rich with the

9

erba luce for the white Calusa passito wine, would also flourish, even to the limits of profit which, for *some*, meant practically no limit.

Like a Jehu confounded by traffic lights, Carrema came to his senses and slammed on the mental handbrake. Such a waste of those soul-destroying religious exercises and observances to damn oneself for eternity by even the most covert display of envy. Sedately, he replaced his hat, settled his workaday features to the tune of piety modelled on Masaccio's *St Peter Healing the Sick,* and plodded on, only just disturbed by a voice of old nagging insistently, "*e ancora!* it's too much for one old woman when Our Lady must dress in rags scarcely fit for an earthly queen."

Thus, far from London, from Clapham, from a disaffected detective called Cherry, the story seems to begin.

For neither he nor Carrema, nor even the aged Madame la Marquise provide those things called temporal parameters to this saga. One has to take into account her earliest recorded forbears and, even then, another thousand years would be too short in the reckoning . . .

To digress with marvelling is to transgress in the telling. But to press on seems, sometimes, too niggardly against the opportunity to retrace steps through the fabled halls of Time where gold and porphyry, jacinth and gonfalons began.

What to do when the past is so insistent, so obtrusive? What else but twine it as best one can with the elusive present and that rogue strand we distinguish as the future?

Carrema advances, solitary in that idyllic landscape, bleating *sotto voce* much like the distant goats at pasture, rehearsing a difficult part to be played with a consummate actress or, likelier, a penetrating critic of others' performances.

He knows from chastening experience, the Marchesa is too shrewd to be fooled by a false note. None, he'd insisted to the Commission, could be comfortable in her presence, because she had the malignancy of those who *find out.* One of the cardinals had smiled discreetly as he made a note: I think he means, "of those who find *one* out".

Carrema's intelligence, let alone his charity, could never allow

10

him to understand that good and simple people were far from malignancy which is nothing more than scurrilous exploitation of discoveries . . .

Her servants and the labourers in her maize fields—he could hear their raucous shouts, from beyond the chestnut groves—loved and respected her, no matter what she did.

And that was the trouble. No matter what!

Che fare?

He might brood on her wickedness from now till—well, till then, but it could never be brought home to one who managed her vast estates, still, with scant help and a will of iron. She who could, even now, dress a vine with the best of them.

Formidable . . . but madness, that cataclysm of the mind beloved of the foul fiend, explained so much to a niggardly nature. It was, after all, a debilitating condition with which he considered himself fitted by training and vocation to deal. But—how did one exorcise demons sheltered by wealth and position? No master of the seminary had prepared him for battle with a strong-minded woman descendant from a long line of bloody-minded Deodatis.

Gift of God indeed! Blaspheming gift of the devil—hand to the brow, hand to the left breast, hand to the right breast and so, we come safe out of that brief flicker of darkness.

Carrema plods steadily towards the grim façade of the Castello but he's not at one with those incredibly beautiful surroundings for which Virgil himself might have added epilogue to Eclogues. Not Carrema, eyes and mind jaundiced, ambition thwarted, passed over on that deadliest of charges brought by his superiors—inadequacy. Just capable enough to perform rituals for rustics, dispense the sacraments, give absolution for peccadillos—in short, the barely run-of-a-mill priest made to measure dead men's cassocks.

Incumbent of this parish, chaplain to Madame, at her service—which was seldom—Gaspare Carrema approaches her stronghold, crowned with those detestable fish-tailed merlons of the Ghibellines, lip-reading a prayer for guidance against loss, the threat of sacrilege, his own humiliation. To be required, at his time of life, to beard a lioness in her den! Wasn't her father still reverenced as *il leone*, bad cess to his brutish soul—and his grandfather wearing the red shirt of the devil's favourite Italian?

A pell-mell of such thoughts plagued this diminutive till sudden rheum made his eyes swim—like marinated mussels as Gennaro would say.

He paused to wipe his eyes, daunted by those great gates of hell that had shut fast against Florentine brigands *and* the Papal armies.

Today, they stood open, courting the sun to stream into the great hall and lap the foot of a marble stairway hewn from Carrara, a cataract of white tumbling alongside the massive grey wall hung with tapestries of incalculable value—which Carrema seldom failed to appraise with an auctional eye. As he gazed about him—he could still be impressed thirty years on! at the funeral room walled with black mourning marble from Varenna, its great ebony doors ajar to air away the centuries of gloom, and at the grand galleria above with its profane statuary—a tiny urchin wriggled out of the shadows shrouding the *camera di morte* and stood, fingers to nose, in doubtful contemplation of the unaccountably startled priest.

Nino, Giulietta's grandson! What was that low-born maid-of-all-work thinking of, to allow her barefoot brood the freedom of the Deodatis' hallowed resting place? The dead, even if they were scoundrels, deserved some due. Such profanity! to let brats so much as breathe that consecrated air, where bishops had once prayed.

True, Giulietta wasn't entirely to blame. Didn't Madame permit the base-born almost free run of the ground level, courtyards and all? At harvest time the place became a veritable slum as half of the village came and went, stinking of garlic, wine laden, picnicking by the fountains, sweaty and clod-covered, little better than packaged tourists crawling over St Peter's poor unfortunate Basilica.

Suppressing disgust, Carrema cloyed his expression with syrup of Mantegna—*Christ Preaching to the Children*.

"Nino caro, you should be either at your prayers or your lessons, si?"

The four-year-old gaped with rounded eyes. Comprehension

12

at that age can go no further. He shifted his attention to the sunbeam hung with dust. That was something he could understand. Then, with a child's unspoilt instinct, he caught at some indefinable mote in the priest's unctuous gaze and ran for all his little legs could manage to the safety of that great and good goldness which knew how to make sunbeams seem like rays of laughter.

"*Misfatto!*"

Aye, and worse. It doesn't do for a man of cloth to be found out by anyone, even by a little demon of Giulietta's ilk. Out of humour, perturbed by what he knew and what he didn't know, Carrema elected to delay his meeting with the Marchesa. A glance at his watch told him the household's siesta had ten minutes more to run; he saw no reason to add her likely annoyance to his problems.

To *the* problem, there to his right. Fifteen paces away to the doors framed by the Renaissance, by Ghiberti himself no less, through which he scurried, in part to still apprehension, in part to strengthen his resolve; most of all to find solace in contemplation of a treasure for which Carrema saw himself as sole custodian.

Entering the ancient chapel of the Deodati he cooled his brow from the stoup of lukewarm holy water and, after a graceful genuflection only years of practice before a mirror can produce, Carrema fell into rapt appraisal of the Presence.

A few treasures were still scattered about the gloom-laden chapel, though *she'd* sold too many more. Reliquaries, paintings scorched by time, rare carvings and, high over all, the threadbare gonfalons of past Deodati who'd known how to fight, damn their souls . . . somewhere, tradition had it, the bones of Dieudonné himself added a mort to the chapel foundations.

These mouldering tokens, reminding of a stronger faith, had long lost their appeal even to Carrema. He'd outlived all they could offer by way of pious contemplation, but what's to do when casual, in a corner, hangs a cunning wrought casque by Negroli no less; its worth, a newspaper proprietor's ransom, plays havoc with one's devotions.

The Presence, as he apostrophized it, was altogether different,

13

a bauble transcending all other earthly vanities. For the insignific-ant little priest it had become a reason for living, a salve to injured pride, consolation for neglect and, ultimately, a subject for research so that his woeful ignorance had found haven under an amateur scholar's stuff gown.

An academic pin-point. Found out once more! Carrema is merely one of a multitude which must breathe in the shadow of the great anyone or thing, or perish.

Such enthusiasts are dangerous. They must kill doubts; force truth to lie, forge evidence and fabricate proof; and sometimes end as panders flaunting their symbiotic trumpery in the market place.

When Carrema stood alone before this Presence it was *his* as indubitably as a concubine bought and paid for by an acquisitive lecher. Yet he, poor fool, belonged to *it*, was in thrall and utterly possessed as only a man plagued by vacuum in heart and head may be. The very *idea* of Carrema took nourishment from this artifact's invisible effluence as a deflated tyre realizes itself under the influence of an air pump.

What are minuscules not capable of in the presence of a symbol? And so much for a subject now on both knees before the object.

Gaze shifts in amazement from the one to the other. Nothing so very special about this over-decorated gew-gaw, surely, before which a man in semblance abases himself, mouthing the words of a favourite scribbler as he does so?

"O Creator and Redeemer of men . . . You have prepared a great supper whereof You offer us, not Lamb dressed as old Law, but your veritable holy Body and Blood to be our food. Out of this divine banquet, You bring joy to all of faith, bidding them drink deeply from the Cup of Salvation."

What *is* he on about? It's only an old cupboard.

But that's to ignore the major clue to a minor mystery. The Cup of Salvation is *there*, somewhere on an altar notorious for its hopeless simplicity—the region was, in byegone days, a hotbed of Waldensian heresy . . .

A notional onlooker would seek in vain for what's at the very heart of this narrative.

Carrema venerates an anomaly, a hybrid, a veritable mongrel variously described—world-renowned objects and mongrels usually are—as the Deodati Aumbry, because it folds into the likeness of a cabinet; as the Deodati Triptych, unfolding to reveal masterpiece paintings of the Last Supper, the Passion and the Sepulture; as the Deodati Altar because it serves when opened as a portable altar. The whole thing is hardly bigger than a standard TV set.

This accretion began life as an altar, possibly fashioned by the Master of Burgundy in the late eleventh century, though others incline to Godfrey of Claire. The cabinet incorporating the triptych was added in the late twelfth century, as was the niche containing St Foy's tooth, further augmenting its function as a reliquary. The whole hotch-potch was refashioned, bejewelled and more or less immortalized by Benvenuto Cellini.

Its worth is inestimable, and yet there's further to tell of a treasure spanning the centuries as focus of a remarkable rumour.

The base of the altar is four inches deep. The significance is deeper. In that base is a secret drawer. How it opens is known only to the reigning member of the Deodati dynasty. This, in itself a small miracle, but fact it is that the secret has passed from the dying to the living, son or daughter against Salic law.

Naturally the Church has done what it could to break the code. Early in the nineteenth century an enterprising confessor installed a crude bugging device behind the death-bed—no more than a speaking tube leading to an ear trumpet in the next room where a confederate priest played the monitor.

Labour wasted. Old Giovanni Deodati took his time dying and the eavesdropper in black, after three days confined to an unheated closet, got to the finishing post first with a fatal bout of pneumonia. There was laughter in the next room and *then* Giovanni died after cursing the confessor—no Deodatis after the eighteenth century were noted for piety—blessing his children and, presumably, passing on the secret.

Carrema had resolved, with fair acumen, no family will nurse a secret so conscientiously for seven hundred years unless it weighs beyond the world's capacity to bear. He also knew of the numerous attempts to come at the truth.

Freely using his position as the Marchesa's chaplain he'd ransacked the castle's extensive muniment room. After years of patient searching he stumbled on the Benedict XI brief written under seal to the Count Flambardo Deodati, which began:

"Amatissime Frater in Christo: tarde cognivimus gestorum exceptionis eorum in servitio Christi contra infideles sceleratissimis"—and so forth.

Ten years after the count's return from Crusade it had come to Benedict's ears, "in the uncertain form of rumour which we deplore in so great a matter, that you returned seized of a cup bargained for, in Jerusalem delivered, which vessel, we are assured, is, in verity, the sacred chalice wherewith our Lord celebrated the serene act of his sacrifice. I beseech you . . ."

That Carrema "found" this appeal of 1307 in 1980 tucked into a massive folio book of accounts relating to estate management may be his sole claim to fame.

It had plainly been used to mark a place.

Six years had passed since he'd reported his discovery. In time one of the Vatican's assistant curators of archives informed the Curial committee that no copy of the letter existed. Would he be so kind as to—?

Kindness itself, Carrema made an excruciatingly correct copy and posted it to Rome where it excited much pondering, speculation, probing and inevitable controversy over the *possibility* of the Cup's existence. It was common knowledge that *something* had a place in the Deodati Treasure.

Another six years might have passed in an elegant round of "sentences", refutation and *ad majorem theorem dei* if the world hadn't thrust its materialistic nose into a matter which was none of its concern.

Carrema discovered and reported almost hysterically that the Marchesa had long ago made a decision, was on the point of selling, *selling* the Aumbry and its holy contents for a mess of polenta, not only in the sweaty market-place for all the world and the devil to buy but, worse, it was to be auctioned to the highest bidder at Peachum's celebrated rooms in London, no less. Auctioned like any commode or common cattle or—speechlessness reigned for at least five minutes as this and that cardinal digested a new definition of bombshells.

16

A matter of such momentousness was too intoxicating to allow sober appraisal until the morning after . . .

The man from Chicago declined to discuss it. "We got one. Why another? This is a whole new ball game an' I don' wan' no part of it. I got my own troubles."

Fairly put, but the game hadn't really changed. A new-found perception of the Aumbry's importance had simply soared into the Cerulean at prospect of its loss.

From a lofty position of calculated off-handedness and even outright—however concealed—scepticism, the Curial few descended more speedily than overnight to finger the space threatened with vacuum by the proposed sale and to cry aloud, "We believe!".

Another spoilsport had to mention Genoa, of course, but he was soon slapped down and semi-lapidated by half a dozen stony stares.

"Of course it's genuine," affirmed Moroni. "Didn't I consistently hold that as my solemn opinion?'

"No," said Albertini. "But I did maintain that St Foy's tooth clinched the argument for me."

"Tooth fiddlesticks! Any fool could see that was no more than a stratagem to conceal the true relic. And no one doubts the Aumbry *per se*."

"You drive and I walk, but we meet at last," blandly from Moroni. "Though I would not go quite so far as to describe a saint's molar as a stratagem."

"You might go further and fare worse. All relics are stratagems."

Thus, the incarnadined key-holes for the Kingdom's Keys, debating towards speculative certainty that there surely can't be holy smoke without fire.

Meat and drink enough to sustain them all in a state of excited presupposition. And cannot a feast of assumptions achieve more than a fast for one's convictions?

In a minor conclave it was agreed every effort must be made to keep the Aumbry *in loco originis* or thereabouts pending its future disposition. But how? That is, how to proceed with celerity *and* utmost circumspection? The sale was very nearly imminent.

17

How employ persuasion so that even a headstrong old lady intent, it seemed, on raising money for some harebrained philanthropical scheme, should see the error of her ways and restore that which belonged *de jure* to the Church Universal?

Someone reminded their eminent perplexities that a Deodati languished in obscurity within the Vatican itself. A Monsignore Francesco di Fonschesca, nephew to the Marchesa, occupied a position of doubtful importance in the office of Bulls and Briefs. Could he not be prevailed upon to use his influence *spiritualis et consanguinis* to bring her, neck and crop, back from the brink of downright sacrilege and serve-her-right perdition?

Intemperate language. A measure of the steam being generated, pressurized and threatening to blow all apart as urbane Caffarelli cautioned.

"We must proceed another way. Recall, that the Monsignore is known for his unorthodox views on Vatican II and birth-control. You do well to throw up your hands, Moroni. To our infinite sadness he has nothing more to hope for in the matter of preferment. Anyway, he would be a lukewarm advocate to a woman he admires, for what he does not, as I hear, believe in. Better, surely, to use the humble labourer who has tended this particular vine for so long."

Caffarelli, encouraged to continue, reasoned in this manner.

"Suppose we build on our conviction that the Treasure indeed contains our Lord's chalice? Is it so difficult to conceive, when so much of the past had been lost in order to be found? The Holy Shroud is an almost too obvious example of God's exquisite sense of timing . . . let's go further and assume that even the most hardened heretic is open to irrefutable evidence."

"But," the head of the Council of the Congregation objected, "this person knows what the aumbry contains better than anyone. What further evidence could persuade her such a miraculous survival should fortify the Church and not her bank balance?"

"Indeed," Caffarelli allowed. "This marvel, if it is authentic, has had time to lose its meaning over the centuries. The Deodatis neglected it till it became—negligible. To persuade her, one must break the cast-iron mould of indifference."

"How break it?" a medley of voices enquired.

Caffarelli, noted for his wisdom and the length of his pauses, even when discussing the weather, let time pass while the mind behind closed eyes sought a fitting reply.

"There is, in Rome, a man of transcending sensitivity to matter, to objects. He's much employed by the authorities to investigate crimes of the most heinous kind. His success, when confronted by material linked to these crimes, is phenomenal, I'm assured. Some talk of his supernatural powers—and if I believed such gossip I would disdain to mention his existence—but I see no reason to deny more informed opinion that he *is* a genuine sensitive."

"What then?" one impatient voice demanded.

"Why," the fine grey eyes opened abruptly: mock astonishment surrounded by wrinkles like the old scars of many cats' claws, "I merely propose a test which kills more than one bird with a single stone. Let the good father Carrema persuade La Donna Deodati it is in *every*body's interest that the aumbry's contents be authenticated beyond all possible doubts. He believes she is ignorant of written evidence that the cup exists."

"She has the letter," Moroni contradicted.

"She has the letter," Caffarelli conceded, "insofar as it is somewhere in the castle. Father Carrema showed a discretion beyond his apparent intellect by remaining silent as to its contents . . . If then, it can, by a graphic demonstration, be brought home to her that she is, indeed, at the point of pawning the Lord's Cup, surely we may depend on moral persuasion to do the rest?" He paused interminably for pure effect. "Because, of course, we would ensure that the findings of a select body bearing witness to a miraculous revelation are disseminated, as it were, from *urbis* to *orbis*—would we not?"

The small coterie heard, and applauded soundlessly with the gentlest of nods, excepting Bauer, the heavy German carper.

"How can we be sure of a miracle?"

Caffarelli smiled, pleased as a spider plagued with flies. "A miraculous revelation is something else and quite within our competence. Father Carrema will convince the Marchesa she owes the world this disclosure."

A rustling of silk suggested difficulties.

"Suppose she refuses a commission of enquiry?"

"Carrema would no doubt point out that a refusal would be noted abroad sufficiently to jeopardize the sale."

"Ah!" said Bauer, and was satisfied.

Unlike Moroni. "I cannot subscribe to an unlikely proposition. If she's the kind of woman you suggest, what's to prevent her selling the Treasure and the Cup willy-nilly whatever we say?"

That was worth a meaningful smile.

"We agree the matter is urgent. I see no point in building a bridge to cross the Rubicon while others swim."

Not so cryptic a conclusion. Caffarelli was no doubt thinking of Giovanni della Paresi who was known to be intensely interested in the accumulating affair of the Deodati Treasure.

Two

CONSEQUENTLY, CARREMA KNEW only as much as it seemed necessary for him to know. So did the cardinals. Why should he tell *them* that della Paresi had favoured him with instructions from the beginning, when news of his discovery reached the Archives?

This extra element of conspiracy combined with a private briefing from Caffarelli, after the minor conclave had flattered his pretensions beyond any man's willingness to satisfy.

Merciful heaven! to be empowered by a Prince of the Church to conduct an embassy of such delicacy, of almost world-shattering significance . . . yet, this brevity who bore his soul in a nutshell could still fret at being employed like a mere *sampietrini* to sweep the way clear for others' glory. His, he realized too late, was the dirtiest job; one fraught with dangers, not to his soul, for which he paid his premiums regularly, but more importantly, to self-esteem diminishing by an inch at each and every encounter with the Marchesa—a woman who'd studied life-long how to put a poor devil of a priest in his place—and *he* was seconded to coerce *her* adamantine will!

Such petulant thoughts dogged Carrema from presbytery to castle, to chapel—to unblinking contemplation of his only god-child, the Treasure.

He never doubted it contained the Blessed Cup. Never doubted she was profligate enough to sell it. How then, with the most perfunctory guidance from on high, could he hope to persuade her to co-operate in such an experiment as Head Office now proposed?

He lifted the Treasure with reverential care. For a snatch of time he saw, behind closed eyes, a vision of self as in an El Greco special, robe of shot silk, bodily attenuated, spiritually etiolated, soaring beyond roly-poly clouds to Paradise assured, bearing in his arms that which belonged to God alone. He heard the voice of the Almighty gratefully remitting the pains and penalties of purgatory for—three weeks? A month? Two with luck.

Blessed are the mean spirited, for they shall be rewarded in their imaginings . . .

Vision dissolved, as his arms began to ache under the weight of that heavenly passport forcing him to replace it on the altar. Then, fingers like lively mice scurried furtively over the jewelled surface, seeking for the thousandth time the secret of a mechanism so cunningly contrived as to defeat generations of tactile experiment.

A stepsound at the half-opened door betrayed his character: that faintest air of a body-snatcher caught in the act, the merest implication of a burnt-out case of *in flagrante delicto*. Even solitary at his table he'd reach for the salt with the contriving air of a shop-lifter.

The red-handed expression gave place to one more accommodating as he recognized the Signorina Petacci, the Marchesa's kinswoman, secretary and general hanger-on.

In her late fifties, the Signorina had long ago abandoned a life's pretence of nursing a beauty she'd never remotely possessed.

Atrociously made up, from years of habit, she resembled nothing so much as an indifferent actress reduced to bit parts in horror films. The upturn of lipstick only emphasized the downturn of a meagre mouth's corners. Eye-shadow cruelly served to reveal occupied sockets and her hair, savagely scraped back, made of it the wretched creature's crowning punishment.

The Marchesa understood better than Carrema how entirely a woman will revenge herself upon herself at last when life plays the three card trick on hapless individuals fated never to find the ace.

She was short, flat as an ironing board and quite without resources of any kind. In a moment of weakness the Marchesa allowed an appeal to kinship, taking the Signorina under her wing "for as long as I can stand you, so make yourself familiar with the front door and the path to the lodge gates". Safer, far safer, to beware of pity.

She'd worked hard to become very nearly indispensable; in

time, the front door lost its sinister meaning and she could begin to dabble in harmless intrigues—to the Marchesa's secret amusement.

Not surprisingly Signorina Petacci had found a kindred spirit in Carrema. Like had appealed to like with a veering glance and hand-to-mouth discretion. There were shared secrets, whispered in the confessional, strengthening the bond between, sanctifying the hours spent in mutual agonizing over Madame's scarcely concealed atheism.

Strange platonics—conspiring to throw veil on veil of concern over their hatred for one whose spiritual well-being was a constant preoccupation.

Carrema had her to thank for his stroke of good luck. She'd insisted he examine every scrap of writing in the muniment room, knowing, by bitter experience, destiny's way of making use of irony and the unexpected men are meant to overlook, or the joke is spoiled. She'd advised him on the petty steps to be taken, cleverly allowing him the impression that he alone was responsible, had acted entirely on his own intentions.

A strange pair indeed: she with the pious roll of those sepulchral eyes, a husky voice diffidently commanding him beneath a show of self-disparagement, while he might have been a bashful lover—for his eyes never sought hers.

"The Marchesa expects you?"

"It's difficult. After all. They want so much of me."

No answer to her question. Only a continuation of solitudinous thoughts. He began to pace the platform before the altar, pausing now and then to genuflect for no apparent reason. She followed his movements with the very faintest trace of smiling irony; but said nothing.

"You see," he stopped, turning to let his gaze just miss her, "they have this extraordinary notion that a revelation will somehow change her mind." He explained all that had passed between Cardinal Caffarelli and himself the day before. "At first," he concluded, "I felt I had been signally favoured . . ."

She listened carefully before surprising him with a singular observation.

"You were in Rome for two days."

So pointedly expressed that Carrema flushed like a lover accused of breaking tryst.

"An urgent summons. I had no time to let you know—no choice but to go at once."

She nodded, a gesture of forgiveness. Set herself to consider the difficulty. "We must save the Marchesa from herself," the Signorina hoarded platitudes as other women save scraps of material for patchwork.

"But how? You know her—I told his Eminence—she's a law unto herself—the eleventh Commandment repealing the rest. Seventy-five and reaping in the fields, dressing the vines, driving a *tractor*! Why, last year she camped out for days in the chestnut groves and Gennaro could scarcely keep up with her—he told me so—with pride . . . sometimes I ask myself what kind of creature she is."

"She is a woman." He missed the hint of pride, too stupidly taking her words at their face value.

"I don't dispute the fact," testily, "but she means to sell and I—"

"When do they propose this seance?"

"It is *not* a seance—not in that sense . . . tomorrow evening. And I'm to persuade her. Suppose she refuses? What am I to say to his Eminence?"

"The Treasure will support you."

Swift, the conversion from a sneer to a lugubrious nod.

"Let's hope so. If she refuses, it will be *my* failure and that won't go unnoticed in Rome . . . I feel hardly used."

"Martyrs no longer grow on trees these days. We're bound to suffer without hope for our convictions."

Carrema showed surprise—and some apprehension. Was she laughing at him? He came near to glancing at her.

"Convictions?" It seemed news to him that he could have such things.

"That's what you told me!" Tartly. "And haven't you demonstrated irrefutably that the Cup of Christ exists, is there, only inches from your touch?"

Reflexively he drew his hand away from the burning question

24

where it had rested; frowned, and tried hard to sidle out of the devil's own cul-de-sac.

"It's no secret is it? The Cup certainly exists. She knows and doesn't care. The blessed Benedict himself had report of it—but suppose we're all wrong? Can I *really* speak for its validity as Christ's own?"

She appeared shocked by this sudden, uncharacteristic explosion of doubt.

"The responsibility's too much!" he almost shouted.

"But you've always said—"

"Here! in the quiet of this chapel, in the peace of my own room I could say what I believe based on faith vouchsafed me by vocation! But when Rome takes a hand—the dimensions become—" he gestured hopelessly. "How can I go further?"

"Let your faith do the fighting," unclothed contempt.

"To what purpose! Will it provide the words? I tell you she means to sell."

"The Aumbry—let her sell. You said yourself she doesn't care about the cup—I don't see your problem."

"Good heavens woman, it's obvious! If the cup is of such momentousness as to invite a commission from Rome—"

"Let them worry about that. You've only to persuade her to accept their proposition. Go to her now—you will succeed."

". . . how can you be certain?"

She had not the faintest idea, for all that she smiled with a sudden gleam of teeth. Those platitudes came to her aid in good time. "I will pray for you."

Much good that'll do me, Carrema reflected biliously as he mounted the escalating marble to the upper floor where he lingered to admire a superb Aphrodite, "a truly beautiful rendering of the female form beyond the usual hackneyed lucubrations" Carrema's words: a stereotyped litany of critics' tripe providing the excuse to loiter and wallow in all that was left to his mouldering celibacy. Distressed as ever by an appalling scarcity of fig-leaves he went on his way, vaguely disturbed that he'd genuflected unthinkingly before a petrified succubus . . .

The Marchesa would be in the smallest room on the floor at the far end of the corridor. She'd never used the great study close to an audience chamber of old where generations of Deodatis had played out their high-flying roles as magistrates, petty statesmen, intriguers, patriots to rebels for good or no cause whatsoever. Behind those doors men had received sentences of death from Raffael Deodati in the troubled times of Charles I. Many were put to the enquiry after weeks in the darkness of dungeons below. Much blood had been spilled by some of them . . . in the next room the Gonfaloniere Alessandro had paid the price for spilling a little too much. Step by step Carrema faltered forward.

A strong voice responded to his fishfinger tap and he opened the door to a familiar room. Or a tale of chaos within four walls, whitewashed to give a light and fresh appeal, furnishing simple and surprisingly modern. To the left of the door stood a large metal filing-cabinet filled with the business of the estate. In a corner, a game bag carelessly flung aside, an old hunting rifle, loaded in spite of a broken safety catch; and a pair of strung rabbits bloodied the tiled floor. More feminine were the bowls of flowers on the desk and several small tables. Less "feminine" were binoculars, piles of agricultural journals, her father's foils and mask, and much else.

Behind the desk a high, arched, French window stood open to the cool Alpine breezes. On the balcony terracotta urns brimmed with azaleas.

Here, for an hour after siesta, she would attend to business, the settling of accounts, meetings with tenants to hear grievances or give orders. They seldom left without a chicken or butter from the dairy, though their ears might be charred by the heat of her ready invective. Not an aspect of three hundred lives dependent on her management escaped her attention, of the children especially. All prospered and wondered what would become of them when the Marchesa was no more.

All that had been taken care of, was being taken care of. One consequence of her plans meant that an insignificant little priest found himself in her presence there and then.

A "presence" will do to describe her. There's no hint of *grande dame* stiff in satin black, ivory-tipped ebony wand beating a tattoo of commands from the very centre of the universe.

This one imposed, dominated casually, in spite of, or because of an old leather jacket, patched trousers and footwear suspiciously resembling cut-down Wellington boots.

Assuredly, centuries of a unique kind of breeding had gone into her total make-up; an eagle sharp countenance, a fire in the eyes might be met with anywhere in the world and not leave a powerful impression of something indefinable and more than the eye could meet.

Can aristo-arthritis account for such stiff-necked bearing? Does age alone explain *hauteur* that likely showed first in the cradle?

Allow some sympathy, then, for Carrema quailing beyond his quota as he goes from foot to foot while she finishes typing a letter soon torn vigorously from the punch-drunk Olivetti's feeble grasp and signed with a flourish almost in one continuous movement.

"A letter to Foscari's, the agricultural bandits. Their quotation for fertilizers is laughable and one must tell them so. What do you want, Carrema? Is it about this ridiculous aumbry which is not a true aumbry? Mutability confounds truth. Sermonize on that some Sunday. Well?"

Carrema wilted first, inwardly squirmed second.

"Carrema!" No respect for his cloth. Addressed no better than her lowliest cowman—it was too bad! One of these days he would make a mental note to remind her who he was. Let's see: it must be all of thirty years since he'd made the first one. Meantime more weighty matters to be thought of. His personal comfort, for example.

"A warm day, Madame," he glanced longingly at a nearby chair. "Tiring to those no longer young."

"Nonsense! I can give you twenty years and *I* was out in the fields from seven to twelve. *And* an hour's shooting at six. Well, what is it?"

The very robustness of her voice fatigued him, but he limped on.

"I was yesterday with his Eminence, Cardinal Caffarelli who is—"

"The *Domini papae camerarius* yes, yes I know all that, and a bigger fool never yet existed—I wouldn't trust him to run a junk shop."

Thomas à Kempis give me words! It mortified that one who'd long ago sold out her single preferential share in a multinational company should slander one of the managing directors.

"The matter has reached a critical juncture, Madame la Marchesa. I—am required by the Committee appointed to consider this affair, to inform you they have no wish to interfere with your disposal of what is lawfully yours."

"Good of it."

"Er—you surely mean 'them'?"

"A committee is an it. Go on."

"They—it . . . they are of opinion that if the article is indeed the Holy Cup, it raises a question far transcending the rights of individual possession—"

"It belongs to the world?"

He snatched eagerly at her seemingly mild echo of Caffarelli's very own words. "Exactly!"

"Or the Church?"

à Kempis or *some*one guide me with this fiendish woman! "There—there are some who would talk of interchangeable terms."

"Well I'm not one of them. I like everything in its proper place, *vous voyez*. Continue."

"Madame, they are the first to admit there is no positive proof as to the Cup's authenticity—"

"Or its existence."

Carrema showed genuine perplexity. "There is surely evidence as to that."

"Produce it."

He began confidently, bearing Caffarelli's instructions in mind. "Age-long tradition. The many letters of enquiry, not least one from the blessed Benedict himself only recently discovered in the Vatican archives," he noted her surprise, and hurriedly pressed on with memorized argument. "There has to be dramatic content in a secret kept so immaculately for so long or the precautions would make little sense."

"'Immaculately'. . . that's not your word." She gazed levelly

28

till his wavered and dropped. "Have you yourself seen this holy mug?"

"You know I have not."

"It *was* a rhetorical question. Time-wasting . . . of course the Deodati knew what the aumbry contains, but the least godly of us could not bring ourselves to destroy an heirloom."

"An heirloom!"

"Nothing more," she insisted. "Bought and paid for in the distant past, a tiresome necessity inherited with all the other baubles."

"A bauble!" The shock and the horror.

"Negligible! Do you suppose I, for instance, have satisfied curiosity, any more than my father or his father did? I've no doubt Cellini did—he had to—yes, I have the power to do so— but you wouldn't understand, Carrema, absolute power resides in freedom to exercise the option of *not* doing. What would it profit me to view this thing?"

"Much, surely, if it be the Lord's cup."

She smiled grimly. "Wasn't it Carducci who said, 'to adorn utility is a lesson in futility!'? You've been through the records with a toothcomb no doubt, but there *are* other documents of far greater importance in the Cassone Deodati. For example, our first and last hero who brought home the 'Lord's Cup' from Jerusalem. He was no fool for all he was wholly French.

"As well as I can remember, he said 'Whether it be the Saviour's cup or no, let it abide in peace and obscurity and be not mocked of the world as with all the fragments of the True Cross, the multitude of thorny crowns and lately, the Holy Shroud of Lirey as to which even Clement bids perpetual silence on the Bishop of Troyes. As it was enjoined on Pierre d'Arcis, let it be so with the Dieudonné's everlastingly . . .'"

She broke off, freed herself of that transforming aura whereby generations of the noblesse had seemed to speak through her, almost at will.

"You're far from understanding, Carrema. It's as well. If you had enough you'd be just one more of many rogues."

"I certainly do not understand what you mean by the Holy Shroud of Lirey."

"What *I* mean!" She waved a hand dismissively. "You're not meant to. But think yourself well used that I've bothered to explain. Now, tell me what you and the Signorina have planned *sub rosa*. Don't look so astonished. I know you're hole-in-the-corner with her and I find it entertaining."

Carrema, inclined to protest, thought better of it. He must stick with his brief, endure her shafts of scorn as Sebastian smiled at those dreadful arrows, and so, a deprecating smile would serve though his heart wasn't in it.

"I value the Signorina's sympathy, but she is not to my purpose here."

She nodded graciously, invited him to come to the point.

Carrema explained in good plainchant the test proposed by the Committee to establish the Cup's identity.

"To what purpose?"

"That I can't say," he admitted so frankly she was inclined to believe him. "If I might hazard a guess, should the test prove positive, they might well recommend a negotiated purchase of the Chalice."

She had a raucous laugh, much like nutmeg to the grater. "Chalice, mug, cup, beaker, crater, receptacle—what shall we call it, eh? How many years of desiccating disputation to agree a term?

"I'll give you the likely scenario. Your friends in Rome will find the mug guilty of existing as a *genuine* relic and they'll proclaim it aloud to the world. They'll pull out every stop, organize a 'Run for the Cup', anything to ensure it stays under their control. They won't *bid* for it—that's beneath their dignity, but they'll cry aloud 'We ought to have it. *Hers* is the moral duty to give us possession outright of what's rightfully ours.'. . . don't you agree?"

Carrema dared not reply. Remembering his most secret meeting with della Paresi, he almost persuaded himself of someone present, disguised as a shadow—listening.

She monitored his silence with sober interest, weighing a situation which, she knew, would not go away with her refusal. Abruptly, as it seemed, the Marchesa made up her mind.

"Very well. As soon as it can be arranged. Tomorrow evening

30

if they wish. Tell them later will be too late . . . yes, it should be amusing. Let them fetch their divine dowser, but no hints or nudges and wink till they have what *they* want for proof. Tomorrow evening. That's enough."

It seemed like a miracle, this problem he'd agonized over to the point of a sleepless night—resolved, at a stroke. He stammered his thanks and was ready to leave when she pointed a finger, peremptory as an RSM's swagger-stick, at the corner.

"Rabbits for the pot. Take them."

He dared not refuse, recovered them gingerly and left precipitately still stuttering thanks.

She called him back when he was already half-way along the *galleria*.

"Carrema!" stentorian, quite unsuited to her years and station.

Heart pounding he returned and ventured the least of him through the smallest possible opening. "Madame?"

"You're so sure of the Aumbry's contents?"

"I would stake my life on it."

She appeared dubious, as though it must surely be worth more than that. "And what effect does it have on you when you imagine you're in its presence?"

Dumbfounded he stared, almost visibly mouthed the question to be sure he hadn't mis-heard. He only just missed *looking* at the Marchesa, let his gaze slide past her instead and out to the balcony.

"Madame, how can you ask? We agreed I have never set eyes on this marvel."

Her smile slow moving—*latet anguis in herba!*—disconcerted more than any frown. A smile filled with the wisdom of one who finds out and so demonstrates the cruelty of truth.

"You are in love with a box, my friend."

"I—don't understand," evident without words.

"I mean, your parents knew what they were doing when they forced you into a seminary."

And *then* he understood; and hated her for it. Rabbit-laden, along the *galleria*, unseeing past the Parian stripper, and down the clash of Carrara stairs, at the foot of which the Signorina stood waiting. She remarked the blackness hard against white,

31

noted the leaden steps of a tired and defeated man, too old to change his mind about the important things. Too old to change.

She was bound to assume his failure.

His gaze rested briefly on her dumb enquiry, then swung away up the way he'd come . . . "She has consented," was all he could manage in tones of deepest dejection, then almost boorishly he pushed past her and out through the great portals, a Chaplinesque silhouette of man and dangling rabbits, and into the life-giving sun which could do nothing more for him except to make him sweat for his living.

Three

GIAN GALEAZZI LEANED with both elbows on the steering wheel of his battered Fiat watching Carrema's approach down the last of a long avenue of lime trees. He pondered how the moving black speck seemed to defy the laws of perspective by remaining just that.

Amused contemplation faded as Carrema came closer—and continued on his path as if the doctor had never been. Drooping shoulders, ground-hugging gait and the defeatist air of hang-dog were nothing untoward; but Carrema at least observed the civilities.

What had happened at the Castello?

He drove on, smiling as he visualized the likely scene between his old friend and the priest with a threadbare soul. Obviously it all had to do with the Deodati Treasure and therefore . . . after all, it wasn't so much to smile about. He'd presumed heavily on their friendship, constantly warning her against steering her worthwhile course over pitfalls . . .

A sudden view of Giulietta dashing after Nino down the entrance steps and almost into the first trees bordering the drive restored him to better humour. He drew alongside as she caught the little malefactor and slapped its bottom till it howled with glee. Everybody in the village knew about the minor miracle who fell about with laughter each time he was chastised. Which was often.

Galeazzi climbed out and watched the pantomime to its end. The enormous Giulietta, a triumph of hearty appetite over his appeals to diet, basted her tiny grandchild doubled up with laughter until, infected herself, she desisted, laughing helplessly.

"Doctor, what am I to do with him? Can't you help?"

Obligingly, he fished in his pocket and brought out a fistful of sugared almonds, thrusting them into a tiny hand grown big as a bear's paw.

"Let's see if these produce tears of penitence."

"You're hopeless—helpless as I am. The Marchesa's no better and *that's* another miracle."

Galeazzi smiled. "We could try an injection of tears."

"What's the good of that! He'd laugh till he cried." She gave the impenitent a push. "Go off with you and stay with mischief or you'll do worse without it."

Hand to mouth he ran off still chuckling at the rewards loose-living can bring—and the sun smiled its approval.

"What was it this time?" Galeazzi idly wondered as he unclipped the sun visor from his spectacles.

"I caught him mocking the Signorina behind her back, bobbing and prinking, tongue half out of his head . . . he did it very well."

Glances exchanged, but nothing said. "And the Marchesa?"

"She's due to help in the kitchen. I said 'no' but she said 'yes'." The voluminous Giulietta shrugged, as though to say, "of course I was bound to lose".

"I saw the padre just now."

"He's gone. She's still in her office. You'll catch her if you hurry."

He ran lightly up the steps, paused at the top to lean over the balustrade. "Giulietta! We could try onions."

"Onions?"

"For Nino's chronic lachrymal deficiency."

She laughed and shook her head as he disappeared into the Castello. Her expression gave a fair picture of the meaning he had for the village and its environs. Twenty-three years of devoted care, for every and any one of 24 hours a day had lodged him immovably in all hearts—excepting Carrema's, perhaps, and a few of the priest's partisans who knew why he skipped his place in church on Sundays. "Let someone else on the brink have it," he'd told Carrema. "I tumbled over long ago." Carrema was not amused, never missed a chance of retailing the only confession from Galeazzi he was ever to hear.

"Vittoria! *Vous-êtes là?*"

Thus, Galeazzi at her door. They'll continue in French for a while. After all, it's the first tongue in this region. They'll drop into Italian, switch to English and back to French, not only for the fun of it, but they know how soundless the Signorina can be in felt-soled shoes on marble floors.

Giulietta, the Marchesa's eyes and ears in the Castello, had dropped the hint many years before. "She can't help herself, Madame," Giulietta extenuated, "she is *sympatica* with doors. In the village we say such women are disappointed key-holes because there aren't keys enough to go round."

"Come in, Gian, and be quick about it. You've a choice. Five minutes here or three hours in the dairy with four females and all the *tome* you can eat."

"Cheese-making? Today?" He smiled. Trust her to have a finger in *that*. Her speciality. What was it the locals intoned? "It sates hunger, quenches thirst, cleans the teeth, and converts the worst." All the same: "No time, *ma donna*. Besides, too many women, too much cheese. I've cleaned my teeth twice already today—and I'm not the worst."

"Gian, will you never grow up? Sometimes you talk so glibly, like—like a young lover."

"What's wrong with life?" he demanded, not so inconsequentially. And gravely asked, in his unpredictable fashion. Full of paradox that seldom failed of its point, as now, shaming the Marchesa herself and melting her heart briefly.

Once more, she wondered, as she watched him straddle a chair, arms folded on the back, had Gian Galeazzi himself inspired her with the idea, the great plan now so near its fruition? Was it through him that she'd found a positive solution to the inevitable end?

Gian Galeazzi, an orphan, partially deaf, with nothing in the world but himself, had fought and worked and *willed* that self to be the only worthwhile thing in a suffering world, an alleviator, comforter, a crusader against so much useless pain and anguish— a doctor if you please.

About such things they hardly ever spoke and that confirmed the meaning and depth of their relationship.

"Tell me what's happened. I just saw Carrema escorted by rabbits. They all looked in a bad way."

She told him, briefly and comprehensively, puzzled that he should appear so concerned.

"And so you've agreed?"

She smiled, but not ingenuously enough to fool him. "Why not?"

"I'll tell you why not!" he flared. "You don't have a spoon long enough to sup with them."

"*Ich diene, Herr Doktor,*" with asperity. "I should have consulted you."

"Consulted your own best interests. If you knew the people you're dealing with—"

"Little man! Our firm has been dealing with them for a thousand years—*and* beaten them."

"Times changed long ago. You've no archers, no cannon to uphold your pride. Believe me, one is useless without the other."

"Gian, much can still be done against presumption. Don't begrudge me a last fling."

"Why not just send it to London and forget this charlatan?"

"I shall have one of my own. You don't yet know everything."

"Well—have your way. Is this an evening dress affair? Those apples look delicious. Or am I permitted to attend?"

She pointed a none too clean finger. "Take one. I positively insist on your presence."

"Why then, I'll be there. Where shall this 'test' take place—in the Salle de Justice?"

"The Deodatis have dispensed justice nowhere else."

"And when it's over?"

"It will go to London." She searched among the medley on an overburdened desk and found a letter which she handed to him along with an apple.

He read it aloud. "Madam: we have your latest instructions regarding the Deodati Aumbry and are pleased to inform you the final addition to our catalogue may now be completed. Preliminary notice to interested parties has attracted considerable enquiry and we can assure you with every confidence that the agreed reserve price should be far below our initial appraisal of market expectations. We await the arrival of your agent and the Aumbry itself with eager anticipation.

"Meanwhile, do not hesitate to contact us if you have any queries relating to the sale."

He looked up, frowning. "When?"

"When what?"

"The agent. The aumbry. When do they leave Italy?"

"Tomorrow."

"Tomorrow! But you say the test is tomorrow."

"When it's over Sarinan goes to Switzerland and flies to London from Zurich."

Perplexity reigned harder than ever. "But if the aumbry is—"

"Don't worry yourself, Gian." She regarded him with a rare mellow expression and almost, she sighed. "Leave intrigue to older hands . . . have I told you what the reserve price is to be?"

Apparently she hadn't.

"Six million pounds."

He nodded morosely and supposed there *was* that much money in the world at which she laughed outright.

"Much more, Gian *mio*. And if we have confirmation of this ridiculous 'test'? Christ's own cup—any advance on six—do I hear seven—eight, thank you, sir—nine, your eminence—going at nine . . ."

He smiled as she imitated the bland tone of an English auctioneer to perfection. But did Peachum's know of the Cup?

That, she explained, would be taken care of by Sarinan.

"And if it fails the test?"

"Sold at six to the Getty museum on the left or the Metropolitan on the right. What do I care? Think of it, Gian—a comprehensive endowment fund for the price of a gilded vanity. Isn't that what we—what I've planned for?"

He considered the apple in his hand. "It's a grand dispensation and you know I'm with you all the way but—even child's play can be dangerous . . . and you're not playing with children."

"At my time of life . . . there's little to fear."

"What, *ma Donna*, do *you* believe the cup to be?" Still he seemed to address the apple.

Really the man was full of surprises today!

"You've never asked till now."

He shrugged. "It never languished anywhere but in obscurity till now. I know what I think, and that's good enough."

"Well, *I'm* not so curious as to ask *you*. Undoubtedly there's an object of some kind locked into the base—and an object is only what we want it to be—its meaning is in us."

"Further?"

"Nothing further. I mean, for example, I'm not afraid of atom bombs, only of what others want them to be."

"Carrema?"

She gestured her contempt. "Carrema and his kind make a mockery of faith. I'll go along with those who believe in what they cannot see or even comprehend, but to pin faith to a tangible object is like—like—"

"Like saying 'I'll believe because it may be in my best interests to do so'?"

She nodded thoughtfully. "Possibly. I've no interest in metaphysics."

"Or in doctors of physic. That prescription I brought three days ago sits there untouched on your desk. I'll get it filled myself."

"Unimportant. The point is, be here tomorrow. I want a trustworthy witness."

"I'll try. If it's difficult, make sure of Giulietta or son Luigi and his wife. Everyone. You mustn't be alone in this business or let the Aumbry out of your sight."

"In England," pensively, "they used, apparently, to count the spoons after the last distinguished guests had left."

He paused at the door and regarded her oddly. "What foolishness. The English eat fish and chips—with their fingers."

"That was in Julius Caesar's time, ignoramus."

The two friends stood nowhere on ceremony. When one had finished whatever he or she had to say, he or she simply walked off, from an office, a public room or wherever. It wasn't incivility, simply a tacit understanding that their lives were a shared continuity, as indissoluble as marriage ties and very likely twice as hygienic.

So, they went their ways with constant reference to the impact

38

made on each other, schemed, these cohabitors, as it were, of a single mind, to enrich the lives of those about them. Schemed with an almost comical appearance of being unaware, of being outside all that had to do with the future prosperity of the Deodati commune.

Much of it depending on the fabulous treasure they sometimes privately referred to as the Deodati grandiosity.

If there was a gathering of clouds, they had their scouts within the Castello itself. A mere shadow of greyish darkness gliding over marble as a skater on thin ice, hiding itself in one of many niches to watch with teeth stapling the lower lip as Galeazzi downs the stairs two and three at a time.

"Invincible ignorance!" Pleasurable, to spit out that echo of the good Father's malediction. He, with mock mournfulness, she with the venom of a woman scorned for, of course, he scarcely noticed her existence—even as a patient—though he took care to see her with a nurse in attendance.

Irksome also, to eavesdroppers, that their names are scarcely ever mentioned. Better to be spoken ill of than not at all. She had a position in the house—vague, ill-defined, but—the Signorina nevertheless.

She hurried forward to keep him in view as he dashed down the portico steps like an overgrown schoolboy, like any sniper, she kept him in her sights till he reached his car and drove away. How was it that, with some, one might almost not have been born?

"Perhaps that's why I don't love him," she mused, half-wittingly, unconscious of the bitter irony that allows the self to find out its fellow under the bed.

Some, in the Eternal City, knew only too well that the Deodati treasure was to be auctioned by Peachum's, an old and long established House still flourishing in one of London's fashionable quarters. Known also, that the Treasure was due to leave the country soon. Much too well known that central government had had no power to prevent its loss by refusing a certificate of export: no one had realized the Val' d'Aosta was virtually an autonomous region. By waiting on the certain refusal of an export certificate they'd lost valuable time, if not the Treasure itself.

The Committee was forced to cobble together a solution to the problem in hours rather than weeks. Secrecy was essential, which meant the least number of people involved the better. Given a time factor of near zero, it could feel reasonably satisfied that, by six o'clock on the evening of the following day, two unofficial-seeming cars were approaching the Castello Deodati.

The first, a cleverly casual Mercedes, driven by a young Vatican priest, carried their eminences Caffarelli and Bauer, very nearly in mufti, a simple black and red-trimmed day-dress. Between them, under guard, to judge by a trapped demeanour, sat a nervous little fellow of middling age, possessed of features so negative as to appear positive.

At intervals one or other of the cardinals murmured reassurance, had even patted his putty-white hand serving more than all to unnerve the poor nondescript who wasn't renowned as a sensitive for nothing.

He felt more relaxed with the Carabinieri.

On the brief plane trip from Rome to Turin and now, on the long, dusty, winding road to the Val' d'Aosta he'd consoled himself mournfully that this excursion counted as a kind of promotion. He, Bartolommeo Saachi, a relative nobody, sandwiched between four-star cardinals, was to be entrusted, so they'd informed him in a splendid parlour of the Palace itself, with a secret known only to God, the Son, the Blessed Virgin— and a few others. He, the humble proprietor of a *gelateria* was chosen and pronounced fit to adjudicate on—he could scarcely trust his recollection more than his present situation—to give an opinion, a verdict on the veritable cup of Christ . . ."only, we must be sure, Signor Saachi, that it *is* as we indisputably believe, 'veritable' in the order of miracle. You are uniquely endowed to substantiate our belief. But we must emphasize, a doubt exists— a mistaken doubt unquestionably, but in a matter of such world-shaking import the Church plainly cannot afford to make mistakes. And so, we are resolved to stake all—that is—to place a weighty responsibility on your shoulders. Poor fragile friend, if you dispute our conviction, we will philosophize our deepest disappointment as finding ourselves in no worse a condition than before. If you gratify our dearest hopes, Signor Saachi, the Church Triumphant will remain beholden to you for all time—and your expenses will, of course, be fully defrayed."

It doesn't take an honours graduate in Doublespeak to sense which side one's bread is buttered. Saachi knew what was expected of him—his sensitivity helped—and with care he had much to gain. It surprised him, poor fool, that nothing had been said about Genoa. Surely? . . .

His nervous system suffered the very deuce as they neared the Castello. The incredibly fertile valley was never green enough to tranquilize anxiety, nor the sun throwing a halo over the Gran Paradiso as it bore away westward leaving the upland fields and pastures ready for the purple passion of twilight.

"They cultivate high in these parts." Bauer's admiration was mild and faintly condescending.

"Potatoes, even lettuce will grow at four thousand feet—the snow lettuce—many other crops too." Thus Caffarelli, the patriot before the priest.

"Southern slopes—advantageously placed." The German, Heidelberg-born, inevitably nicknamed "Grosse Fasse", yawned and closed his eyes. Caffarelli smiled reminiscently, overtaken by a boyhood memory: a field officer of the Reichswehr coolly directing the siting of artillery—"*gänzlish passend!*" Abruptly he turned to Saachi busy with his own thoughts.

"I have it, Signor Saachi—I knew to have heard the name before. There was, in the Vatican library, a former citizen of Cremona—Bartolommeo Saachi—he wrote and published one of our earliest books of recipes—*Platine de Honestate Voluptate* etc., you have heard of him?"

"I can't say I have, your Eminence. I don't read much."

"The poor fellow is now only remembered as Platine."

"Why?" Bauer opened his eyes disconcertingly wide.

"Why? Because the man is become the book, the book has become the man."

"That is heresy."

The Italian raised his eyebrows, unsure of Bauer's drift of

41

humour. It didn't strike his eminence as being particularly funny.

At the dreaded word, Saachi hunched back into the seat and could not be drawn again until they were safely arrived, while the cardinals, recalling yet another Saachi, argued about his "Mass of St Gregory" hung in the Vatican. Bauer insisted it was a Pesellino.

"Will this take long?" Bauer wondered, minutes later.

"We shall abbreviate. Just a short prayer for·guidance."

"The shorter the better," Grosse Fasse muttered in Bavarian patois as he climbed stiffly out of the car. "And why della Paresi had to be included, I can't think."

"He included himself." Drily from Caffarelli, more disconcerted by the fact than he cared to admit.

The little group waited on the portico, too conscious of a seemingly deserted house. "You'd think they were not expecting us," Bauer grumbled.

Nobody relished the apparently studied affront.

"Where's Carrema I wonder?" irritably from Caffarelli, "he's supposed to be here at least."

"Fra della Paresi is arriving, Eminence."

The senior cardinal favoured his chaplain with a benevolently withering glance. "Sometimes, my son, it's not a bad idea to tell ignoramuses something they *don't* know."

Peace and tranquillity descended as the second car came to rest behind the larger vehicle. Or was it an uneasy silence shared by these churchmen conscious that a peer beyond his peers had softly closed his car door and now approached like a lime-washed shadow, robed as he was in the Dominican habit.

His part in the whole affair is unclear, ambiguous—and indisputable. By someone he was appointed Monitore, to hold a watching brief over all concerning the Treasure. In spite of official denials that he had an executive role, Caffarelli and Bauer knew his reputation too well to alter their private opinions . . . after all, they were privileged to watch him in action that evening.

Which is now, as he makes of his noiseless approach a deafening moment of drama. That—emergent countenance, unframed canvas of deathly repose, not easily looked upon.

Saachi dared not: the chaplain, young and darkly handsome, full of responsibility without power could afford nonchalance. But Caffarelli and Bauer?

The former masked unease with an urbanity common to scions of old Roman black nobility. But the effort, so to speak, very nearly snapped the elastic securing the domino.

"You see we are being treated like pariahs, Signor Monitore. What do you say to that?"

Fire kindled and died in already scorched eyes. No danger. Merely a touch of resentment at the salutation. The Dominican answered in curiously *de profundis* tones.

"I say she must one day wait at the gates of hell, long enough to endure the torments of the damned in her imagination."

Saachi shuddered. A Saturday night TV horror film could never shake him so badly.

"Extravagant," Bauer ventured. Yes, ventured! He who could lumber like an untracked panzer over all opposition to his way of thinking.

"I state a fact—economically. My vows require me to leave extravagance to others—Eminence."

Bauer's confusion and an attempt to bluster a protest died with the appearance of Carrema bustling forward to welcome them as effusively as he could manage given the poverty of their reception.

"Your Eminences, gentlemen, my apologies, but so much to do—and I could not be sure to the minute of your—"

"No inordinate hurry, Father Carrema. Let me introduce you. Fra della Paresi, appointed by His Holiness to see fair play as I understand. My chaplain, Father Ciccio, his Eminence you met in Rome of course. Signor Bartolommeo Saachi, whose extraordinary gifts are known to you?"

"Indeed, I'm an avid admirer of your powers, Signor. The case of the dismembered corpse was most—"

"Perhaps you'll do the honours if the Marchesa is tactically indisposed, Father," curtly from Caffarelli who'd scarcely give good time of day to Carrema's breed swarming in Rome.

Shedding more of his self-esteem Carrema ushered the party into the great hall where he paused, uncertain as to what next. Caffarelli prompted him.

"We shall proceed at once to the chapel—as I think we agreed—and there pray for a happy outcome for our labours. The place seems utterly deserted!" He glanced about him, disconcerted by the silence, by the lack even of elementary ceremony.

"The servants and tenants are—are at supper in the great kitchen—they will not come to chapel."

"Will not—? Have they no interest?"

"There's no doing anything with them—the Marchesa never supports my attempts to—the Signorina expresses a wish to be present." Briefly, he explained the Petacci woman.

Caffarelli, mollified, nodded condescendingly. Anything was better than nobody. "We shall be delighted. And the Treasure?"

"As you requested, it is in the *Sala di Giustizia*."

The Dominican restlessly moving here and there, examining everything, missed nothing. "A relic of ancient pretensions. There's an odour of peacocks about that woman."

Carrema saw a chance to fan flames. "She holds court once a month to settle differences between her tenants."

"A feudal heretic . . . too bad these are not feudal times."

"Tolerance for the time being at least," Caffarelli suggested.

"No tolerance at any time!" To snarl a rebuke at a cardinal is power indeed. Not one of those present but felt it. "I wish to look about me for a while; shall come to the chapel in good time. It's there?" He gestured towards the funeral chamber, glancing at Carrema who felt the full weight of someone walking over his grave. At least, he shivered and shook his head, not trusting to words but pointing in the opposite direction.

In a moment the Dominican had, as it were, dematerialized, for he left no firm impression of corporeal departure.

Caffarelli watched the minor phenomenon with half-closed, speculative eyes. "He smells a rat," he murmured.

Bauer grinned. "It's a matter of taste."

Carrema, overwhelmed at sight of great men baring their teeth in public, somehow stammered that refreshments were available at their pleasure.

"I will not break her bread in this house." Caffarelli walked briskly to the chapel.

44

The rest, lack-lustre, followed, subdued and silent except for Bauer, mumbling at some being too finicky to touch manna in the desert.

As the chapel filled with high-powered prayer and incantations a noiseless pillar of darkness wandered in the immediate environs of the castello, pausing at intervals, not to listen especially, but to come at the catch, to sense precisely how they were all in process of being fooled.

In spite of his plans.

The Dominican is no ordinary man. Maybe a meritocrat *par excellence*, heart and soul in God's service however much his enemies demand "Which one?" Admitted, he knows almost as much as the devil he believes in when it comes to sin and such.

Of course mankind is suspect, so naturally he must garment in a hairshirt worn over his conscience, underwear a shroud of suspicion about motives and hoary dealings, anathematize those who mouth honour and practise everything but. In the eyes of his god, whichever one, he's often correct. Mankind being what it is, black hatred may well shoot in the dark and never miss.

This man, who holidays in ruins, revels in shattered lives, master of the broken pillar, would conduct Caffarelli himself to hell if this venture goes awry. He senses all is not well, but cannot put a finger to the iota. As a skilled technician of ritual and the solemn sarabande of high intrigue he's bound to look askance at a precipitate and crudely planned charade . . . in which he has no part.

Spectre-silent he prowls through the grounds, merges with shadows, scarcely leaves his own on the moonstruck sward, always an eye to the castle in which . . . the slightest scuffle distracted his thoughts; from a bush close by a small form emerged; swift as a snow leopard he pounced and held fast to nothing more than a tiny boy, face tilted, terror-stricken at sight of a tortured countenance where none should be. Shadows are funny, the moon is friendly, and things smaller than his hand rustle and chirrup. This was something different and too much.

Loosed from that clammy grasp, the child scuttles away calling "*Mammia!*" at panic pitch.

That night Nino met with his first nightmare.

Four

THE DOMINICAN HAD something to prowl about, but it had nothing to do with Sarinan, who'd been closeted with the Marchesa for an hour or more. Not even the Signorina could break their privacy, even if she'd known of Sarinan's presence.

By the time she returned from some trifling errand in the village Giulietta's son-in-law was mopping the floor of the *galleria*; took so long about it that she had no chance to listen in depth though she could hear voices coming from the office. High-handed she demanded to know who the visitor might be. Gennaro, civilly, had no idea. She stifled her ready temper, too aware of her standing with the servants, and wondered pointedly at pains taken to clean a floor at such an hour.

He smiled politely. "Illustrious visitors, Signorina. The Marchesa was most particular, any dirt in the house must be no more than they bring with them."

She thought how far down in the world she had come to not dare screaming at him for his insolence.

"Where are they?"

"In the chapel I think, Signorina."

"Already! Tell the Marchesa I shall come for her when they're ready."

"Understood, Signorina. You will come to her when she is ready."

She turned back, eyes flashing with fury having no other vent. Began to speak, thought better of it and stormed away, too high heels at the tic-tac tempo of a death-watch beetle, while Gennaro mopped industriously, whistling *sotto voce* and out of tune "Giovannezza", an old Fascist marching song.

Its rhythm exactly matched the clatter of footsteps down the grand staircase.

★

46

"Well, Sarinan, your last undertaking—for me, I mean."

"I'm saddened and honoured all in one, Madame."

The Marchesa shook her head, smiled despairingly. "You're too old still to have a way with you."

"Without it I'm out of business."

"Times have changed. Could you *still* sell Trajan's column to a dumb American?"

"It *was* long ago, but you know, I wasn't so smart—I didn't sell it!"

"But he paid for what he didn't get?"

"Let's say the transaction was not completed."

"I hear my trusted agent is in trouble with the authorities."

"A technicality, that's all. Believe me, I've never profited by a single lira in *our* dealings."

"Funnily enough I believe you."

"It's even funnier that I have too much respect for you—d'you know why?"

Apparently, she had no idea.

"Because I know what you intend. May your remaining days be more than those of Ma-hal-a-leel, but why spend them in selling one by one the Deodati betrothal jewels, the Madonna Biondo, the Bellini sketches, the Malatesta Cassone and—?"

"And, Sarinan?"

A shrug and a shrewd stroke of his nose.

"Whatever else has netted a profit of four millions . . . So I make a few enquiries and I discover Madame is laying the foundations of a fortune, realizing assets, to endow a home for handicapped kids, here in the Castello Deodati. Madame, I kiss your hand on behalf of all that happy laughter to come. You alone have saved an oldish rogue from becoming an ageless cynic."

And who the devil is this fashion-conscious chunk of glib assurance, air of a long-serving diplomat, scraping the bottom of his empty cornucopia for words of praise while the Marchesa listens and looks on with unveiled amusement soaked in irony?

Unpublished by *Who's Who*? Safik Sarinan may be more widely known than most contemporaries laid to rest between its covers. On a day when life is getting him down with its heckling insistence on scruples he'll admit to fifty-four winters. When the gods wink and he's made yet another coup, he'll blithely deduct ten per cent and stick at forty-nine summers. Somehow he gets away with it, mainly because this cosmopolitan, of Syrian/Armenian parentage, born in Lebanon, has a total disdain of life's conventions, its slavish adherence to the tyranny of time and, above all, of its utter gullibility. In the melting entrepot of the Westernized Middle East he quickly learned how to weigh scruples against the weighty assurance of fools.

Yet, the desire to profit by gold-plated stupidity came second to a more sincere, worthier quest for the rare and beautiful.

Coupled together these motives helped build his reputation over the years till now he had the entrée to every fortress sheltering plutocratic connoisseurs and the major museums of the world, as well as dealing for lesser individuals, not to be despised because they possessed only an item or two to be disposed of at the best possible price.

A useful epitaph for one who knew how to get exactly that. By fair means sometimes, by sheer effrontery, others.

He really did try to flog Trajan's column. Rome almost died laughing. But it characterized the man, his methods and his motives: the luxury of perpetrating an exquisite practical joke consorted with a high-class con man's need to make ready money.

Cincinnati museum still smarts at the price it fell over itself to pay for a splendid, highly authenticated van Gogh *Wallflowers* which Sarinan knew to be a *pitturaccia* by the uncelebrated pre-war Berlin artist, Wacker.

They still talk about that genuine tour de force by a genuine rogue.

With negotiations near to completion, Sarinan worked himself into a state of near apoplexy by suddenly announcing that, *in his opinion, Wallflowers* was, after all, a genuine Wacker "with stylistic affinities".

Those italicized words guaranteed his success. By presuming to know better than his peers, as sure as night follows day, the worthy curators were bound to consult *their* opinions and discover what Sarinan already knew they knew—which had nothing to do with Messrs Wacker and Gogh—viz., their's was superior knowledge to the point of total blindness, deafness and downright ignorance. Thus, fools were served and Sarinan who, for once, acted as principal after a carefree investment of a few hundred marks in Berlin's flea-market, flew out of Cincinnati with reputation intact *and* the kind of cheque which, like a highly readable novel, is difficult to put down.

"To business then," the Marchesa abrupted, "my guests will be here soon. You'll leave before they do."

"You make something of the timing then?"

"Eight hundred years . . . the Deodati's have had plenty of practice." She pushed a document across the desk, a square of exquisite ebb and flow in the Italian hand seen under Lamplight. "My final authorization to Peachum's. They expect you tomorrow or the day after?"

"And my part?"

"Agent and courier. I hold you responsible for the Treasure's safe delivery."

Sarinan smiled or, rather, he fabricated a coward's accommodating grimace.

"Normally, dear lady, Pickford's bullet-proof wagon and a dozen armed guards would be employed when the stakes reach six or seven million sterling."

"I can't afford it. And you seem enamoured of that figure."

He nodded in more serious vein. "I told you when I first inspected this thing. And I have never been wrong in a valuation—never."

"Perhaps you could be wrong at last." She leaned hard against the desk studying him with an eye to flaws. "You must have heard rumours about the Treasure?"

"It contains teeth—yes, you pointed them out." He affected carelessness while resenting a suggestion of ignorance.

"St Foy's tooth . . . it's of no significance." Then, as if she too had something to resent, she spoke curtly. "I didn't ask you here to play postman or pass the time of day." She selected another, but sealed, letter and placed it with the first. "This tells something of the Treasure obviously unknown to you. Now— give me your hands. Hold them out."

49

Surprised, Sarinan complied.

She took both, manicured to perfection, disgracing hers, nail-torn and none too clean.

Once, she squeezed his left hand gently. Thrice she exerted pressure on his right, then released both with the faintest chuckle.

"The line is broken at last . . . it's as simple as that, Sarinan."

Bewildered, he protested that he didn't understand.

"Of course you don't. For generations that simple action has protected the true meaning of the Deodati Treasure. Now, *before* I die, it goes to a stranger—to you. Remember, one left, three right."

"I'm honoured, Madame," he added whimsically, "I think."

At which she laughed, as if relieved of an ancient burden. "Well said! But be sure to tell them what I've told you. Give them this letter with the enclosure. It will explain everything."

"This to Peachum's—not to me?"

"You'll have to know sometime . . . the aumbry has a hollow base. By pressure, as I showed you, a drawer is activated . . . it's reputed to contain the Lord's cup, the one he mentioned at that last supper."

Sarinan ran the gamut in ten seconds, a whole catalogue of expressions studiously collected over more than forty years of peddling, from the Beirut bazaars to the souks of California.

First, affected astonishment, then genuine astonishment, then outright incredulity switching back to affected disbelief, then genuine amusement at a joke succeeded by a frantic realization that it wasn't and so on, all so inextricably mixed that he ended with a slight headache and a frown of perfect perplexity. *Someone*, his expression seemed to suggest, might have given him warning of this—startling development.

He now fully understood why he was here.

"I'll—I'll assume you're serious; but one or two factors occur. I can't believe you've—"

"Name them."

"A, the question of provenance. *Nobody* can authenticate the possessions of one, two thousand years dead, unless they're recorded at the time. Egyptology has that advantage. B, the

50

authorities would refuse it a certificate of export. C . . . the Church would certainly take measures to prevent its sale."

"Easily answered. A, you know as well as I, a mere allusion, in the collector's mind, is almost equal to documentary evidence. Ideation, and then the materialization of that idea. B, mine is the right to dispose of the inheritance as I think fit. As for C . . . the Church has the same right to bid at the sale as others have."

Sarinan showed little sign of being convinced. Suddenly, and badly, he was troubled by this out of the celestial blue bombshell. Why, he wondered aloud, had she made no mention of it before? After all, she'd summoned him at least ten months ago.

"I thought nothing of it at that time or any time, till our priest had to poke his nose into the business and alert the Vatican."

"The Vatican!" so that explained—much. Sarinan looked distinctly uncomfortable.

Sight 20/20 she was not the woman to miss much. "The commission no longer appeals?" and *he* was not one to miss a hint of contempt.

"I'm entitled to time enough to come to terms with the dangers inherent in a new version of an enterprise. I have no more than other men's share of courage, so I don't have much to spare . . . if I'm to carry out my part of the bargain *with conviction* I must know all there is to know—historically."

He paused, as if to summon reserves of wisdom seldom needed when a ready wit would serve. "If there is one thing I've learned in a lifetime of what the Yankees call wheeling and dealing, it's this: in respect of 'treasures', masterpieces, coveted junk of all kinds, your pieces of paper, certificates, letters, manuscripts, what you wish, are worthless unless they are fortified by word of mouth—yes, even mine! *especially* mine if my success in business is a stick of the yard."

"Why?"

"Because," flared Sarinan, master of maybe, prince of perhaps, Sarinan at the top of his bent, "the spoken came before the printed *or* written word . . . did the Cross depend on the Bible? No say-so, no Church! Therefore, if you'll briefly tell the history of what you call the Lord's cup I'll double the price you expect. If not—I leave the Castello and, with regret, your service."

51

Well, the Deodatis had always been noted for their sense of fair play. You can't throw a man from the ramparts or hang your enemies in chains without a bit of a trial *and* not expect trauma to curdle the blood of those yet unborn. The Marchesa's inheritance saw his point and she easily conceded in her own right.

Minutes later the dumbfounded impresario of *objets d'art* knew very nearly as much as the Marchesa herself as she finished her précis of the Treasure's second history.

"But why so much secrecy for a cup? No, I don't understand."

How could he, lacking religious convictions *and* denied a sense of continuity? As an urchin of the streets his mouth seldom saw a spoon, never a silver one—which is a symbol of continuity. The Marchesa tried to explain.

"It's impossible for me to know *how* a man of his time arrived at a decision. I'm sure he feared the consequence of advertising the possibility. He fought hard in the Crusade, saw how blood can be shed for an ideal so powerful that splinters of true cross could change hands for money, defiling the reality. Piety or principle, he refused to play the market but, obviously, he simply couldn't destroy the faintest likelihood."

"And—you have *never* seen it."

"Very few of us have. That much of the Conte de Dieudonné's good sense we all inherited it seems."

"But it *was* known to the Church?"

"The Church affected to ignore its existence—and there was Genoa . . . an attempt was made in 1531 to steal the treasure. Certain conclusions were drawn and Maestro Cellini was engaged to re-create the hotch-potch as we know it, adding 'a secret place of infinite cunning to lodge the wondrous article'."

"It's nowhere mentioned in Cellini's memoirs!" he checked at some hidden thought and fell silent long enough to change tack. "And it doesn't concern you what happens to this—this wondrous article?"

"You question like a priest."

"I put the questions they will ask."

". . . no, Sarinan. I've no earthly interest in the fate of a telesma—you understand what I mean by that?"

He nodded uncertainly.

"My line dies with me—a good run for our money as the English say. If the object must lose its legal guardian—better to be rid of it. Let others foster the illusion if they wish—but they must pay a price sufficient to support a worthier cause." Some strange anguish brought her to her feet. "Don't you think, Sarinan, a Christ would have nodded to anything, real or spurious, that might relieve the wrongs visited by Providence on so many unfortunate children?"

Sarinan, also standing, could nod abstractedly while casting about for some avenue of escape, for it was borne in on him by a series of jerks, of other considerations, how much more complex his mission had become.

In his semi-pagan eyes, the cup's value was negligible, but he saw with angry clarity that the Marchesa took too simplistic a view of an artifact tailor-made to rock nations, create new sects—even topple a government or two and not do him much good either if fate thumbed its nose at the whole transaction. So many questions coursed through his mind that he found himself short of mental agility to formulate any one of them. He was distracted by the Marchesa thrusting a variety of papers into his hands.

"And last of all my written authority to the Crédit Suisse—and the key. Take care of it. It will unlock the door to seven hundred thousand pounds sterling."

His business sense responded to the carrion call of figures. "And the added value of the crockery—plus expenses."

Contempt showed at last—naked and unashamed. "As much as you want, *comme d'habitude.*"

"London gets more expensive," a flabby attempt to defend himself and they both knew it.

They paused to listen as someone outside drummed discreetly on the door.

"That's Gennaro's signal. They've just arrived. He'll take you the back way through the second courtyard. You'll find your car parked outside—he'll show you—from then on . . . let me know when you reach London."

"Understood, Madame. But please—a last question. This

53

visitation by the Church—what does it mean? What do you plan to tell them?"

She gazed beyond him, pensively, as if other, more important questions might have occurred—to either of them.

"I shall demonstrate that—"

"Demonstrate?"

". . . suggest, that true faith ought not to depend on what's left of a dinner service."

Sarinan shrugged, stuffed the papers into his document case and took his leave.

Maybe she *is* crazy he concluded, on the far side of the door.

Five

IT'S TRUE, SAFIK SARINAN clutching a slimline portfolio containing his fortune—this was to be his last throw against the advancing years—quit the Castello Deodati without incident. Guided by Gennaro he threaded innumerable passages, climbed and descended a stone stairway or two before they crossed the courtyard with its elaborate well-head at the centre. Moonlight flooded the galleried enclosure, made a pretence of cloisters carved in chiaroscuro, while a bat chanced its blindness against the arches, went a black course in and out, unfailing.

Yet, the timelessness, the peace and the silence, even the innocent presence of Gennaro inspired in Sarinan an almost superstitious sense of menace—imminent—for which he could not account.

Sarinan had his share of sensitivity, not all of it in hands that could distinguish Chinese from Japanese Imari porcelain, blindfold, for example. For the rest he could only agree with a snap impression that all this back door clandestinity was typical Italian intrigue . . .

Nearer the heart he sensed it came to more than a trite reaction and, as he stepped through a wicket gate at the end of a short vaulted passage, Sarinan was so far cowed by some pending apprehension that he actually debated the wisdom of retracing his steps and cancelling the whole business.

Figures have been the destruction of many men—a few noughts can, in certain circumstances, spell the unwritten warrant for execution. Better, sometimes, to turn back and choose mere existence against the prospect of living dangerously on the interest.

Sarinan did not turn back. He gave goodnight and a handful of lira to the faithful Gennaro and watched the door close softly to a click.

Before facing his car he stood listening intently—the receding steps of the manservant, cicadas sawing the air in two, a cowbell tolling in distance pastures—yet he heard nothing. Glanced about him, uncertain, frowning at intuition tugging his sleeve, flicked at a sudden moth and chuckled as if to reassure—himself.

Safik Sarinan, world famous mountebank. Hesitant? He who never refused a challenge from the meanest *tombaroli* to the meanest curator. And won! nine out of ten times. He tapped his forehead, still self-persuading. "It's all up here. So why should I care about them? I know how to outwit—it's all up here . . ."

With the batteries of his resolution newly charged, apprehension controlled, Sarinan climbed into his car and drove away with the easy air of a man with much to gain.

As to what he had to lose, intuition had done its best for him—and failed.

Sometimes, miasma can be the unacceptable face of charisma. A deadly combination in men like della Paresi. He's been that way not so long before Sarinan's departure. Noted the car, and assumed the visitor to the Marchesa—from Rome. All was as it should be, and yet, he could not shake off a suspicion of some off-stage scene playing counterpoint to the total drama pregnant with a single theme—how to redeem a sacred anomaly from profane hands . . .

He returned to the chapel in time for final prayers shared with an almost non-existent audience. He noted Saachi deep in his orisons and, at a distance, Father Carrema with the Petacci woman. She might be useful . . .

The two cardinals, uncomfortably cramped, prayed at the modest sized altar, while the young chaplain lounged in the wings, yawning occasionally behind his hand and glancing a prim rebuke at the Dominican for his late-coming.

Paresi genuflected perfunctorily, glowered at the presumptuous priest, then openly inspected the Renaissance splendour of the Deodati chapel, as if the rest were at play.

Smiled bitterly. He knew their history well enough. Liberals and heretics, inimical first and last to the Church. True, one of them had fought for Jerusalem and a doubtful pope or two when it suited their deeper purposes.

Aspects of this affair dogged and disturbed him. To use a sensitive was surely malpractice, against all canons? What could be gained when ice-cream sellers are schooled to discover an echo of the truth? Strawberry flavoured! The Dominican scorned such evidence and, so he suspected, did that miserable brace of cardinals.

His smouldering gaze hovered over the wretched Carrema, still doubled like an awkward foetus over his devotions. The fool hath spoken! Brought forth a mouse from muniments—harnessed to a mountain *ma foi*! And they must dance to the piping of this negative . . . a venture, he reflected, can only prosper if the ship of fools sinks in good time—weakness, folly and good intentions badly mis-handled, today's ingredients for this polenta world. *Crosta!*

Eyes made to scorn twisted and lingered on the Petacci woman. And the "progressives" would ordain such creatures as that! Women shaped like piety, 36-24-36, in charge of the sacraments God save us—don't overdo it, Caffarelli, or we'll be here till All Souls' day—how much did she know as her mistress's confidante? Yes, she could perhaps be useful . . . later.

Endless speculation, endless dissatisfaction, because it was all wrong. None of this hung together. No incense could disguise odours sans sanctity. A test!

Prayers were done with at last. The small party approached the door and the Dominican.

"You hardly joined us, fra Giovanni," mildly.

"I had other things to think of."

"Our Dominican is uneasy. Should we be uneasy too?" Bauer wondered.

Perhaps but not openly, in the presence of fools. He stared past them. "Their tree bears no fruit."

Surprise, even consternation. Caffarelli recovered first and nodded once, smiling. "The plain wooden cross. Yes—one would expect better in a chapel of this magnificence. That bronze by Riccio—mouth-watering. And Bernini had a hand in the refurbishing I believe."

Too arrogant to bother with comment della Paresi turned to Carrema, tentatively warming himself at this unaccustomed blaze, but fearful of sparks.

"You will conduct the Signor and this lady to the *Sala di Giustizia.*"

"Oh—had we not better wait till—?"

"At once!"

Clangorous as hell's door slammed.

Outside the chapel four players watched three supernumaries ascend to the first level. Paresi turned to Caffarelli keeping an eye fixed on the last resting room of the Deodatis.

"One of us is an unwilling participant in a farce, Eminence."

Such insolence! from the lowest to the highest. But Caffarelli, the Vatican's champion bridge-player and second only to The Gorilla at poker, knew the rules of the game, knew enough not to betray his feeling.

"*Absolvo te.* But does the head have its reasons?" Who, he insinuated, would credit such a man with a heart?

"All this for a rumour."

"My dear fellow, the Church was founded on rumour." Caffarelli checked and coloured damning himself for facetiousness before a man who had the third ear of the Pope no less. "I quote our detractors as an antidote to overstrained sensibilities."

Crafty della Paresi said nothing to fill the faintly shocked silence, edging Caffarelli further into isolation. His urbanity fled long enough to leave a frightened political-animal which could still snarl from its corner. "You would do well not to be in too many places at once, della Paresi!"

Brilliant, Eminence. Thus you came by your red hat? By St Jerome that's clever, that's paradox, that's the response saying all and risking nothing. At a stroke Caffarelli retrieves his authority with a busted flush. Bauer breathes a little more freely and the young chaplain smirks openly at this put-in-his-place dogsbody.

Who hangs his head in shame? Not della Paresi! At a good distance that facial spasm might just resemble a smile.

"While you have prayed for light, someone has come and gone. While you prospect for a miracle its future is decided by

58

the Marchesa and another. In fact, I doubt it exists here—in the present."

"You must have reasons," Bauer insisted.

"I don't require reasons! I look for proof that we're wasting our time."

Caffarelli, troubled by the monk's misgivings, all the more because they were too vague to be disputed, saw nothing untoward. "Carrema tells me there will be witnesses to this affair, the doctor, Galeazzi, will be present."

"He will not be here. I rang him from the village."

Caffarelli frowned, glancing at the others. "Rang? Why should he not be?"

". . . I think it best." No more words. Only a vision of a habited figure, gliding soundlessly up the marble cataract, thunderous by comparison.

Grave and sober countenances below, not too scarred by browbeating and a brush with the sinister. A moment of immobility served to underline defeat of a kind.

Caffarelli moved first to break from an impotence that—uniquity could induce by a mere throw of the eye. Ill at ease, the others followed, deep in preoccupation with fugitive thoughts that tend to flutter over self-preservation.

They could find time to marvel at a *galleria* made for procession to the taffeta rustle of vestments and the silky susurrus of *cappi*—an icy grandeur for floes to glide unremarked.

But why was della Paresi storming at the solid-seeming Gennaro standing like a sentry before the bronze doors of the *Sala*?

"So what? The Marchesa must dispose herself before I can allow entry."

"Do you know who I am?" the Dominican hissed in a blind fury.

"I don't care who the devil you are—what does *that* signify?" Gennaro, never in awe of his mistress, could hardly be blinded by a smokey-eyed monk. Nor did the prospect of two cardinals closing to starboard bother his phlegmatic soul.

"We are to be kept waiting by this infidel!" Eyes blazing, eyes of a man who brooked nothing like this from many above him, eyes of one who saw no difference between two worlds apart.

"If the Marchesa is mistress in her own house—then we shall wait as she directs." Affable Caffarelli, glad of any ally against della Paresi's perpetual warfare, even this unlikely major domo in blue dungarees and sweat shirt.

Gennaro grunted and muttered his favourite comment on that other world and all its doings: *Ci fa schifo.*

The Dominican felt sick too, was ready to launch a stronger verbal assault when a command came from the other side of those massive doors, bronzed with the chronicles of Sigismondo, and Gennaro at once wrestled them back, pulling and tugging with a horse-coper's vigour, the hinges screaming like a whinny of bloodstock mares.

Magnificent perspective! Theatrical as a set piece by old Bibiena—twice as cunning too. For a seventeenth-century Deodati had decreed mirrors galore to make a mockery of some old maxim that justice must be *seen* to be done. Wit from the Attic with a grain of truth . . . so much can be done with mirrors.

A blaze of light reflected, making visual echoes to the vanishing point, illuminating a chamber rivalling the grandeur of the Equestrian Hall in Mantua's Palazzo del Te.

Two massive quinquecento chimney-pieces—Rovvezano's, they say; the dominating statue of the almost condottiere Faolo Luigi Deodati—scapegrace of the House—lost-wax cast in that very room while engineers sweated below to strengthen the sagging joists. Only unimportant paintings remained, the rest had long since gone to Peachum's wrapped in Aubusson tapestries so to say.

The very floor was a masterpiece in marquetry, unique of its kind—a giant tree, branched to give name and reign of every Deodati from then till yesterday, each cunningly lodged in the foliage.

Not easily seen, even by the diamond light of six paired electroliers, for the whole floor space was filled with three hundred chairs, plain but comfortably cushioned, row upon row, stretching from where the newcomers stood to a long and highly ornate table ready-made for a hundred games of shove ha'penny.

Along the aisle dividing the two blocs of seating the newcomers had their first view of the Aumbry. Perspective and distance

60

enhanced first impressions. The stones flashed a spectrum response to the lights, the gold chasing and casing hinted at the presence of some hidden content paradoxically both near and far from attainable. Undoubtedly it deserved an involuntary "Superb!" from Caffarelli.

Bauer peered stolidly, wondering what Luther would have said of it *after* the Annunciation in the Cloaca.

The chaplain clasped his hands in mute adoration of what he knew it was supposed to contain.

Paresi's scowl said nothing out of the ordinary, but the knuckles of his involuted hands showed white under a clenching pressure.

As for Carrema, the Treasure out of its time-honoured place flowered into an object of indescribable transcendancy. His intelligence failed to understand the effect of a sense of occasion. Instead, searching feverishly through his repertoire he hit on Giotto's Scrovegni dedicating his chapel to the three weird sisters.

The Signorina watched them in turn: her eyes, half-closed, jerked rapidly from one to another with not a single movement of her head.

Saachi's years seemed to weigh heavily in this presence, this setting, the august company, a composition of cross-roads confounding his journey to fame and possibly fortune beyond the modest returns from ice cream. His total personality, not downtrodden so much as ground into the dust, seemed the worst possible choice for drawing a bow at so sublime a venture.

A door opened at the far end of the hall, the mistress of the Castello Deodati appeared with a retinue of—her servants!

Too obviously they were domestics; that fat woman had to be a cook, her face red as Treviso's *radicchio* from roasting over the kitchen fires—the lean and hungry looking fellow behind, a pure and simple peasant, the old man God knows what, and that young woman bursting with child—and there were more, all of them so pleased with themselves, laughing and chattering as if a circus had come to town. Disgusting!

The Marchesa went almost unrecognized, resplendent in an ancient sweater, *slacks* and a sleeveless sheepskin jacket, *boots*

61

cast off by a gamekeeper—God in heaven what was this place!. . .
but she had a patrician's carriage, no denying it.

"*Approchez, messieurs*. You're welcome." Firm, loud and full
of authority she waved her company to the front seats close
to Gargantua's table. They realized too late—these were her
"witnesses". How dared she make theatre of this solemn occasion
with sweaty menials for audience.

Caffarelli heard the sharp intake of breath from the man at his
shoulder. "It's intolerable! Eminence, she is degrading you,
demeaning your office."

The Cardinal bit his under lip with vexation, divided between
the truth and the presumption. Who was this friar to play proud
when he, Caffarelli, knew the world, the score, the stakes and
how to play his hand?

"If you don't care to muddy your footwear for the Faith invest
in a pair of galoshes, good Friar!"

"Madame," he called aloud, progressing slowly at the head of
his party, "the warmth of your welcome is proverbial. The whole
of Italy rings with tales of your hospitality and we're suitably
grateful for the generous share we receive." He continued in this
vein, trading mockery for mockery, slight for slight, contriving,
at the same time, to introduce his companions with the utmost
polished civility.

Arrived at the table he affected a close scrutiny of the Aumbry
while seeming to ignore her studied silence. Which grew too
long for comfort.

"I'm overjoyed that you permit your dependents to witness
the possibility of miracle. Blessed are they that—"

A snigger converting to a cough from somewhere behind him
left Caffarelli silent and confused.

"My dependents as you call them, are Ghibellines of old. On
their behalf I welcome the Guelphs."

Her eye caught the Dominican's as she ended and, unaccountably, her air of absolute self-possession fled and returned in a
breath. "There you have it, Caffarelli. What you requested. Let
the Judge of all answer your requirements."

"Amen to that . . . but I had hoped to venture a question or
two."

"As many as you wish."

". . . in private."

"These people are some of my family. There's nothing to hide."

She pointed to chairs ranged along the table's length.

"No reason to stand. We prefer to sit on our ceremonies as they say in these parts."

There was delighted laughter from her partisans as Caffarelli hesitated, debating whether to sit or stand on his—ceremony. With a concessionary shrug he took a chair and the rest followed suit.

"Madame, the question uppermost in our minds is why you determined to sell a treasure of such hidden significance with-out—if you'll allow the harsh note of criticism—informing the Church of your intention."

"No doubt *you* will allow," evenly, "my right to dispose of my property, given under section 114 of the 5th article of our Constitution."

"Your right is unanswerable—much like my original ques-tion," smooth as the dagger from its sheath.

"It's the numbers game isn't it, Caffarelli? How many shrouds to begin with? How many tears of Christ dropped in Lazarus' grave still remain? How much of the Virgin's milk has survived in how many vials? Why was Pius shamed to dedicate the head of the Apostle Andrew? Why did the abbess claim possession of Santa Reparata's hand and arm when all sanity and senility could see it was a thing of plaster and wood? Why the need to make mystery of history, to muddy the clear water of life with senseless myth? There's nothing wholesome in teeth, splinters of wood, filthy grave clothes, blood soaked shifts."

". . . we must work with what we have, according to the times."

"The tools of a trade are not the words of a Christ."

"Vehicles of a faith are transport like any other, they carry the people to the Man with a Message, but like those others, be it an infant's tricycle to the very latest Fiat, they will break down, be outgrown, become redundant."

63

"How would it serve your purpose if this cup 'broke down' in time?"

"Authentic or not, it is mutable."

"And if our good Father Carrema hadn't taken a stroll beyond his nose would you be richer or poorer?"

"How can you ask? The Church, dear lady, is strong precisely because it refuses to deny meaning in all things. *Nothing* is significant until its significance is sought for and inferred—an atomic physicist would understand as much. Consequently, do you imagine we could safely ignore the *fact* that he came by chance on material evidence of a possibility?"

Bauer coughed discreetly, just enough to attract their attention. "May I ask as a practical consideration, do we have an equitable right to bid for this Treasure at the London sale?"

"Why not?"

"Then surely it makes sense to avoid a commercial contest by selling outright to those with a professional interest?"

Why should she dissemble her amusement. "You must have graduated from a school for business studies—in another life perhaps. The Aumbry is valued at seven millions sterling—I accepted that—cup thrown in for good measure. I hardly mentioned it. But, if Carrema says it's priceless and you agree, I'd be a fool not to look to the highest bidder!"

"Money!"

". . . you're treading a minefield, Cardinal. What is Peter's pence, and why do bankers die?"

"That is not to the purpose! We ask why you refuse to sell to the Church?"

"There is no selling, no giving! How can I sell a lie!"

"But you can't be sure that—"

"You know, and I know, this cup, if it exists, cannot be *the* cup."

"Again, why?" Caffarelli demanded.

"The commonest of sense, Cardinal . . . where, in the history of the Apostles, in the very chronicles of the Church Fathers, is mention made of a cup preserved?" She paused for a reply that never came. "Nowhere . . . it was—unimportant."

"The cup from which our Lord drank!" the chaplain tried and failed to restrain indignation. "How can you say that!"

"Go back to the nursery, young man, and learn that he did *not* drink from the cup."

Scorn from the Marchesa, laughter from her people, mortification to the priest and carefully concealed amusement from Caffarelli.

"Unimportant," she repeated, "because *life* was too earnest, these items were too everyday, too stale to memorialize, too insignificant to clothe with meaning, too far removed from hindsight . . . when Christ was a modern, who would search for antiques? And when they did, it had to be too late . . . that's why we ignored it."

Paresi leaned forward, gaze nailed to an old woman who dared—! "You have no room for surprise that there's a curse upon your house."

Two elements at war: his raging fire against her icy disdain . . . they had more than their reasons.

"Then you're doubly welcome under my roof, Dominican."

"All very interesting, but we're here for a purpose, *ja?*" Bauer preferred the cut and dried of things. And there's Saachi at his side sinking deeper into gloom while the menials behind enjoy themselves too much at our expense . . .

Caffarelli was glad to agree. "With your permission, Madame?"

The chatelaine nodded. The cardinal turned to Saachi, smiled encouragingly and patted his hand, a gesture light as snowfall. "You have a small condition I believe?"

"Only, your Eminence—*ma Donna*," dry in the mouth, marvelling at his temerity in such company, "less light would favour concentration."

The Marchesa signed to Gennaro who quickly doused all but one of the electroliers.

Well chosen; the single efflorescence struck this curious scene an oblique glancing blow and the Treasure, defined and isolated, coruscated all the more, and, more than ever, Renaissance was in the air.

A Verdi opera without music, casting its spell on this tiny

collection of susceptibilities. There is an Italian rapport with signs and portents, finding much in little, from Trajan's spoils to the fetishism of a Veronican handkerchief.

Spell-bound or not, most eyes were drawn to the drama of a gilded bauble summoned to the inquisition.

The Marchesa, inwardly concerned at Galeazzi's absence, kept an outward composure, surveying all with a mouth line lengthened by some secret bout of humour.

The Dominican's last rush of blood to the head had impelled him to rise, to take a few steps away from company he could not bring himself to keep. A gaze restless, divided between the huddle of rustics and those at the table, a *monitore* extraordinary, believing nothing but his own rancorous suspicion of men and motives measured against a credo more extreme than say, Bernardino's or Loyola's or even that of "Peter Martyr".

A brief mumble of prayers provided a ragged overture to the business in hand.

"Signor Saachi," firmly from Caffarelli indicating a chair immediately before the Treasure. Saachi tried miserably to forget hunger—he'd eaten nothing since early morning and his stomach protested too audibly to improve the occasion.

He followed his usual procedure, head bowed, eyes closed, as if in prayer or deep concentrated effort to become a sponge, a receiver for lost wavelengths . . . or even nothing of the kind.

Yet, when he raised his eyes at last to the goldsmith's work, Saachi suggested a dramatically different creature. At will he seemed transformed from unassuming self to some incomparable being instinct with the kind of vibrancy that shimmers like sunlight poured on a forest fire.

The generality recognized as much, suspended its disbelief for the time being, found enough readiness to believe in his apparent capacity to inform out of the depths of his being.

Problematically he *saw* the Aumbry, but who could tell from a blank regard that seemed to pass through it with X-ray indifference?

So far, a stunning performance.

Even a Dominican must strain forward to catch a burgeon of incoherencies, the babble one might posit in earliest Man, starved

66

of means to express a sunset's glory, incomprehensible problems of existence, whimpering infantile as he peered into the nameless night . . .

Thus Saachi, seeming to strive after the unknown, until he found what he was looking for, and a medley of phrases to go with it.

"No greater gift, friend . . . bought with blood . . . I shall not see Tuscany again, but I have seen Jerusalem and fought for her salvation as Christ the redeemer fought for ours . . . I knew a man, a very honest man who showed me many things . . . wonders such as none have looked upon . . . but of all, no greater was this Christly cup . . . he loved me, I say, because I fell down and worshipped what I had no direction of . . . I worshipped in ignorance and he . . . a holy man, pitied my lack and marvelled at my faith in I knew not what . . . smiling, he told me I knelt to Christ's own cup, Giacomo . . . and when I learned of this, my heart leapt with joy . . . and I slew for possession . . . I have paid the price and with my death, the interest . . . take counsel from my misfortune . . . blood will have blood . . . I cannot seek my ransom from hell while I live encumbered with a witness to my sin . . . take it, and let time wash it clean of sacrilege till it be born again to the light of day . . . immaculate, as I hope for my soul . . ."

Well yes, a plausible story, deftly tying dead circumstances into a neat, brown paper parcel, Sellotaped and all.

Intense silence proclaimed the over-awe of the supernatural. Who, apart from the Marchesa, could not be impressed by a tale told by a sensitive, a snatch of monologue come smoking hot from the sound archives of History?

Let the hidden camera range a little.

Bauer believes, heart and soul, that's evident.

Caffarelli never doubted, if the beatific spread of his fine drawn countenance means anything. A performance he could never have dreamt of if he hadn't planned it waking. A tapered finger to that lofty brow, eyes closed, he muttered a little Latinity to relieve overwrought feelings, while his chaplain's eyes seemed to start just a shade vulgarly from his head.

Carrema's doubts were long dead. Now, he buried them,

borrowing his expression from Sasseta's St Francis and the Poor Gentleman. He spoiled the effect by more nearly resembling the pious-looking horse.

The Signorina, seldom given the opportunity, abandoned herself—that is, dropped to her knees praying fit to bust and crossing herself like a semaphoric railway signal gone berserk.

A large white cat chose this moment to wander in, jump on the table, sniff at the Treasure and miaow violently or critically, at which the Signorina broke from her devotions with a comical display of startled surprise.

The Marchesa chuckled. The handful of tenants, expressionless till then, grinned broadly, realizing their mistress was quite unimpressed, after all, by tomfoolery. Much more interesting, this feline diversion, circling the Aumbry before stalking off to where della Paresi stood.

Oddly, head tilted back a little. Curious too, his expression of mingled bafflement and fear. As if he fought to ward off some premonition.

Which proved him to be more "sensitive" than Signor Saachi who now showed signs—like a bad actor after a successful first night—of complacency.

At this point another, minor circumstance raised the drama by a notch or two. The cat, cautiously curious about strangers, approached the Dominican, slowed to a halt, arched its back, and spat viciously before turning tail and rushing out by the way it had come.

The Marchesa viewed with some interest the effect on a man criticized by a cat. No change of expression, except that the eyes flickered from the animal to the Treasure and back again, as though searching for some link between the two. Her barely perceptible nod seemed to say, "Yes, as I thought".

It went unnoticed by Caffarelli and the rest, all agog to see truth verified, proof revealed as the Marchesa prepared to break an ancient family secret.

Caffarelli stood, benign and radiant with satisfaction. It had all gone so well, so convincingly well.

"Madame, I hope you will agree, we have been privileged . . . a voice from the past . . . not lightly to be dismissed."

"Perhaps. But who was Giacomo?"

Caffarelli's smile dissolved into something like perplexity. "Giacomo? Er—your illustrious ancestor who received the cup finally."

"His name was Flambard."

"That's of no significance," tetchily. "The position remains, what is to be the fate of this miracle after Signor Saachi's masterly revelation?"

"You're so sure of it?"

To cliché or not to cliché, the knitting of brows *is* absurd. But Caffarelli's puzzlement was genuine. "I do not understand, lady. You have witnessed—"

"Nothing. I *have* heard how to square a circle."

"Very well then! Assuming its presence and its meaning, do you still contemplate this sale?"

"If I say 'yes' what then?"

"Allow me to reply, Eminence . . . betray our Saviour's chalice into hands stinking of the market place and you must answer with your soul."

Renaissance realms indeed. Where language grows extravagant and pensive Borgias finger rings while high born ladies draw themselves up before a churlish priest too *papabile* for his own good.

"Dantesque, Dominican. You've moved in too many circles."

Caffarelli gently asserted his authority. Things could so easily get out of hand with these two; glance for glance he saw they were at daggers drawn. "Madame, we must depend on you . . ."

Not a brocade or Mantuan silk in sight but striking all the same this woman worth a column in the Almanach de Gotha, resplendent in the workaday clothes of her meanest *capoccia*, passing them all on her way to the glittering gew-gaw, masking a moment of fear before she remembered: all was well, her dispositions were made. Let be what must be.

The tenants and servants pressed closer, even the Dominican must take a step nearer as she clasped the Aumbry pressing once, three times and, as if by a kind of sympathetic magic a drawer in the base slid forward. And there, on a lining of badly faded blue velvet reposed an old and gleaming set of dentures.

Democracy at work. Everyone, high and low, ecclesiastic or rustic, had a glimpse of that staggering anomaly. Reactions differed. None was prepared for what happened next.

A sibilance of unnatural intensity filled that massive space resounding again and once more with two mere syllables.

"*Strega!*"

Even the women among the Deodati servants, reared in modernity and the soul's emancipation, came near to crossing themselves at mention of witches.

The Signorina had no such inhibition.

"My second best—I'd mislaid them for years." Imperturbably, lowering the temperature by degrees. Her people relaxed and laughed outright as they realized how Saachi had led the Church party straight into the trap.

"You will burn in hell for this." Conversationally judicial, all passion and malignancy spent in the force of that single imprecation.

"I pity you, Dominican. Born too late to outdo Sprenger, too soon to see the world's end."

"But why?" Pitiful Caffarelli, hands fluttering, urbanity gone to the four winds, gaze rebounding from "Treasure" to the Marchesa, from Aumbry to Carrema, from a portable altar to Bauer stolidly staring at nothing with an I-told-you-so expression, from that superb tripytch to the Dominican who seemed to know before the devil himself, from that ghastly parody of a relic nestling in its velvety niche to Saachi reflecting on the sure and certain rewards of ice cream after all, and so, reduced to repeating the only question worth his pains. "Why?"

"From confessional to calumny your people have thriven on secrecy, are in love with secrets, their own and other people's. You set out to possess mine . . . well, Caffarelli, you have it. Go back to Rome, make the best of things and be thankful we had no press, no television to expose you and your clumsy tricks."

"But where is the cup!" Caffarelli almost shrieked. Her indictment scarcely bothered him. The Church was continually under unmerited attack these days, but he saw now with della Paresi's eyes, how dangerously she'd duped them all. Saw himself as a laughing-stock in the Cruel City—knew he must answer for it there where they remember eternally and forgive never.

70

Six

AT A SIGNAL from his mistress, Gennaro shepherded the retainers out of the hall. With the doctor's breathless arrival she had no need of witnesses. They left, excited and satisfied by a performance beyond their expectations. A kind of *Il Trovatore* with conjuring tricks . . . too bad about the orchestra. It took time for the babble of excited chatter to sink into distant regions of the Castello.

Gian Galeazzi appeared just when her fortitude needed support. Anger she'd bargained for, but black cowled, white hot dementia is hard for flesh and blood past the prime to withstand.

No one troubled to heed Carrema's muttered "Dottore Galeazzi". Hostility paid all its attention to the Marchesa.

Galeazzi looked none too pleased. He peered angrily around searching for a culprit as it seemed. His eye stopped short at the Dominican.

"I might have guessed . . . Giovanni della Paresi. The man who studied how to do mischief *before* he left his mother's womb. I warned you, Vittoria—never catch a tiger by its teeth."

Hostility briefly transferred to the newcomer. Carrema's censorious expression owed much to Ghirlandaio's *Christ rebuking Judas*. Economically minded, he decided to share it between the doctor and that awful woman.

Galeazzi took off his spectacles with a sideways lunge and began to polish them vigorously, ignoring an assortment of scowls and black looks from those about him. Caffarelli, demoralized by events beyond his control, struggled out of a mild coma, vaguely enquiring "Who is this man?"

The Marchesa told him—once more.

"And 'this man' is extremely angry at being sent on a wild goose chase," Galeazzi added.

Approaching the Treasure he puzzled for a moment over its

71

unlikely contents, then smiled with such muscularity that it very nearly ended as a chuckle.

"So that's what you had in store," he glanced at the Marchesa before snatching another look at the travesty. After all, there wasn't much to chuckle about. He quickly diagnosed the collective reaction and found alarming symptoms of malignancy, one of the incurable diseases.

So much for the patients, so much the worse for the victims, as he explained tersely to the Marchesa. "You're lucky to be alive."

"She is anathema. What has that to do with life?" No hesitation, no consulting with superiors on so grave a matter. With a swishing stride or two he brushed past the doctor and Bauer, snatched the offending dentures and flung them hard against the nearest wall where they fell clattering with an odd tinzle, much like the violent scatter of pearls.

"Hocus-pocus, Dominican, and you know it—and because you know it you're twice at odds with the world you hate and ten times more enchanted by the death you love . . . I knew the old doctor who helped deliver you—he remembered how you damned nearly kicked your mother to death, tantrums before you saw the light of day. 'Watch out!' you were screaming incoherently. She died, but here you are. So, Vittoria—watch out."

"I know what I'm dealing with," calmly.

"Madame, all this is nothing to the point," from Caffarelli who'd found his voice once more. "I wish only to know what has become of the cup."

"Are you begging her to make a fool of you twice over!" the Dominican came perilously close to striking the startled cardinal, came close enough, in any event, to overwhelm him and his faction with a burning sense of outrage.

"*I* can tell you what's become of it! This wretched woman has already sent it to market—to London—to be sold!"

Caffarelli peered about him for scattered wits. Glanced aloft for enlightenment. Was forced back to own resources. "It would make no sense to dispatch an object still in doubt for sale. Surely it's inseparable from this masterpiece."

72

"*What* masterpiece!" He paused, not for effect, but to command agitation. "This is *not* the Deodati Treasure!"

Can a man of peace drop bombshells? Take another look at Giovanni della Paresi and dare to doubt his readiness to toss a grenade for the Faith if it would serve.

Stupidly, Bauer, Carrema and the young priest gaped at what was and was not. Whose sanity was at risk? His or theirs? Caffarelli opened his mouth, closed it, and made one more attempt.

"Fra Giovanni, one might think you had taken leave of your senses."

"In such a world my punishment is to remain sane . . . she had a visitor tonight . . . it had to do with the genuine Treasure—this is a copy."

"That's none of your affair, Paresi." The doctor spoke with a quiet and compelling authority. "The Marchesa didn't ask you to come. You begged to play a part in this ridiculous farce and you might as well abide by the result. All of you."

Caffarelli tried belatedly to take his cue from the Dominican. "I had some idea—" he broke off as Saachi dared to blow his nose louder than the social graces are inclined to allow. He frowned and tried again. "Do you concede the Marchesa's authority to speak in her own house?"

"To what useful purpose?" she wondered. "If your soothsayer had divined a set of dentures I'd deserve your reproaches as you've earned my contempt."

But Caffarelli must finish with at least half a query. "A copy?"

She nodded. "Search through Cellini's unpublished memoirs—if you can find them." And that was all she would say on the subject.

Defeat conceded. In silence Caffarelli bowed and retired trailing the shreds of dignity. Bauer strode out as though he knew all about upshot, the Signorina allied herself with the disorderly faction, favoured the Marchesa with a look Anna Magnani might once have envied, viciously dug Saachi in the ribs short of someone to stab in the back and followed him out with a defiant air. The chaplain turned dolorous shaking his head sadly and processed out with a mincing gait. Carrema, lacking an image to suit a personal crisis, let his sleekabout eye slide past the Marchesa, started to genuflect to the bogus treasure, realized his mistake and hurried away as if to an appointment with aftermath.

Leaving Giovanni della Paresi to return, as it seemed, from tryst with some mind-haunting familiar, a mien cast in a mould of implacable enmity against all the world—and its wife.

He moved with a measured step to stand before a travesty which he contemplated briefly before raising his eyes by a flicker or two to regard the Deodati witch.

"Confessed . . . I did not foresee the possibility." A curious twitch of a scarcely tonsured head brought his attention back to the false quantity. To which he spoke, in the gentlest of tones.

"You haven't won . . . the tactics of little men never yet beat Holy Mother Church's strategy. In time She will subjugate all— and the bonfire will . . . discriminate."

Sublime and superb—if one cares for that sort of thing.

No more words, not another glance to spoil the ghostly exit of a man who *used* silence as some might use a handgun.

The small knot of defeat and dejection lingered outside the bronze doors. Paresi appeared as the Signorina was assuring all and sundry, under no circumstances could she possibly remain under the same roof with vile sacrilege and blasphemy. To her great relief he objected.

"You will remain, Signorina," brusquely.

The cardinals were utterly forgotten as she flashed a kohl-covered glance of admiration and gratitude. So handsome, so vibrant, so dark and menacing. And so lost to a woman's arms.

"If you think it best," meek as a novice threatened with more.

"We need a friend at court."

For the price of that shop-soiled smile she was his forever. Had she known his true thoughts—it would have made little difference . . .

Not one to hover, to confer, he went rapidly down the stairs followed by the cardinals and the rest, dragged, as it were, in his wake.

Condescended to await them at the very centre of a great hall still hung with weapons enough to furnish a company of mercenaries. A worthy backdrop.

"It must be obvious, Eminence, this woman has so far played a game to her satisfaction and our discomfort."

Miserably, Caffarelli couldn't deny it.

"Had I been in her place," the Petacci broke in fervently, "I would have bequeathed such a holy treasure to the Church outright."

His mind still full of false teeth, Bauer, logical to the point of stupidity, frowned uncertainly.

Carrema smiled like a seraph beaming on a favourite cherub.

Paresi nodded, believing none of it. "I shall not return to Rome immediately. But his Holiness must learn of this," he raked the rest with a comprehensive glower. "As you value your hope of salvation, not a word, not a thought of all that's passed." His warning seemed to include Bauer himself, or why should the bulky cardinal shuffle uneasily?

"Signorina, you'll accompany me to my car. There is a matter I wish to discuss."

Rapture can so nearly end in rupture. And who could deny such a masterful servant of the Lord, even if his celibacy must needs respect her chastity?

In a way, the Dominican now disappears from our chronicle. His hand will seem to be evident in much that follows but who will ever know for sure?

Caffarelli, at least, greets his departure with relief. Good riddance to one who was to trouble as the hound to the truffle. Even this unprecedented catastrophe seemed to recede with him and become a bit more tolerable, and Caffarelli could dwell on events as they affected Caffarelli. Began with one who couldn't answer back.

"I had expected better from the Val' d'Aosta, Father Carrema. And I suggest, in future, you research thoroughly before you play at antiquarian scholarship."

How to quail in a split second. Carrema managed it. Stuttered and stammered words of *mea culpa* to end lamely enough: "You see, Eminence, I could not foresee—"

"Certainly, certainly. I accept prevision is in *very* short supply," which reminded him to cast a speculative eye on the totally ignored and wretched "sensitive". "Catania produces a very fine ice cream I recall, *gelato di compagna*. Would we find it in your parlour, Signor Saachi?"

The man mumbled nothing very much—knew it was all up with him. Caffarelli turned back to Carrema.

"You will notify our Office of any scruple of evidence explaining the Marchesa's dreadful behaviour . . . attend most assiduously to her confession."

Carrema stared in total disbelief at this new role being thrust upon him. Hard to explain that he wasn't very good at doing the impossible. "Eminence, she has not attended mass or been confessed since her father died, more than forty years ago."

Caffarelli heard this startling admission as if it had to be Carrema's fault. Plainly, he'd had enough of too much and with a finger-flick of impatience pattered down the broad steps with his companions in tow. Deigned not at all to acknowledge the returning Signorina's breathless promise, "I will do what I can, your Eminence."

Whether her outburst made sense to him or anyone else mattered nothing. The Curial party was gone, leaving the priest and the lady's companion to watch those cardinal red rear-lights accelerating to the vanishing point.

"What did he say?"

"I am bound to secrecy," proud *and* pensive.

By a rascally monk! Well, he wished her joy. He had his own cross to bear and he could have sworn it had turned to lead.

"After all," pensive still, "what's to be done?"

Light spilling from the doorway fell on his surprise and, for no apparent reason he thought of Verdi's Lady Macbeth contemplating the death of someone or other. He felt the chill of the night air briefly invading his heart. For one unrepeatable moment Carrema experienced the wisdom of a visionary sage.

"Everything has been done. From now on, Signorina, only consequences can flow. And with those I have nothing to do."

Wishing her goodnight with a lowered glance he set off on the long road home, like a man who's pawned a load of mischief, lost the ticket, and had it returned to him by an officious busybody.

The Signorina returned to the hall, out of temper despite her

76

understanding with della Paresi. Or because of it. His fascination was all very well, but would it pay the rent? Dangerous, to promise princes more than she, a beggar woman, dependent on another's charity, could perform. Not their discomfiture bothered her, in secret she could relish the joke played on men not noticeably less stupid because they wore birettas; but she knew how to suffer the torments of St Lawrence at thought of so much wealth concentrated in one old woman's hands merely by selling a few trivial bagatelles.

She began to ascend the stairs—*la scala*—her thoughts drifted away to a never-to-be-forgotten, never-to-be-repeated visit by an eighteen-year-old—La Scala—so many years, so much hard-saved money for admission . . . and there was that Cerberus Gennaro, hovering at the door to the *Sala di Giustizia*! She bit her lip with the force of vows imposed on her by life: ignominy, poverty and frustration, went another way, thinking of telephones, to her quarters in the oldest, most romantic part of the *castello*.

"You really must be mad!" this from Galeazzi to the Marchesa.

Carrema's outburst on the little bridge had expressed the self-same idea, but the difference between them! The doctor's explosive opinion had to do with friendship and real concern for another's well-being.

He'd listened in stunned silence as she sketched vividly enough, in a mixture of French and Italian, the whole scenario previous to his arrival.

He could understand and applaud the simple unmasking of that mountebank Saachi, but to fool all of them, all of the time, over the cup and the copy was pushing an appointment with fate on the eleventh hour to an unpleasant conclusion. He'd scarcely allowed her to finish before pronouncing, angrily and with traces of a stutter, on her state of mind.

Well, the Deodati blood was never less than up. In fact, the Marchesa "drew herself up haughtily" as some will *still* insist on saying.

To tell the truth, she thrust hands deep into her old sheepskin's pockets and pouted dreadfully. "You weren't here to stop me."

"I wasn't meant to be! Vittoria, do you know what stop-at-nothing means? Paresi!"

"They meddled in what was none of their business—through that stupid Carrema of course. Had to be taught a lesson."

"By dangling the cup before their covetous noses—for heaven's *sake*!"

"I'm selling *a* cup. They wanted *the* cup. Nothing said about *another* cup. If the one in Genoa is genuine why should they bother?"

Galeazzi dismissed the argument, the logic and very nearly the question. "If there were a dozen cups it doesn't alter the fact—a suit of reinforced asbestos wouldn't protect you against that man."

She could appreciate his concern enough to forget her satisfaction at spoiling their game, cared too much to see him upset on her account.

"Well, it's all over. This time tomorrow the Deodati Home for Handicapped Children will be safe in London. Sarinan was here tonight."

That cheered him up no end. "You put a lot of faith in that rogue."

"Not much. He has enough in himself."

". . . I wonder if he knows of della Paresi?"

"Why should he?" sharply.

"Something our Dominican said . . . how did he *know* you'd already 'sent it to market'?"

"I—don't see that it matters."

". . . I think I do. After all—he knew this was a copy."

They regarded each other awhile, swapping significances as it were, till she was bound to smile away misgivings and, in her coarse, peasant way, the Marchesa slapped the good doctor on the back.

"Gian, *mon cher*, what is this room of stupid dimensions called?"

"The *Sala di Giustizia*, I believe."

"Well, justice was done here tonight—and I have a long day ahead of me tomorrow."

"Good. I take the hint." He paused, unwilling to sour her

cumulating pleasure at thought of the happiness her death would one day bring. "It's worth remembering Monsignore, your nephew's, verdict on della Paresi. 'A man who has never looked at his image in a mirror'."

She shrugged, "That's not particularly imaginative—even for poor Carlo."

"More than you think," gravely. "It implies a man who is afraid of nothing but to find his image is not there."

The delicate chime of the ancient clock from the Battista Alberti campanile deferentially joined in the dying moments of their converse.

Galeazzi took his leave, gruffly advising the Marchesa—to her infinite amusement—to bolt the Castello doors well before the darkest hours.

PART II

LONDON

Seven

THE DETAILS OF Sarinan's journey to London are explicit, implicit, confusing and not exactly reliable.

It's believed he drove back to Turin, stayed overnight, oddly enough, in the Hotel Castello on the Via Rovello, caught an early morning flight to Zurich and had himself taxied to Crédit Suisse on the Bahnhofstrasse. He spent an hour with bank officials complying with the formalities needed to give him legal custody before contracting with a security firm to pack and convoy the Treasure to Zurich airport.

He took lunch, *rösti* and *geschnatzeltes* apparently, spent an hour or so in the bar of the Bergamo hotel, loudly ordering Cardinal lager, was seen in animated conversation with a dark-haired man, described as "possibly English" by a barman. He left in time to board a flight for London.

Air hostesses attending to his section, Executive Class, were quite definite he'd shown signs of nervousness. Trained to recognize symptoms, they recalled frequent uneasy glances, alerting them to the possibility of trouble, "but nothing came of it, thank goodness".

At Heathrow customs officials also noted his "strained behaviour", took greater pains to discover all was in order. They knew Sarinan well. A regular traveller. He left the airport after arranging with a second security firm to freight the treasure to Peachum's punctually at ten the following morning.

A taxi took him to his pied-à-terre in Chelsea, rented permanently for his many flying trips to the capital but, for some reason, and *very* obviously, he changed his mind. The relief porter remembered him entering the foyer, and recognized him as a regular. He was about to greet him but . . .

"He just stood at the door, looking white and shaken as you might say. I don't think he heard me call 'good evening'. Just turned on his heels and went out without another word."

In fact, Sarinan stepped straight into another taxi and was driven to Grosvenor Square from where he eventually found his way, walking presumably, to Park Lane's Dorchester Hotel.

Here, again, he was not unknown. Occasionally he used the hotel as a setting to impress clients during some complicated business deal.

He arrived there somewhat wet and dishevelled—it had been raining heavily all day—carried a minimum of luggage and booked a room for the night. The Desk could hardly forget an interesting snatch of conversation as Sarinan glanced restlessly about him at the crowded foyer.

"I hope your security's good."

"More than adequate, Mr Sarinan."

"I'm being followed."

"I hope not, sir."

"I've got to let them know."

"Who, sir?"

"The cops—how do I get in touch?"

"I hope that won't be necessary."

"That guy who's just come in—he was on the plane! I tell you he—"

"He's just gone out again—as you see."

"I'm damn sure I'm right. Send the floor waiter up—I'll eat in my room."

"Very good, sir."

Confusing? Unreliable? Certainly it's an itinerary composed of the true and the false of fact and fiction—and that's life.

We, to some extent, have the benefit of hindsight. Cherry has no such luck. How, in London, should his dexter know what someone's sinister is doing somewhere in Italy? As for those indelible impressions of an increasingly frightened man . . .

Of all this the Inspector has not the faintest idea when he's called to the Assistant Commissioner's office some time after Sarinan showed up at Peachum's. Nor could Sir John know so very much. It was all, he felt, rather vague. Not orders, but a recommendation from the up-line to take note *was* just a little too official to be ignored. As he explained.

"Sledgehammers and peanuts probably. Sit down, Cherry,

84

and kindly remove that scowl from your not particularly prepossessing features."

"I can't be held responsible for my face and the scowl may have a connection with toothache."

Not a "sir" in sight. Does that suggest a Cherry in decline, insubordinate to the point of don't care, no man's master but his own, a *maverick*? Well, yes, it does.

There's more than a grain of truth in spit and sawdust, as they say. So, look on Cherry as one heartily sick of searching out wickedness in a world surfeited with the stuff, and that's nearer the mark.

But, and this was Sir John's strongest card against an eccentric who sends in his resignation on Michaelmas and Lady Day regularly as rent, he can be re-animated, re-motivated, and very nearly rejuvenated by a case fractionally out of the ordinary, especially if discretion is more desirable than any other part of valour.

Sir John knew better than to trot out the old cliché, even if it *was* one of those; so he looked grave, fiddled with that disreputable pipe, fingered the discreditable ball point on the end of its chain and seemed to wonder how else he could enthuse the miserable looking bugger facing him.

He was unsure why the crass inspiration took him in such a non-sequiturial way, would spend a few nights of wakefulness trying to establish the connection between peculiar 999 calls and Cherry's personal well-being.

"Ever thought of getting married again, Cherry?" flicked off the cuff as it were.

Cherry stared his surprise, then bridled, forgot his toothache, started to say something like "It's none of your damned business" but it was far too late. His expression said it nicely, very nicely indeed.

"Interested in the welfare of my officers, that's all." Stiff as starch the A.C. sounded—and looked.

"Thank you, sir," cleverly, in the 'umble tones of Uriah knocked all of a heap by such noble and affecting condescension. "But I *do* think marriage is *rather* a drastic remedy for toothache. I find Boots' oil of cloves cheaper and just a bit more effective."

The retort magnificent it was. That is, Sir John felt insulted, rebuffed, baffled, outraged and, well, thoroughly put down. It made things no better that he'd damned well asked for it.

"Suit yourself," gruffly, as he carefully memorized every word for his wife's delectation with the dinner cheese and biscuits that evening. Lady June had a soft spot for Cherry, God knows why. The deuce of it was he'd find himself sharing the joke—against himself of all people!

"Let's get on with it. It isn't much, but then again—"

"One of those," Cherry supposed.

"For heaven's sake, man! You're supposed to be too intelligent to mess about with clichés. Yes, one of those—but this one's a piece of cake . . . what do you know about the Dotearti Treasure?"

Cherry adjusted swiftly. The Deodati Treasure—quite so. Not that Cherry was slumped in his chair, but he seemed to sit straighter than usual. "I know it exists. And I think it's supposed to contain a cup. Something to do with the Last Supper."

"But that's a painting isn't it?"

"I mean the original."

Sir John's mystification was comical and complete. "Is that a fact?"

"Er—the supposition is a fact—yes."

"You could knock me down with a feather—how do you know that?"

Cherry looked evasive. "I—I've been reading about it—there was an item in the paper and—"

"Reading." Solicitous as senna-pods. "Cherry, are you sure it isn't too much reading that gives you toothache?"

The Inspector opened his mouth and left it that way. He simply couldn't think of a reply.

"It *may*," grudgingly, "help to have some background but I doubt it. We've had two calls from an individual called Sarinan."

"Safik Sarinan?"

Sir John glanced up from his notes. "Yes. You know him?"

"I know of him. He's about one of the most audacious characters in the world of antiques and fine art. A kind of roving commission operator—brilliant, but unscrupulous."

"He's in a blue funk somewhere in London. It seems he came over a couple of days ago bringing this treasure thing with him.

First he phoned us from the Dorchester, then he rang again from Peachum's. They're handling the sale."

"Both followed up of course."

"Both. The officers concerned made comforting noises and that was the end of it. Or would have been if Peachum's hadn't phoned to say they were worried."

"I see."

"Apparently he told them he was going straight to his hotel."

"The Dorchester?"

"No. He stopped there for one night, then moved out. The idea was, he would ring Peachum's about an hour after leaving to confirm he was safely at a new address. That was two days ago."

"But he didn't ring back."

". . . how do you know?"

"I mean, if he didn't, is that significant?"

"Only if you accept Chairman Condamine's opinion that Sarinan was in a very bad way—quote, close to hysteria, unquote." Cherry nodded thoughtfully and said he wasn't surprised. Into that mild comment was packed some days of research by his intuition into a certainty that the much publicized Treasure spelled trouble. Nothing, these days, that intuition concluded, be it a man of no consequence, or a priceless artifact of little importance, carefully coated with charisma, or smeared with mediacoloured aura could possibly escape trouble.

To begin with, Peachum's had made sure of its future by going vulgarly public, press-ganging journalists into puffing its "historical importance", not so much to dazzle a public always eager to gape at week-end wonders, as to alert the world fraternity of megamillionaires and museum bosses to the importance they should attach to this superbity.

Nothing missed. After Cherry's "thoughtful nod" came a lengthy silence. The A.C. fidgeted a bit with his comforter, the briar, replaced it on the desk with a grimace before regarding Cherry with no great change of expression.

"You're probably asking yourself, why should that old bastard disturb my morning slump over the crossword on the strength of two phone calls from some foreigner sporting a persecution complex?"

"Yes."

Eyebrows hitched to the heavens. "Cherry, I'm all for honesty but you do tend to carry it too far."

Cherry mumbled something which Sir John took for an apology.

"Danvers thought I should know after he got word of an anonymous call early this morning. A man with what's described as a faint Latin accent said exactly this: If you have a fraud squad you would do well to look twice at the Deodati Treasure. He then rang off."

Cherry regarded the A.C. sombrely, his tooth problem quite forgotten in a heated moment of rubbing two and two together.

"A long distance call?"

Sir John nodded.

"Rome?"

"Rome. Yes."

"And the Fraud Squad—?"

"No. They're not looking into it. You are. And that's all I have. You can find the 999 officers can't you? You're supposed to be a detective."

"That," a truculent Cherry's response, "is why the world in general and this country in particular is falling apart."

"Oh? And what's that supposed to mean?"

"It means incivility is the downward thrust of the upward crust."

"And that includes me!"

Cherry sighed. "Sack me if you like. I could do with three million friends."

Not on your life, said Sir John to no-one but Sir John. Not after comprehensively smashing that video ring . . . all the same, he's going down a rugged hill somewhere in his mind. I'll try being nice to the arrogant swine.

"Nicotine works."

". . . I'm sorry?"

"Toothache. Smoke two gaspers in quick succession."

". . . thank you, sir. I'll try that."

Miss Fitt sniffed. "Glad to see you're still in one piece, Inspector."

Cherry bore down on her, all guns blazing. "No you're not!

You can't wait for the day when bits of me come flying out of that door followed by him with my head stuck on the end of his ball-point and you clumping around doing the dance of the seven onion skins!"

"Living in the past, Inspector. We only use carbon papers."

The door slammed mightily on doughty Miss Fitt but she cowered in her chair all the same.

"How's the tooth?" Duff's anxious enquiry was well-intentioned. Cherry in a foul mood and plagued by tooth trouble could make life—difficult. A pint of oil poured over the lot might help.

"Two cigarettes. One after the other."

"Ah!" Total mystification.

"That's what he said." Bitterly, from a man totally at odds with all and most of the sundries, lax at his desk as a sack of Seville oranges, plagued by a mere abscess and the merer thought of humanity. Duff knowing a no-win situation when he saw one, coughed delicately and edged towards the door.

"Where do you think you're going?"

"Er—solitude might help. I'll come back later."

"Don't bother . . . two he said—why not three?"

Duff hesitated, then found a pack on the cluttered desk, took one and lit it. "You'd better start now. I've heard it helps."

Cherry eyed the gesture, relented and smiled apologetically at a man doing his level best. "I'm sorry, Duff. Take no notice. Just a passing cloud."

He inhaled deeply, stared into space for long enough to order disordered thoughts, extrapolating things of which he had, at that moment, no real understanding.

Duff, long-time friend and collaborator, watched his superior carefully, more concerned by deeper portents than present surface irritability.

The last dirty business had scarred them both. No one involved with a skein of porn video merchants escaped scot free. Not coppers, not the child murdered by a father bestialized by their foul products.

Bad enough, but what really depressed him, Duff knew, was his certainty that sociologists, drugged by their misconceived theories, would spring to the defence of a pernicious industry, insist, in the trial to come, that scenes of horrific, mindless, sadistic violence couldn't possibly have a "quantifiable effect on a man's inhuman behaviour to man—or *kids*"!

That aching tooth could just as well be a symptom of an anguished heart for a man who'd once believed justice meant retribution—especially where conscience was dead.

In time, the inspector gave the best gist he could manage of Sir John's meagre summary. To Duff it hardly seemed a matter for special treatment and finally, that's what he said.

Cherry nodded, "My first thought—but Danvers doesn't nudge Sir John unless someone nudges him—and that's without an 'anonymous'."

"What gives you second thoughts?"

"A very frightened man is nothing uncommon—especially nowadays, but connect it with a call from—faraway places and you've got indistinct possibilities of *some*thing untoward."

"Especially if the frightened man goes missing."

"Not that I've the faintest notion of what we're supposed to discover."

Duff muttered about carts and horses. Cherry didn't think that was helpful. There were circumstances. Which ones in particular the sergeant wondered.

"The Deodati Treasure to begin with. Peachum's to end with. A firm with that kind of reputation does some in-depth homework on authenticity—so who questions it—and why? Sarinan turns up in a blue funk and then appears to disappear. Why?"

"Natural causes? Why should Peachum's worry?"

"When one's trying to sell a multi-million pound eye-opener, a spanner in the works can hardly be welcome."

"If they know about the Italian spanner."

"Danvers must have mentioned. I mean, they're entitled to know."

"So, panic at Peachum's."

"Which is where we'd better start, I imagine."

"Now?"

"No time like it. And we might even see a Post Impressionist you could bid for. Just the thing for Marjorie's birthday."

Duff struggled into a raincoat two sizes too small for comfort.

"Funny thing, I used to think Post Impressionists were those distressed gentlefolk who wrote begging letters."

"How very imaginative," Cherry murmured.

Duff, not a bit put out knew, as they quit the Yard, that he'd forgotten his toothache and was very nearly in tune with the times—if only for the time being.

Eight

DUFF DROVE PRIM and proper, to the rather splendid premises occupied for two and three-quarter centuries by Peachum's, an exclusive firm of auctioneers that had everything—or had had everything—except a Royal Warrant, for obvious reasons.

Congleton Street was one of those two-sided vistas of rare pre-Georgian design that has tourists from California to Kyoto staggering, with reason and wide-eyed admiration.

Preserved by and reserved for the *haut monde* it remains a place of see and be seen, mostly for the well-heeled, thick-souled *jeunesse dorée*, the Prince Otto von Grottos and sons of Supermarketeers who've already left their mark . . . their molls all have a look-alike affinity with Diana; in fact, they're part of an élite of which, we, the lower levels of this yob get-on-your-bicycle-and-stay-there society, had better be proud.

Not that you'll find Marks and Spencer's *here*, or MacDonalds, or Curry's; only saddlers By Appointment, a sort of Gunter's, Constance Spry's and all that sort of thing don't y'know?

No room for downmarket hucksters in Congleton Street. Can't be, when Peachum's, for example, had four of the frontages knocked into one vast emporium before anyone could read the Town and Country Planning Act which didn't exist anyway. As business burgeoned it secured a fifth adjoining property early this century until now its corridors and general ramifications seem more endless than ever.

A succession of rooms and connecting passages leads to the holy of holies, a vast auction room in which Josiah Peachum first knocked down the household effects of "ladies and gentlemen of quality made indigent by the vicissitudes of life". (Nell Gwynn was an early client.) Wily as a Charles James Fox and wide as the Mall, Josiah founded a repository, providing a rich reserve of valuable articles, unclaimed, unpaid for, or simply unwanted, which were processed through his sales at 100 per cent profit. Wider yet, and wider, were his successors until . . .

But so old-established is Peachum's, buttressed by its blue-chip quotation in 'Change, so weighed down with know-how pickled in *gravitas*, it easily rides all criticism and competitors' sour-grape accusations of being the highest fence in the business over which the Law standing on a chair on a table can't see.

True or false is not to our purpose. That Peachum's is currently in ferment, couched in well-bred undertones, ought to be.

Crises are not uncommon but the present affair concerning the Aumbry is proving out of the ordinary, even for Peachum's. The sale is only ten or so days away and suddenly the Treasure is suspect and Sarinan, its legal custodian, has disappeared into thin air.

Into this atmosphere, lush as a hot-house, hushed as an undertaker's on a go-slow, past "dead" items of superb pedigree giving Peachum's that unique lived-in feeling of a Pharaoh's tomb, walked Cherry and Duff preceded by a yellow plush flunkey garbed in early Peachum style even to the powdered peruke and buckled shoes. For sheer showmanship this world-renowned feature of the place put it one step behind Madame Tussaud's and two ahead of Sotheby's.

On the upper floors they read the doors in the many passages, name dropping the Byzantine, the Pre-Columbian, Art Nouveau, English 18th Cent. and many more scattered throughout that rabbit warren. As they passed Fine Art—Religious, a young precious dressed in the height of Lombard Street Deco rushed impetuously into their lives tossing an agonized squeal over his shoulder to some left-behind.

"I *told* Jeremy—it's infinitely worse than the Filippo Lippi fracas!"

And he scuttled away leaving Duff frowning at what he took to be foul language. Cherry decided he was Pre-Raphaelite with a soupçon of pretensions to the Directoire—not bad for one who'd never before set eyes on the expert from Ormolu and Blue John.

Duff returned to a state of bemusement. Had never seen the likes of their yellow-liveried guide snapping its white kid gloves over bare knuckles as it pavanned ahead of them. Maybe once, in a film with Stewart Grainger—but that was years ago . . .

"What's it supposed to be?" hovered on his lips and luckily stayed there.

They came to rest before an imposing doorway on the second floor: pedimented and architraved in Georgian mode, white on powdered blue. Lounging to one side, another, considerably younger, yellow-plushed attendant tried hard and miserably failed to look the part. A few words passed between them before the first turned, superciliously snapping his gloves, and went stately down the stairs.

"You the fuzz?" came from under a wig sizes too big.

Cherry nodded.

"Lucky sods. Wish I was in your shoes, then."

"Whose shoes are *you* in?" Duff wondered.

"One's Boswell's the other's Johnson's far as I'm concerned. Buckles on the bastards I *ask* you."

The young forlorn explained he was on a Youth Opportunities Con.

"Passes the time," Duff supposed.

"Yeah. I spend most of it wondering how I'm broad'nin' Britain's industrial base that old cow's always on about."

"You'd better announce us."

"Oh yeah. What was it again?"

Cherry told the Y.O. recruit exactly. He flung open the door and announced:

"There's two C.I. Dicks to see yer. Inspector Duff and Sergeant Cherry."

The door closed behind them with the faintest hint of a sigh and "what a bloody carry-on".

Cherry's initial impression: borrowed opulence. Everything in the Chairman's office—excepting the light fittings—belonged to other periods, other countries and probably, other people. The rosewood Louis Quinze desk and a Saryg carpet from Bokhara will suggest the rest of the inventory.

To which period the man behind the desk belonged seemed problematic. Somehow he brought a whiff of Petticoat Lane to his mid-sixties, his baldness, his courtly air; but one can say with certainty, Mr Condamine had more than maintained Peachum's at its high pitch of perfection.

With his kind of administrative ability, a knack of choosing the best experts for the many departments, his superficial knowledge of every valuable object of art about him mattered not.

For the moment, anxiety predominated, a puckered brow spoiled the overall effect, but he waved them to suspect Chippendales with an extensive gesture of grace proper to dukes or old-time floor-walkers.

"This is a sorry business, Inspector," he confided to Duff.

"Vice is versa, I'm afraid. Your—young man got it wrong," Cherry explained.

"He'll have to go," darkly. "Only yesterday he announced Her Highness Princess Maria Charlottenberg von Micklen Hiundloe der Stadde Griesewold am Farschneckken Gratz-Krappe, as 'some German bird'." Mr Condamine recovered and turned his attention to Cherry with a nicely balanced apology to both.

"I take it you have not yet located Mr Sarinan, Inspector?"

Cherry conceded the fact.

"His disappearance is very inconvenient and not a little disturbing."

"Why, exactly?"

"The sale is ten days away. If things should go wrong . . ." he contemplated the awful prospect which seemed to be hovering somewhere over their heads.

"Do you have reservations about the Treasure itself?"

"Good heavens, no. The Marchesa is not in the business of foisting spurious objets d'art on anyone, least of all Peachum's."

The very idea! And who doesn't know about mysterious phone calls from Rome, then, and who's expecting me to tell him, Cherry mentioned to himself.

"I think," he said, "we'd better have a recap, Mr Condamine. I'll explain later why we're taking this gentleman's disappearance seriously indeed. It might be helpful to have a full account of your dealings with him over this treasure—and any details you can recall—his state of mind particularly."

"It may take some time."

"As much as you care to spare me."

Condamine, charmed by signs of *noblesse oblige* nodded graciously, sat back with closed eyes to order his remembrance of things past.

The Treasure, extracted with the greatest care from its packing case, the wrappings removed, rested on a fine *bonheur de jour* table imported from the Peachum reserves for the occasion.

Whatever merit it possessed seemed to present the three onlookers with a conflict of reactions. For Condamine, magisterial at his desk and just as gravely ignorant, hands arched to frame the prize, it amounted to just that: a prestigious acquisition snatched from predatory competitors. Of course he recognized it had an intrinsic value but preferred roughly to translate it into seven millions plus, ten per cent from the seller, eight from the buyer. Business first, connoisseurship—eventually.

J. H. Cuthers, head of the Mediaeval department, contrasted badly. Only appeared to be stunted because he was down on his knees like an adoring Magus. The silence had a reverential quality thanks to Cuthers alone, a lean, wispy man whose readiness to enthuse far outweighed his scholarship. (He was known to his colleagues as the *auto-da-fay* and not without cause.) A rare work of art released in him a tremendous and unquestioning admiration, simply because it *was* rare.

Romanticists can afford to respond with effortless ease to antiquity materializing before their very eyes. Experts can't.

Fortyish and fair, eyes blue and slightly prominent, hands constantly in motion, nervous and birdlike, lips moving as if recalling a half-forgotten litany.

Positively no relation to Sarinan who stood aside like a showman, appraising with benefit of long experience others' reaction to reality; but he had a deeper preoccupation having most to do with Sarinan, his increasingly complex connection to that magnificent medley presently outfacing him. Tric-trac! Nothing more; a made thing of wood, gilt and mineralogical throw-outs; nothing more, the gleam in a psychollector's eyes, nothing more but, suppose life turns all of a sudden serious . . .

"It's magnificent." Cuthers breathed uncritical admiration as if he'd never seen the thing before, determined to infect others. Aimed a dumb appeal at Condamine.

"Very fine, very fine indeed," Condamine agreed with the faintest hint of censure. Bad business ploy to flatter in a third and very interested party's presence. He quickly changed the subject.

"You have all the documentation, Mr Sarinan?"

"I have it here—including the Marchesa's letter. You—you'd better read it first."

Condamine frowned, sensing that all was not as it should be. A *je ne sais quoi* air of ill-concealed anxiety about the fellow . . .

"Is anything wrong, Mr Sarinan?"

Sarinan, fascinated it seemed by Cuthers' extravagant behaviour, transferred his attention with an effort, freed a lower lip from clenching teeth and scowled his doubts of Condamine's intelligence.

"Of course there's something wrong! Sarinan is in danger." He was inclined, at critical moments in the conduct of his affairs, to invest himself as it were in the grammar of royalty. "Sarinan guarantees this is Etruscan", "Sarinan never lies". "We will not take less than a million."

So, "I tell you, Sarinan is in danger!"

Cuthers continued to gaze raptly at the Treasure, too far gone to be concerned with trivialities. Condamine smiled knowingly. Sarinan's verbal extravagancies were generally accepted coin of the never-never realm. Everyone knew Sarinan.

"You exaggerate I'm sure," soothing as cough mixture.

Had Condamine taken leave of his senses? How could *any*one exaggerate the paramount question of Sarinan's safety and well-being? Certainly not Sarinan, or what was the world worth? Bloody British! He meant in his thoughts—these sanguine British, but his English, though excellent, lacked finesse. "No exaggeration! Sarinan is followed. From the moment I boarded my plane at Zurich—to London—to my hotel. I am changing my hotel . . . even now there will be someone out there—waiting. I know it."

Genuine fear communicates itself. Delusions revenge themselves by exploiting others. That something beyond mere words got through to Condamine. Even Cuthers managed a desultory glance.

"What evidence do you have?"

"That!" A sudden pointing of the finger at the Treasure was pure Wilkie Collins.

Condamine frowned. A man's life—one thing. A business opportunity—another. He wrinkled his nose at this sudden whiff of brimstone.

"*You* accompanied it from Zurich. It didn't follow you, Mr Sarinan."

And *merde* to British logic! "You don't understand. In my Zurich hotel I am drinking an innocent Cardinal, this man I never see before in my whole life calls me 'Mr Sarinan'. I think nothing of it. I am known. Why not? But when I think twice, I remember that *I* know the thousands of people who know me. This man I do not know."

Too bad! So much else to discuss and none of it concerned Sarinan as such.

"Well then?" With mustered patience.

"Don't you see—he began to discuss the Deodati Treasure. *Congratulated* me on handling the sale of the century, always with the smile of *double entendre, vous comprenez?*"

Condamine held up a hand, anxious to prevent the parley degenerating into French.

"Cause for satisfaction, Mr Sarinan. We have made it our business to internationalize awareness of this sale. Was this man an American?"

"That's the crunch! His English was excellent, but Sarinan does not smatter in a dozen languages to be fooled by pretenders. He had to be Italian, black hair, black eyes and what do you call—a schwarz complexion."

"I can only repeat, the Treasure is hardly shrouded in secrecy."

"I grab your point—but he seemed to know as much about it as I do." Sarinan paused to let this sink in, to mop his brow and generally cope with agitation.

"If everything is in order we have nothing to fear."

Sarinan bridled, badly resenting the "we" when "you" might have been kinder to his personal well-being. "You don't know everything already, any more than I did when *she* told me, *she* gave me the secret, *she* showed me."

The notion of a "secret" got through at last, strengthening Condamine's perception that perhaps all was not quite as it should be. He took the letter flourished by Sarinan, and read with growing alarm, that he might possibly be aware of a small mystery attaching to the Treasure, that it was a matter of indifference to her except that the "bauble" had been given a recent importance beyond its merit, but if an examination of the accompanying photostats and Mr Sarinan's explanation might lead Peachum's to feel it could enhance the Treasure's sale potential, she hoped to hear of a successful disposal bringing honour and profit to "your house and mine".

Condamine stared from letter to Peachum in total bewilderment. "What is this, Mr Sarinan? The Marchesa never mentioned a—a bauble till now. Can you explain?"

Briefly Sarinan did so.

"And *she* has never seen this cup?"

"The Marchesa has said."

"Why not?"

Inspiration came to the agent's aid. "Because it is a telesma—you understand?"

Condamine nodded uncertainly, glanced at the letter and quoted aloud, "A relic, authentic only as far as it goes?"

"Do you doubt her word—or mine. The prize is exceptional or why do I risk my life? I am followed because of this thing."

"Of course. No one doubts—" he broke off, utterly at a loss. Here was news from nowhere—and how did one come to terms with a breathtaker of such magnitude. By now, Cuthers had wrested his attention from the triptych to follow an intriguing development with some interest.

"Cuthers, here's Mr Sarinan informing us we're possessed of the Holy Grail."

"With respect, I don't think he quite said that. The cup used at the last supper is something else."

"You mean—you mean the one—" not religiously inclined, but overwhelmed by the prospect of a holy jackpot, Condamine could go no further. He puffed a little, cleared his throat a great deal and glanced apprehensively at the Treasure as if white rabbits might suddenly pop out for a bit of exercise. Thank God it wasn't the Holy Grail. Irrationally he felt *that* possibility would be the death of him.

"Do you know anything about this, Cuthers?" Severely, an implication that *some*one had to be responsible.

"Cobwebs of rumour, nothing more. I know the Deodatis kept very quiet about it. Of course the Genoese version is more widely known but no better authenticated."

"You mean there's *more* than one?" Condamine's eyes were outstanding to a dangerous degree. In a mad, mercifully fleeting moment he saw the whole supper service in Leonardo da Vinci's wall-to-wall representation gathered up in the white tablecloth and hurriedly sold to the first bidder as a job lot . . . there could be cups and platters all over the place. And the irreproachable name of Peachum might . . .

Just in time reality took over from feverish speculation. "You say it's in there?"

Sarinan nodded impatiently.

"Then we'd better—you've seen it of course."

"No."

Portrait of a man now utterly out of control of normally disciplined features. "Not!"

"Why should I have? It is only to be opened in your presence. Once you've taken the steps to verify—"

"That could mean weeks—months!"

The sale was less than a fortnight away. What in heaven's name was the Marchesa thinking of, saddling him with something stuck like a bookmark between the New Testament's pages!

"It might help if we could see it," Cuthers suggested.

Condamine looked as wilted as the out-of-season carnation drooping in his button-hole. He gestured in an uncertain manner. "Mr Sarinan?"

But Sarinan had eyes only for Sarinan's predicament. "If I do not show up here tomorrow you will be good enough to contact the cops."

"Yes, yes," irritably. "I'm sure you have nothing to fear."

"*I* cannot afford to be so sure," he drew a finger across his throat as though to illustrate the high cost of living. Condamine's resentment broke the bounds at last.

"Mr Sarinan, I must remind you, we have a contract with the Marchesa to dispose of a property for which you are an intermediary and we recognize you as such. But there is nothing in our

100

agreement requiring us to guarantee your safety. Now, since you *are* here, shall we proceed?"

Sarinan shuffled ungraciously to heel; crossed to the Treasure, folded various panels including those forming the triptych into the semblance of a scintilla-covered box, then applied the faintest pressure according to the Marchesa's instructions: he stepped back, mildly surprised by the sudden thrust of a drawer seemingly propelled violently from behind by some cunning illusion.

Even Condamine leaned to the mystery like a child drunk on pantomime. Undeniable the element of stagecraft, the conjuring of an expectant air prompting all eyes to focus on centuries of secrecy and benign neglect.

It reposed, coated with the green of Greece, on a scrap of Milanese velvet, time worn and colour-tired to the point of exhaustion. Cut from the cast-off blue gown of some Isabella d'Este?

Reposed, or lay negligently aside, jolted from its niche. Sarinan reached forward to right it, then, as an afterthought, he drew back the flaps and the hinged top, placing the cup before the triptych with its trinity of exquisitely painted scenes from the Everlasting Drama.

Which came alive, as it seemed, in that poor presence of a drinking vessel, shaped in dull bronze, to a recollection of cupped hands, surpassingly beautiful in its simplicity, mute with the message that it was deep in time, had been present, had touched a secret.

Almost a shared impression. For an unrepeatable moment not one of the trio doubted its origin, the high significance of the word made material.

"You see," said Sarinan on the sly, "the Marchesa did not exaggerate—the Deodatis concealed no fiction for so many years."

Condamine nodded solemnly, but his wily mind was elsewhere, careering and cavorting among percentages and potentials. Enhanced value, new laurels for Peachum's, New Year's honours list, security requirements, P.R. mobilization, new catalogues— even perhaps a separate booklet; metaphorically, Condamine was busily polishing the sunshine with Brasso . . . Sarinan, a hard bargaining romantic streaked with Middle Eastern mysticism, nervously regarded the tangible reason for any man's death. Men would kill for that holy hotch-potch, which bothered him; some would gladly sacrifice themselves for the sake of its contents—which didn't bother him one bit. He would like to have explained this to the Marchesa but it was far too late for *sagesse*.

Without rhyme or reason Cuthers believed. In the beginning there's always a word. When it's made as manifest as, let's say, an unearthed telesma, emotion takes over, overwhelms and makes a fool of reason.

Cuthers believed.

Condamine, his thoughts turning more commercial by the minute, watched Sarinan lift the cup between his hands and sniff vigorously like a Benedictine exploring a liqueur for an elusive odour of sanctity.

"It stinks," he pronounced firmly, "of antiquity. As to its origin I don't see why not."

Condamine agreed in silence, still regarding Sarinan who'd replaced the cup and closed the drawer. He turned to the Chairman, not missing the cash-register beam in his eye, the mouth slightly open for business.

"The sky's the limit," he promised.

"I don't see it," Condamine argued as a matter of principle.

"I do," Sarinan contradicted. It rather reminded of a TV hackney show starring those ancient comedians, Wheeler and Dealer. "Sarinan's life is at risk—so—the sky," he pointed upwards before explaining.

"You have there the copy of a letter written seven hundred years ago to the father of the Deodatis. That is what began this rumour. The Marchesa includes the original letter in the deal."

Sarinan handed over the rest of the documentation before snatching another look at what promised to be his greatest coup. He turned to Condamine with a furtive, indirect eye.

"When I say I am followed, I mean it is now as clear as fine lacquer why I am followed."

"Oh?" Not noticeably on a rising note of interest.

"It will be trouble for all of us."

Condamine appealed, half-jocularly, for expert opinion. "Cuthers, d'you think there's a curse on this thing?"

"Has Mr Sarinan ever been wrong in his assessment of a work?"

Both were surprised by Sarinan's instant vehemence. "Yes! Yes I have been wrong and I have known I was wrong. When I am right, that I also know. You and I—we deal in half-truths— that's business, but the whole truth is not business . . . it's something none of us can outwit, right?"

Condamine glanced at Cuthers whose interest seemed to be elsewhere: signs of sincerity in Sarinan! Ah well, they were all getting on a bit. "And so, Mr Sarinan?"

"I shall phone my next address. If you still hear silence by this time tomorrow—please contact the cops."

"I could hardly do otherwise than promise, Inspector. In fact, I gave him forty-eight hours."

Two days . . . what could not have happened to them all in two days, including perhaps Safik Sarinan?

His thoughts turned to bricks, to brick walls, to blank brick walls—all of them made from bricks without straw. He tried and failed to conjure a sense of foreboding on Sarinan's behalf. Yet even by Condamine's pedestrian account the dealer's ill-concealed panic had come across.

"Do we know where he first stayed?"

"Yes. He mentioned the Dorchester."

The Inspector, knowing as much, was automatically testing Condamine's ability to remember details.

"Are you quite sure he meant an innocent Cardinal?"

Condamine smiled, not to be caught out. "I don't care for it myself—a Swiss lager."

"Ah! And can you recall offhand any other address he's used or might use?"

The head of Peachum's shrugged. "These dealers live out of suitcases—here today, there tomorrow. But Sarinan *is* a cut above most of his breed. Pied-à-terres in two or three capitals— let me see—he used to have a place in London, Frensham Court—one of those Chelsea superblocks."

"We'll take a look."

"I very much doubt you'll find him."

Both detectives eyed him blankly, forcing him into justification by waiting for one.

"It's a feeling I have—nothing more. Plainly Mr Sarinan fears something and well, you know, he drew a finger across his throat *most* expressively."

Cherry took this in good part, nodding gravely at the strong possibility. Most people enjoyed playing the sleuth at times. Figuratively, Condamine had donned deerstalker and Inverness and, brandishing an outsize magnifying glass, had tracked down a Lebanese corpse slumped in a classic pose somewhere in the bowels of Frensham Court.

"We must hope for the best." Very late Victorian he sounded. "By the way, I'd like to see this—Treasure."

"Would that be necessary?" Rather early Edwardian was Condamine.

"Isn't that what the mystery's all about?"

"Well, yes, I suppose it is but—"

"You've been good enough to explain at some length why you feel you should fear for a man's life sufficiently to contact the authorities. You've taken the trouble to persuade me this work of art contains a significance somehow bound up with Mr Sarinan's whereabouts dead or alive . . . it seems reasonable to examine an accessory before or during the fact, even if I can't question it."

"Er—yes—I take your point, but we can't be sure it *is* relevant to his disappearance can we?"

"Only if we discount an anonymous call from Rome suggesting the Deodati Treasure is not all it should be."

"God bless my soul! Whoever made such an outrageous suggestion?" *Indisputably*, echoes of *The Speckled Band*.

"Do you, or your experts, have any reason to doubt its genuineness?"

"None at all." Firmly. "But why should—?"

"That's all I wanted to know. One last question. How much credence do you give this—cup?"

Condamine sat back portentously, closing his eyes to consider deeply *and* relish the experience of holding two lawmen in breathless expectancy. Ten seconds later he was regarding Cherry with the frankness of one who can't afford special little treats *every* day of the week.

"I'll be plain with you, Inspector . . . I apprehend the cup to be as authentic as the highest bid we can get."

Which, Cherry concluded, was about as honest an answer as the Hammer of the Lots could manage.

"I'll have a man conduct you to Mr Cuthers' room. He has the Treasure for examination presently."

The "man" resplendent in plush, buttons and bows conducted them through more passages and up another stairway to Mr Cuthers' room. Outside a door labelled "Mediaeval, European" they were handed over to yet another yellow anachronism.

"Yers gen'l'men?" came from the large and sweaty bouncer-like visage under a wig scarcely covering the bull-like head.

Cherry identified himself.

"Is that a fact, squire? In the same line of business meself." Plus a nudge and a wink. "Special surveyance—makes a nice change to wage deliveries."

So Peachum's used outside agencies?

"There's not much in-house security, but every so often they ask for Bovril as you might say—specially after that raid on the Goya at Christie's."

The sentinel knocked at the door, opened it and announced the visitors.

Who found themselves in a cramped and crowded attic room. A ceiling sloping mightily on one side allowed them to stay upright on the other.

Cherry's first impression seemed severe. So much guilt? Man caught in a discreditable act? Head well turned over his right shoulder, wispy golden hair awry and that exophthalmic glance of startled enquiry. Reluctance to straighten up and turn when he had so much else to think about.

After introductions, Cuthers disarmed the Inspector's impression simply by admitting he had all sorts of problems on his hands as he placed two chairs with polite indications that they might care to sit. Room enough, but only just. They settled down among the shavings and watched Cuthers roll down his sleeves, retrieve what appeared to be an ancient velvet smoking

105

jacket from a packing crate, struggle into it and perch on the crate's edge wondering aloud how he might be of service.

Cherry noted the old-world courtesy belonging backward and concluded one couldn't spend a lifetime cheek by jowl with the rare and the beautiful without a touch of patina clinging to the persona—as woodshavings to a jacket.

He explained about Sarinan.

Cuthers tried hard to seem concerned, gave up and settled for superficial interest. "Yes, I know. He *was* in a state—not the old Sarinan, all poise and irritating self-assurance."

"You know him?"

"He's much too devious to know, but sooner or later everyone in the trade 'discovers' Sarinan."

"Why?"

"Because he's just about the world's best dealer—has the touch, the flair for producing the totally unexpected."

"Scruples?"

"I forgot to add—he's also the best *double* dealer in most of Europe and all the Americas."

"Where does that leave him with Peachum's?"

"Cordially wary relations at all times—our bread *is* buttered on the same side."

Cherry nodded and supposed he stood to make a lot of money on the deal? A lot, Cuthers agreed.

"Not the sort to run away from the likelihood?"

"Definitely not," emphatically, fingers combing through untidy hair as if in a fruitless search for lice. "Sarinan once concluded a sale at gun-point. New York, I believe."

"Who was holding the gun?"

"Never Sarinan. He makes his killings the painless way."

Cherry let his eye wander over some of the room's contents. "Tell me, Mr Cuthers, do men kill for things like that Cluniac candlestick, that ivory Virgin and Child over there, or the stonework on the bench, carved, I suspect, by the Master mason of Moissac? Or whatever?"

Vulgarly expressed, Cuthers goggled. Cherry, Duff's discreet grin suggested, was at it again.

Deeply versed in a whole age of, let's say, mysterious edification, the expert glanced at the items suspiciously, as if they'd dare to whisper their secrets to a total stranger. He reconsidered the Inspector much as he might have revalued an oversight.

"You *did* say you were from Scotland Yard?"

Cherry's amusement had to do with those comparisons everlastingly made between coppers and the thickness of their boot soles.

"Do they?" he repeated.

"Er—do they what?"

"Kill—to possess the otherwise unattainable?"

Cuthers considered the possibility. "One thing we soon discover in this business, nothing is unattainable. It's the perfect corollary of the phrase—"

"Everything has its price."

"Quite so. There's only one weapon of consequence between those who have and those who want—and that's the cheque book."

"Destructive but not lethal," Cherry supposed.

Cuthers shrugged. "It depends where the money comes from. A lot of people have to die if works of art are purchased from drug-traffickers' profits—which they often are."

"I think," Cherry amended, "I was in mind of middle-men such as Sarinan. Don't *they* get caught in the cross-fire?"

The expert removed a delicate spiral of wood from his sleeve and appeared to address it. "That's known and allowed for. Shearer in the Eastern department can tell you of any number of poor devils murdered in the Gandhara trade. The *tombaroli* are none too scrupulous and the trade war in pre-Columbian artifacts is—deadly."

"So Mr Sarinan's disappearance and 'sinister implications' could go hand in hand."

A conjecture aimed at no one in particular.

"And if that's the case," Cherry pursued, "the Deodati Treasure must share some of the responsibility."

"Mr Sarinan appears to think so."

"Yes . . . I'd like to see it."

"Readily. It's on the table behind you."

Both men turned to view the Cause of it All for some moments. Still keeping his eye on the Treasure, Cherry invited Cuthers to summarize its history.

107

"Long and complicated, Inspector. Its very nature is contradictory . . . for example, it isn't a true aumbry—only loosely referred to as such. Originally it was a portable altar with space beneath for sacred vessels—and the Host possibly. That's how it appeared in the late eleventh or early twelth century, so it could easily have seen the Crusades. One thing's certain, it's Burgundian in style and that ties in with the family's origins—the Counts Dieudonné. From then on, the simplicity was marred or enhanced by magnificent accretions. A cabinet was added to the base, highly ornamented possibly but we can't be sure. The back and sides were lined with panels creating the triptych—they remain as you can see, and they give this piece its unexampled value."

Cuthers hesitated, let his eye dwell speculatively on the Treasure and the policeman before he dared. "You appear to have some knowledge of mediaeval art, Inspector. Perhaps you'd care to hazard a guess at the hand responsible for the triptych?"

Cherry could appreciate even the most diffident challenge. Had never forgotten Doctor Cherry's forceful assertion: "Take this as an axiom common to all walks of life. The elements of detection go beyond bloodstains, fingerprints and can you give an account of your movements on the evening of? Only yesterday I visited fourteen patients on my rounds and discovered I'd left my umbrella with one of them. Which one? The third. Why? Because that's the only house of them all with a hat and umbrella stand in the hallway. Which I use as freely as I do my own—familiarity breeds forgetfulness. Deduction copulating with induction breeds—detection."

"But, Dad, it was fine all day yesterday."

"If you want a career with the Meteorological Office say so! Must've been the day before."

Cherry left his seat, fished for his spectacles, and dropped to one knee bringing him more or less eye level with the masterpiece.

Three scenes from the Passion, boldly executed albeit in comparative miniature; to the left, a cenacular scene, fingers shaped to the cup, an ambiguous gaze bent on someone deserting the story while another fawned cloyly at his shoulder. Strictly logical, the limner had disregarded tendencies to centralize the execution. Next to Passover came the trial. A bewildered figure, deserted and indicted, an enigma watching at safe distance, Caiaphas unyielding and History's best recruits, the mob, gaping at reality for something to do, for lack of invention of the easy option, TV in every hovel.

Brilliant, Cherry decided, that crown of thorns *balanced* on the head like a crude fool's cap, not pressed to the point of bloodshed. Masterly.

As for the third panel. Well, the man had his fair share of insight. The rookie legionary, bored silly, tracing graffiti in the dust with his spear point while a crazy trouble-maker, dead to the world, slept off the effects of intolerable anguish. None of it seen, head sagging forward, for who could support the sight of death before life? As for the perched crown of thorns tumbled to the ground like an abdication of mockery . . .

Cherry noted the one or two angels with unfurled scrolls like new's placards, laboriously sorted out the stop-press latinities.

He straightened up after five minutes of close examination.

"The quotation from Matthew—it seems to give the game away. Giotto's influence—but he never worked in a nutshell . . . so, a disciple of Giotto, torn between the Byzantine and the new wave of realism."

Cuthers nodded, momentarily at a loss for words. He glanced at Duff, who showed no surprise at the verdict—as was right and proper in one who'd been known to confuse Michelangelo with a man from the Mafia.

"Do you agree?" Cuthers was tempted to ask.

"Yes," promptly with total loyalty to Cherry's view of things *and* total ignorance of what he was on about.

"Astonishing." Cuthers' bemused expression had to do with discovering three art experts crushed into a room never designed to hold one—not comfortably at least. "We only—er—attribute of course, a pupil *is* possible."

"Or an avatar—unless Masaccio is too late," Cherry murmured. "And yet those thickish lines suggest Giotto."

Which stopped the unfortunate Cuthers rather dead.

"Go on, Mr Cuthers. Presumably it doesn't end there."

"No. That is we come to a curious combination of circumstances. Until Cellini's day, the cup had been under a primitive lock and key . . . it's believed an attempt was made more than once to steal it. The Deodati of the time commissioned Cellini to restyle and ornament the fabric and create a foolproof security system—Cellini was only too successful."

"All this is on record?"

"Not all Cellini's memoirs were published." Cuthers tried hard not to sound smug. "I had the pleasure of meeting the Marchesa some months back. She told me much of what I've told you."

". . . and what was your impression of this lady?"

"A remarkable person—no question."

"She showed you the cup."

"It was hardly mentioned."

"Odd?"

"Not really. These autocratic types can be full of foibles. I was there to discuss the possibility of selling the Aumbry as such. The trouble is—" he ground to a halt bedevilled by some more immediate problem he'd laid aside with their arrival.

"Yes, Mr Cuthers?"

"Well, suppose Sarinan really has disappeared? You see, in the excitement of the moment we forgot to ask him precisely how it opened. He showed us, gave a demonstration—the drawer shot forward. He returned the cup and closed it—I've spent hours trying to—I mean, the advertising is out, the viewing day isn't far off and Sarinan vanishes."

"Why not ring the Marchesa?"

"We've tried a dozen times and got no answer."

Cherry frowned, at circumstances grave and gay enough to support any number of theories equalled by the same number of natural causes, as he briefly assured Cuthers, leaving him with a promise to return, who knows? perhaps with Sarinan in tow. In less than two minutes they were back in the heavily perfumed air of Congleton Street.

The Inspector stayed strangely mute. Why, Duff privately wondered, when nothing had happened, nothing could be foreseen, little understood about a situation too fluid for hefty speculation or weighty theories to float upon, why was Cherry on a curious *qui vive*, eyeing the scene with the darting motion of a creature intent on survival.

He stopped suddenly at an antique dealer's window and gazed fixedly at a fine Regency mirror such as dandies might have used to compare the cut of a cravat with one of that dog Brummel's second best.

And when he turned, a madman must have envied the gleam in his eye. Duff also caught a glimpse of a none too clean pair of heels, so to speak, an impression of jeans and a scruffy jacket in flight; Cherry restrained his instinct to give chase.

"Don't bother."

"We're being shadowed!"

"Or observed."

Duff waited, at a loss to do anything else.

"Maybe, after all, there *is* something—untoward."

"They'd have to know we—"

"Not we—not anybody. Someone's simply watching Peachum's."

"Do we have any idea why?"

"Not really. Except, that's where the Treasure is."

"Therefore?"

"Therefore, things are happening, elsewhere . . . I think we're in business, Duff."

Allowing for the usual snarl of traffic they reached the riverside block of flats in respectable time. For once Cherry, a keen riparian, scarcely glanced at the Thames. Not that he was missing so very much. Lacklustre now, the mighty river symphony, fallen on hard times to the scrape of a down-and-out's one-string fiddle; all tourism and pleasure craft, no commerce. Just one more service "industry", a wasted liquid asset.

"Tell me," he invited Frensham Court's head porter, resplendent in brown company livery with its orange-trimmed lapels and cuffs—but mercifully unwigged, "what you know of a Mr Safik Sarinan."

Scenting trouble, with luck, maybe a tragedy, even a ten second flicker on TV, the porter turned solemn, switched off the company smile, tucked one or two of his chins into the knot of his tie and thought stertorously, hands folded across a waistcoat plainly under severe strain.

111

"Mr Sarinan is a nice gent, very nice. But he's a Lebanesian you know."

"Ah! A Lebanese."

"Exactly, a Lebanesian. I've personally always thought he was a terrorist, but as I tell everybody, I keep it to myself. It doesn't do y'know. It doesn't do."

"Doesn't do what?" Duff felt bound to ask.

"Why—involvement, y'see. *Involvement*. If he's pushing drugs it's safer to keep one's nose clean."

"Drugs—or terrorism?"

"It's like I say. He's a Lebanesian. It's got to be one or the other—and very likely both."

Cherry decided it might be worth another try. "Does he come here often?" Only just suppressing a giggle.

"Once or twice a year. On business. Very well spoken gent considering. Only stays a few days at a time."

"Maybe he leaves forwarding addresses—for anywhere in the UK?"

"No need. He comes and he goes. Paris, Amsterdam, New York, you name it."

"When was he here last?"

"Er—about six months ago if memory serves. I can check if you want."

"Don't bother. Could he get in without being seen by the staff?"

"Well—he *could,* I suppose, by the rear entrance. He'd have a key of course. But he isn't a backdoor man in my considered opinion."

"That doesn't suggest a drug-pushing terrorist," Duff observed.

"There's always the white slave traffic," darkly.

"Would it," Cherry wondered, "surprise you to know Mr Sarinan is highly regarded in the antique dealers' world?"

The brown and orange head porter cringed and all but threw up his hands to ward off the inconceivable. "That's worse! My gawd that's passing the time with old Nick and his granny if you like! I could tell you a thing or two about antique dealers never mind a penny for a song. We've got one of 'em living on the premises. When it comes to poofs give me a terrorist anytime."

112

"Why?"

"Well you don't know, do you? All this automatic immunity disposal systems going about and—"

"We'd like to look over his rooms."

"Who? Oh, Mr Sarinan. Yes, I think I can accommodate you. One large room and kitchenette. If you find him done in, let me know as soon as possible—there's a waiting list for singles."

"The key," Cherry, with an extended hand.

"Third floor, turn right, right again and through to the back lift and fire escape exit end of the corridor."

He handed them the key attached to a mugshot in a transparent plastic sachet. "A security procedure," he explained—in case the Inspector wondered. Cherry thanked him, studied the miniature likeness briefly and they set off for the lift. Duff turned with an afterthought, calling to the porter just as a dear old lady stepped out of the lift wheeling a shopping trolley.

"By the way, I shouldn't worry about your antique dealer."

"Eh?"

"They say you're all right if you don't kiss and cuddle and that."

Cherry and Duff had reached the third floor before porter and elderly lady had *quite* sorted out badly mixed feelings.

"Odd, when you think of it," Cherry reflected aloud. They were walking through the last claustrophobic corridor—a dreary carpet-covered street of what seemed like a thousand doors. No response from Duff. None expected.

"An international dealer of some repute comes to town hawking an antique worth millions presumably. One would expect him to use the temporary accommodation he's paid for."

"One would," Duff agreed.

"So, if he chooses actually to stay at a *very* expensive hotel . . . it does rather reinforce the apparency of a badly frightened Lebanesian."

They reached 178, stood backs to the door taking a mild interest in the limited scene; a single lift, the stairwell and papers outside 176.

"I don't see it," Duff had finished thinking over Cherry's last point of view. "If a man's scared stiff and can't get B and B at the Tower of London, one place is as good as the next."

"Savour the atmosphere of this morgue. Then think of a large hotel, better security, more life circulating, a small army of servants, floor waiters, instant communication. In a place like this you could cry 'help' for hours . . . and I can't see our Mr Porter moving further from his cubicle than possible. Unless he takes it with him."

The sergeant agreed.

Cherry unlocked and pushed open the door. A comprehensive darkness easily repelled the faint corridor light struggling to gain entry.

The Inspector still gazed persistently though he could see nothing very much. Once more the antennae were out. He remarked casually: "Someone's been here."

"Cleaners?"

A shake of the head. "They don't usually draw the curtains." He thought about this before adding: "That window in the corridor, behind us to the left, unobtrusively watch the street while I go in."

He waited for Duff to position himself before switching on the light.

Nothing. And no body.

A middling-sized room furnished for fly-by-nights; sparse, tasteless and sufficient unto the day, but no sign of occupancy— at very first sight.

An opened carton of milk stood on the draining side of a sink unit half-filling a tiny kitchen. Almost empty. Still fresh and drinkable. He glanced at the sell-by date and smiled a little. What, he wondered idly, had he really expected to find?

While he peered into the inner courtyard three floors below Duff appeared.

"That's right. Seconds after you switched on a blue Volvo parked in Marsh Street opposite took off on a kick start."

Cherry nodded thoughtfully. "Could be coincidence."

"No sign of Sarinan?"

"We might try that wardrobe."

Duff resisted the temptation. Cherry didn't. Not one to believe in fairies, he never doubted there are skeletons at the bottom of most cupboards.

Nothing. Not even a fairy's skeleton.

Duff smiled evilly. It was all, he came near to hinting, rather a waste of time.

"Why?" a preternaturally sharp query from Cherry.

"Why what?"

"Why are we wasting our time?"

Bloody mind reader. "You gave the reason. If a man's feeling vulnerable he won't cut himself off in a cul-de-sac like this."

"I was right in essence, wrong as to substance."

Oh Christ! A metaphysician should practice on metapatients, not down-to-earth CID sergeants badly in need of a square meal. Six o'clock and nothing but canteen coffee since breakfast.

But Cherry had taken the two steps to a small table, half concealed by the curtains, on which a telephone and an open directory. He stared down at both, again with the hint of a smile.

"Our Mr Sarinan is terrified maybe, resourceful certainly."

Duff grunted non-committally.

"The A to D, carefully folded so the pages can't flip over." The Inspector was examining the fine print. "Quite so. The Burlingham Hotel, Rosamund Street. No doubt he called a taxi and was picked up at the back entrance."

"He's not even supposed to be here in the first place."

"Can't help that, old friend. The facts stutter for themselves."

Duff hesitated long enough to calculate the risk, but his superior *did* appear to be in reasonably good humour. "Aren't you rather suggesting he *knows* we're looking for him?"

"A man who's scared doesn't *know* anything. He simply hopes. Look at it from his point of view. He tells everyone 'I'm being followed'. Everyone makes comforting noises including our people. Tactfully he's given to understand you need to be a VIP indeed to merit twenty-four hour cover."

"Therefore?"

"Wiliness. Very well, says Sarinan. I shall leave a trail. I'll deal in signs and portents."

"A carton of milk . . . then why not advertise by coming through the main entrance?"

Cherry frowned. "I admit that *tends* to dent my theory but if—"

The telephone's peremptory shrill startled them both and, surprisingly, increased Cherry's erratic good humour.

"Hullo, yes?" He managed to sound nondescript, vaguely foreign and slightly strained. After listening to the response he replaced the receiver in positively a holiday mood.

"Someone said 'You've got two days, Sarinan'."

"Oh good. Everything is now crystal clear." Duff, on the other hand, seemed to be answering from the deep end of the slough of despondency.

"It really is most interesting. In short order, we learn no end of facts. Principally, Sarinan appears to be justified in claiming persecution of some kind. The Treasure is a factor and . . . I think they've lost him."

"How *could* they be so careless." As ironically as he dared.

"Or why ring here with a powerful ultimatum? He's not here—we are."

Duff looked vaguely consoled. Duff *hated* not to know where he was.

"Possibly," Cherry concluded, "he came in at the front and left by the back entrance before someone thought of covering it—with a blue Volvo for example."

Duff felt he had cause to look dubious. Why should anyone terrorize a more or less honest broker in a deal that appeared to be as good as settled? He decided to postpone the question until they knew a little more.

Which little was, as hardly anybody says nowadays, vouchsafed to them back in the foyer of Frensham Court. The porter, pointedly ignoring Duff, took a few stately steps towards the lift and held up a hand inflated enough to bar a bus.

"You were right, sir. I have just held converse with my under porter, Tomlin, a most observant and conscientious young man. His mother came sixty-fourth in the 'Run for your life' marathon last year." He paused, as if inviting a round of applause from the two blank-faced officers, but nothing transpired. "Tomlin says he saw the Lebanesian quite definitely three evenings back. I'm telling a lie. She came sixty-third. Turned up with a small hold-everything, didn't say a word and went straight out again."

"Mrs Tomlin?"

116

"Er—no, Mr Sarinan."

"That's useful. And if anyone calls for him, asks to see him—*anything*—contact and quote me at the 'Yard', you understand?"

"Yes, certainly."

"Mrs *Lavinia* Tomlin?" Cherry asked, *à propos* of very nearly damn all.

"Why? Is she in trouble?"

"No, I just wondered."

"It's all that orange braid," Cherry explained, once they were outside. "Pomposity increases in galloping proportion to the yardage."

Otherwise, they drove in tired but thoughtful silence to Burlingham's, a small family hotel in the Victoria area, made enquiries of the management, a harassed-looking middle-aged gentleman still hugging some shreds of old world courtesy about him while co-existing uneasily in a world of terrorist bombing and police questioning. Mr Sarinan, he stammered, did indeed register yesterday, paid for a room with adjoining bathroom for three nights, but had not reappeared. Cherry seemed taken a little aback by this news. Yesterday? Did he mean today? But the proprietor could show him the register *and* the receipt counterfoil. Quite definitely, yesterday. Had he left belongings? No, positively nothing.

"I do hope it's not another of those awful terrorists, Inspector. We have an excellent reputation and—"

Cherry reassured him, adding with matching courtesy, "Don't hesitate to call us when he does turn up. It's really nothing serious—simply an irregularity in his visa—none of his fault."

The sigh of relief almost wafted them through the polished brass and glass doors of a cosy-looking, somewhat old style hostelry that simply did *not* know how to keep up with the times.

Cherry doubted whether Mr Crayfoot would ever set eyes on Sarinan again. The Burlingham had been chosen very much at random.

"Let's go home, Duff. Heartburn and homeward footsteps turn."

"You mean you're tired, fed up and hungry like me?"

117

Cherry smiled a bit, here and there, in patches. "I mean, Sarinan's safe enough for the nonce."

A few minutes shrouded in silence brought them back to Clapham.

Nine

IN A GENIAL, almost relaxed mood, Cherry was climbing out of the car in his usual clumsy fashion when his face seemed to congeal into a mask of utter incredulity. A hand shot out to clutch Duff's arm.

"What's up?" He followed Cherry's line of sight but saw nothing more gruesome than the old Victorian family mansion.

"There's a light on in the house!" whisper enough to wake dead drunks.

Well, yes, Duff had to admit there *was* a sliver of light just visible from the basement window in the kitchen. He grinned apprehensively, remembering what it was all about. "Mrs Craxton, I'll be bound," joviality sincere as a false nose at the carnival.

"Who else?" Cherry flared. "Am I at home to the Duke of Swaziland? Do I entertain Felicity Murgatroyd from Page Three when no one's looking?"

"Who am I to cast stones?" Very sententious about it Duff was.

Cherry glared, burning to ashes his hitherto good humour. Mentally the sergeant cowered.

It all had to do with the benign bane of Cherry's widowerish existence.

For some years the gentlest of conspiracies, master-minded by Duff's well-meaning wife, had been afoot to bring the recalcitrant Inspector and the unavailing Mrs Craxton into a bloodcurdling approximation to holy wedlock. If "bloodcurdling" sounds out of context—it's worth remembering Cherry had profited too well from his marriage, and lost too much, to view any further match as likely to be otherwise.

Duff spoiled all. Duff was Marjorie's despair. As a matchmaker he was, in her opinion, as useful as two sticks rubbed together by an idiot arsonist. Being no respecter of persons she applauded

Sir John's subtle persuasion of Cherry to get married *and* ridiculed his sledge-hammer.

So, the sergeant was presently conscious of his defects, including a total incapacity to deal with the plan hatched by Marjorie and billed for that very day. She'd reminded him time was short, that she'd arrange for Mrs Craxton to be at the house and, *however late* they returned, Duff was to broach the idea even if he, Duff, had to stay for a meal while they talked it over. It's a marvellous idea, she'd added with grim finality and Duff had nodded dubiously, conscious only of the word "disastrous" elbowing "marvellous" into limbo.

It recurred now, and only loyalty to Marjorie and a sneaking suspicion that she might just be right, poor intuitive, interfering wee soul, could launch him into a more or less prepared statement.

"Oh yes, it *must* be Mrs Craxton. I'm glad you mentioned her."

"*I* mentioned Miss Murgatroyd!"

"Yes, well I'm glad I mentioned—I'd almost—it nearly slipped my mind. It's Marjorie's night at the Ladies' Guild. She wondered if I might share a bite of something at your place."

"What does that have to do with Mrs Craxton, my charring woman?" Pompous as a porter.

"Ah! I was coming to that—all this Sarinan caper drove it out of—she—that is, Marjorie, arranged for Mrs C to be at the house *however late you—that is we returned*."

Cherry stared, as if one of them had taken leave of his senses. "Very well, but why shout?"

Duff had bawled the last because Marjorie had done just that as he left the house, but he couldn't very well say so.

Cherry, being no fool, suspected something. "You're sounding stilted, a sort of cardboard cut-out of John Snagge on an off-day." Cherry nodded slowly, pleased by his analogy.

"Just as you like," stiffly. "I'll pop off home and carve a sandwich."

"And won't you half get it from Mrs D when you tell her you failed in your mission *however late we were!*"

Fairly yelled at a poor devil wondering if the neighbours had

120

heard. By which he meant *his* neighbours in the street round the corner.

"Come on—let's get to the bottom of this."

Not another word or rearward glance. Cherry strode full of purpose through the rusted iron gate, up the path and three steps to his front door while Duff, searching through his mind's undergrowth, could find no other option but to follow. His reflections on women at that moment must have intrigued Marjorie no end had telepathy struck her in the middle of the Ladies' Guild lecture: How to Use Natural Colouring to Tempt a Husband's Appetite . . .

But Cherry's key slowed on its way to the latch, the door opened niggardly, inches at a time, the eye wavered as it ranged over the long passage and a determined chin sagged under the weight of irresolution.

"What's it all about?" Weakly.

Duff passed him by, head impaled high on a point of principle one might have thought.

"I'll let you know in Mrs C's presence and not before."

"Damn!" half aloud, as not to waken old and worn out sensibilities. Just then, it seemed more important to think of treasure resurrected and a man who might die, might be dead, because of it. Something, he would insist to an inner self, invariably came of nothing, however little came of something. Life . . . such a junior proposition against the senior death of all that had gone before simply to sustain . . . that proposition.

A sad, angry and bewildered man went the length of a passage consoled by a hall-stand, the feel of old, old velvet portières still palling doors left and right—the breakfast room, the surgery— his study, the only room in the house he really cared about; his share of the world, truly defined.

Downstairs he found light and human warmth enough to counter the chill of *weltschmerz*. Duff was already at his accustomed place exchanging pleasantries with Mrs C who stood politely but without deference by the kitchen stove waiting for her employer's appearance.

"Ah! Mrs Craxton. Just as I thought. I was only saying to Mr Duff not moments ago, great Scot, I do believe Mrs C is in the offing."

He glanced at Duff, who was mouthing to the very edge of the vocable: STILTED. With a sudden loss of temper Cherry mouthed back a word casting grave doubts on Duff's legitimacy.

Mrs C's concealed amusement almost got the better of her. Miraculous, the grave expression on a not unattractive face. "If you wish to characterize each other vocally I'm quite happy to leave the room, otherwise I'll serve your meal, Mr Cherry."

"Oh, ah, quite. As you please, Mrs Craxton, but I—I had some idea this—"

"No, it isn't my day—not this bit of it—but Marjorie—Mrs Duff told me you and Mr Duff had something to discuss with me—so I prepared something while I waited."

Plainly she was at a loss; Cherry felt he could relent. Obviously had nothing to do with—with what? He slumped into a chair opposite Duff and pinned him to his place with a stern regard. Duff steadfastly read the maker's name on the cutlery.

"Much obliged to you for your trouble of course. And now, Mr Duff, a word from you to resolve this mystery would not come amiss."

"God bless my soul! The Wimpoles are still toughing it out in Barrett Street and no mistake."

"Turning Victorian literary history upside down suggests mistakes all over the place!"

"Carrots, Mr Cherry?"

"Eh?"

"With the meat course."

"Er, yes. Thank you, yes. Carrots."

There came a huffy, dignified silence long enough for both men to appreciate a meal Lucullus might gladly have shared with Lucullus; Mrs C busied herself with kitchen-sink matters hoping the air would clear enough to discover why she was there at all.

Duff, as usual, was the first to finish, the first to compliment the cook.

"Thank you, Mr Duff."

"*Wasn't* it, Mr Cherry?"

"Eh?" Cherry surfaced from the depths of contemplating a treasure locked within a treasure. What *kind* of cup?

"Excellent! the supper."

"Indeed. First rate, Mrs Craxton. Much obliged to you. The crust was just a little overdone for my taste but otherwise—"

"Biscuits and cheese at your elbow. And I'd esteem it a favour if you'd both kindly explain why I'm here at this hour while I prepare coffee."

"Ask Mr Duff. It's nothing to do with me."

Cherry looked so insufferably smug they *both* wanted to hit him.

"It's Marjorie's idea. We've got this bit of leave coming up in a fortnight y'see. The children are staying with uncle and aunt near enough for them to go on schooling—Mr Cherry has kindly condescended to accompany us for a trip on the Norfolk Broads. It's a four berth cruiser booked for the 24th and her idea is—well, we'd be delighted if you'd care to come along and make a foursome, my dear."

Mrs Craxton was plainly touched, less by the invitation, more by his unfeigned and homely tact never far below the ruggedness when occasion genuinely demanded.

Quite otherwise with Cherry on whom she'd kept an oblique eye. His expression lurched from utter incomprehension through dawning realization to flower at last into sheer aghastness. Some emotion close to horror seemed so manifest, neither was left in doubt as to what he thought of the plan.

Duff frowned angrily on her behalf but she stepped in quickly to remove the wedge, the thin end of which almost visibly showed between them.

"Please tell Marjorie I'm glad she—I appreciate a very kind gesture but it's out of the question. Mr Cherry *is* my employer and I couldn't expect him to take kindly to my presence in the circumstances."

"Oh? And why shouldn't I? Am I a monster—the scourge of domestics, an enemy of democracy!"

The perversity of man—well, a man called Cherry. If Duff was agreeably surprised by his *volte face* and rhetoric favouring the enterprise, Cherry was downright astonished. He even gazed furtively about the kitchen to discover where unforeseen words had been hiding themselves. Even Mrs Craxton seemed to doubt her hearing.

"Yes, in a way," and with total honesty, "an unfledged

123

monster, an unthinking scourge and no friend to the modern substitute for democracy—and I agree to that but—but that has nothing to do with it."

"Then what has?"

"I—don't know. All the same, I think I'd better decline—with thanks to all three of you."

Cherry stood, indecisively, fumbled with the chair back of him and addressed no one in particular, all clear signs of his inner confusion. "To be taken aback isn't necessarily to be wanting in courtesy—especially to a lady I respect too much to behave worse than awkwardly. You see . . . I had this Sarinan affair in mind, so I became confused with visions of boats and cups and bits of stone and—and so on. Believe me, no discourtesy was intended . . . I'll take my coffee to the study . . ."

His departure left a void of silence slowly filling with a little embarrassment and much sadness. Better words to describe their feelings may exist but dictionaries don't necessarily know all. Truth to tell, both felt they'd been unfair to him and that, at least, made a nice change.

Duff could even sound a touch resentful. "All very well. But he didn't say you'd be welcome to join us."

"He couldn't."

"Oh?"

She sat at the table, dispirited as it seemed, or unequal to the trivial play of forces briefly weighing on all three at the end of a long day.

"*You* know Mr Cherry is not the usual man, not altogether . . . he deals in verities as others deal in commodities or stocks and shares. That kind of dealer is a deeply unhappy man, excruciatingly sensitive. If he can he'll retreat and find his peace in some inner world, or the wrongs he tries to right would drive him mad. He was right you know, a confusion of realities—that's all . . . as for four in a boat, it's—an intimate situation—not you and Marjorie, he feels safe with you both. But I'm an unknown quantity—no, it wouldn't do."

"Delicacy?"

She regarded him with interested surprise in those exceptionally fine eyes. "That's it exactly . . . I'm sure Mr Cherry appreciates you—he should. Now, it's rather late, I must be off. I'll deal with all this debris tomorrow."

The sergeant ignored her protests and drove her home, returning to Cherry's place in less than ten minutes. He re-heated the coffee and slopped two fresh cups upstairs to the study.

Where else but in that cavernous room myriad with books, partitioned by alleys and quiet cul-de-sacs of shelves, would the Inspector be found, somewhere on the floor, with a volume of Godtsz and Vasari's Lives of the Painters at his back, head deep in a ponderous-looking volume . . .

. . . Now there was a certain man, a Frank of Amiens in Picardy, one Peter called the Hermit, not well favoured but of a quick and flashing eye, who went before with Urban's blessing over all Italy out of Jerusalem and thence across the highest Alps to proclaim crusade and tell of unimagined desecration of holy places by the infidel Turks in that city of glorious memory till every man was impassioned to zealousness with blazure of his exhortations and nowhere than in France and Normandy did they more embrace the destiny of the Cross.

To Auvergne came the second Urban himself, for the great Council of Clermont wherein he left no passion unstirred, and many were his promises:

Facultates etiam inimicorum nostrorum vestrae erunt: quoniam et illorum thesauros exspoliabitis.

Truly, the promise of treasure and great plunder weighed in the scales close to some politic hearts which had need of absolution sans penance of all sins. Good it was to know, whether fallen by the way, or in the hell-mell of holy battle, the gates of Paradise would fly open to their dying breath.

Now in that multitude which cried aloud "It is the will of God" was a high vassal of Burgundy, Count Dieudonné who had followed his lord to the territories of the Savoys in Piedmont. The Count, it is said, had given shelter from the storms ravaging the Valley of Augustus to the hermit called Peter who, though small of stature, "bore himself high as the Cerrino" labouring to bring men heart and soul to the foot of the perilled Cross.

125

Thus came Count Dieudonné, much prepared in his mind for the great Council and, in good time thereafter, sought leave of his liege lord to take the Cross under the banner of Godfrey of Boulogne.

Legion are the tales told of Flambard Dieudonné's prowess *in partibus infidelium* till, on the glorious 15th of July, 1099, he rode, not distant from Godfrey's side, into Jerusalem resurrected.

From this time, or soon after, the Count, full of exploits, earned to bear upon his shield and standard the Trinity of Tasses d'Or. These semblances gave rise to a curious circumstance on which all Italianate Deodatis have evermore kept silence so that no man may come at the truth. Only, it remains to say, ever after the Count's death in the 47th year of the 12th century, rumour has graced his name as first guardian of the sacred chalice from which Our Saviour denied to drink at Passover.

What truth may be hid I know not, but let others tell the meaning of a device conferred so soon after Jerusalem Delivered wherein a wealth of holy relics might be preserved a thousand years—scarce more than a wink in the eye of eternity . . .

At which point, enter Duff with coffee, to find a body slumped over its book. He smiled a friendship smile, shook his head a time or two, then settled with some difficulty on the floor, his broad back against some opposite shelves.

Cherry, he mused, the armchair traveller with a window-sill for horizon. Never moving, physically, from A to B with conviction so much as from necessity . . .

"So what did little Red Riding Hood do next?"

Cherry glanced sharply, at something of a loss. "I think she grew up and married the wolf who turned into an ugly, thick-headed sergeant in the Metropolitan CID. So there!"

"Coffee?"

"Yes . . . I think we're getting somewhere, Duff."

"I see." Laconically from one who *knew* the world was round.

"Shall I read you the nub of this business? It's quite fascinating."

126

Duff, unwisely, nodded consent. Concertina'd as he was, coffee cup balanced on his knees, he was in the wrong position to refuse and he gathered from Cherry's schoolmarmish eye he was going to be read the damned thing anyway.

Revealing, the facets of utter disbelief lighting up the sergeant's homely countenance as he listened to "whereins" and "thereafters" and who the hell was Godfrey off the ferry from Boulogne? That's to say, he struggled desperately to interpret ancient rigmarole into terms comprehensible enough to beat bewilderment . . .

"There you are," from Cherry triumphantly snapping shut the book.

A long, a very long silence followed.

"What," Duff plucked one of a dozen questions from his reeling mind, "*what* in Godfrey's name, has all that to do with Sarinan's disappearance?"

"Haven't you listened to a word of this!" sharp as a pedagogue's rap over the knuckles.

"I've listened to a lot of crap about crusades, Turks and short-arsed hermits, and I do *not* seem able to find a connecting link between, for example, crossing the Alps and the man we're supposed to be looking for. Of course, I speak as a peasant to a pedant, but I can't for the life of me see what Walter Scott has to do with—"

"Walter What!" Cherry could go no further. Indignantly he brushed aside Duff's mistaken remembrances of *The Talisman* and all but hissed at the hapless peasant facing him. "*This* is from 'The High Annales of the Great and Glorious Crusade Proclaimed by His Holiness Urban the Second, with divers Chronicles of the Most Noble Exploits of Multitudinous Lords and other of High Degree by Johannes, Chronicler of Blankenburg, set down in 1270 Anno Domini and published in 1497 by Meister Hueghtmeer of Antwerp'."

". . . with a title like that who needs to read the bloody book?"

"Duff, I despair. For once we're deep into the realms of mystery redefined as history, and you fail, obtusely, to see a connection."

"Sarinan is modern history, or at least, current affairs, that I

127

understand; but I can't, metaphorically, go riding on a horse bearing a banner with a strange device, looking for a missing person. People would draw certain conclusions—and they'd be right."

Cherry frowned but took the point graciously enough. "It's hard to explain . . . we've brushed History's skirts before—Shakespeare, Judas—skirmishes, no more. But it goes deeper . . ." he stirred his coffee dreamily, much like a reflexive act of divination.

"Mankind," he continued, "was never a lonelier phenomenon than it is today—d'you know why?"

Duff shook his head, but tuned himself to Cherry's mood.

"One foot in the present, the other in the future. No matter what—we count ourselves too smart to bother with the past. It hurts too much, because it reminds us of what we *are*. And yet, five thousand years of recorded wisdom—and folly—could give us the golden age. So where are the computer freaks able to iron out those mistakes and supply a print-out of perfection? No, the past is dead, murdered by good riddance—therefore, long live the future . . . but we give ourselves away, Duff. The hankering after gaslight and crinolines, grown men restoring old steam-engines, the archaeological surge. Subconsciously we know what we're dismissing so lightly . . ."

"And so?" delicately, to bridge the long, contemplative silence between them—and Sarinan.

"And so," more matter-of-fact and down to earth, "to borrow from current parlance, what's wrong with hacking into the data book of history and doing a little retrieval?"

Decisively he tapped the book in his hand. "I'm not saying it's the key to a mystery. At most it proves the lock's existence: a set of facts that end up in Peachum's hands—now, today."

"Do they tell us much about Sarinan?"

Cherry appeared to ignore the question. "The Deodati Treasure is dynamite with a slow-burning fuse, about two thousand years long. Or an unstable element with a diminishing half life, radiation unseen—you smile—well, more Europeans died from the effects of two juxtaposed pieces of wood, during the 'people's crusade' alone, than were murdered at Hiroshima and Nagasaki put together . . . there's no reason why Sarinan shouldn't join them . . . *I* didn't draw a finger across his throat—he did."

"I see your point, but shouldn't we come out of the cloisters and cross at the traffic lights?"

The Inspector smiled. "I'm not sure we shouldn't cross in the other direction."

Duff saw that he'd learn nothing more substantial till Cherry fell out of the cumulo-nimbus and that, he knew, could take hours. He took for granted Cherry's faculty for living a more intense existence far beyond his ken, while going through the motions demanded of an efficient police officer. What puzzled him was that knack of sintering one with another life producing, to everyone's astonishment, a hard-wearing solution.

Yet, Duff driving home that evening, could recall that Cherry loathed his job . . .

No one else was possessed of that secret.

Not even Cherry.

Intense, perhaps. A different existence, certainly.

From ten till almost two next morning Cherry ransacked the huge old house with its store of seemingly limitless information. He spent much of it in the long attic filled with a huge filing system containing at least a million items. The quarters below had grown too small to hold it.

Whether those hours contributed much to his purpose may not be here or there but, by bedtime Cherry knew more about Genesis, as it were, than he did about Revelations.

By concentrating on the letter D and so, coming to the name, Deodati, he discovered by cross-reference a fact which, while it told him something about an illustrious family, was also paradoxically sensational enough to escape him altogether.

Cherry's father had started the collection of cuttings in the war years; his system of indexing was a model of Dewey-eyed clarity. Hardly surprising then that Cherry unearthed the following item from an ancient *News Chronicle* of 1945.

With the cessation of hostilities in Europe reports are increasing of reprisals and revenge killings in those countries recently delivered from the iron grip of Nazi occupation.

In Northern Italy, where resistance to foreign and domestic

Fascism was strongest, the killings have been on a large scale. Last week in the Valle d'Aosta, a region dominated by the old nobility, Count Ignazio, head of the della Paresi family, was abducted by former partisans, summarily tried and shot under the walls of his castle.

According to local sources the Count, a staunch supporter of Mussolini's régime, was responsible for the execution in March 1944 of the much loved Prince Eugenio Deodati. No one in the area doubts he was betrayed by della Paresi who knew of his efforts to save intended victims from the gas chambers. The Castello Deodati became a haven and a staging point for fugitives en route for the Alpine passes to Switzerland and safety.

Count Ignazio is survived by two sons, both former members of the notorious Babilla, a junior branch of the Blackshirts.

The article briefly mentioned a surviving daughter, rumours of a treasure of great religious significance, and it ended there.

And so to bed, in company with a supreme irony.

The man he'd so narrowly missed at Heathrow some years before had passed in print, or like a waking shadow, over his putative grave once more. Because, of course, the name della Paresi meant absolutely nothing to the Inspector.

Ten

BY TEN O'CLOCK that same morning Cherry had questioned the officers called to the hotel by Sarinan. He learned nothing useful beyond a detailed description good enough to be hawked around with a general alert.

While he was considering another face, one without features called the future, things were otherwise at Peachum's. Once more the Treasure had been brought from the high security basement store-room; once more, a quietly desperate Cuthers wrestled delicately to open the shy and retiring drawer.

Peachum's, in fact, presented a picture of daemonic activity much of which centred on the Treasure. Telex messages were transmitted in all directions, phone calls were made in numbers enough to bring tears of joy to the eyes of BT shareholders, while the Press and PR department noisily added its quota to the general pandemonium. Even now, Fasely, the PR chief, was gladdening Condamine's heart with news of TV's willingness to introduce the nation to the greatest sale piece of the century. Only that wretched drawer posed anything like a serious problem. And repeated calls to the Castello Deodati were simply not getting through.

Duff was suggesting coffee to Cherry when word came from Marlborough Street Magistrate's Court. Inspector Finney explained he was holding a window-basher by the name of Sarinan, Safik Sarinan. "Must be your man."

After a ten minute dash to Oxford Circus Cherry was still smiling. Duff thought it made a nice change and refrained from saying so.

Two minutes more found them alone with three chairs, a table, a sort of bunk bed—and Sarinan.

"So, you are Inspector Cherry. I know of you. I am Safik Sarinan—you know of me."

Cherry nodded, sat at the table, invited the dapper, perfectly groomed Lebanese to do the same.

It took a moment for each to size up the other. The one warily, as if he had a doubtful Ming to sell, the other, with that blank regard dissembling intense professional interest. Duff prepared to take notes in the restricted background.

"What," Cherry wondered, "have you got against Selfridges?"

Sarinan shrugged. "Their windows are too damn hard. Three times I had to throw my brick. You English are peculiar. With the first throw they criticize, the second, they advise, on the third they cheered. Spectator sport I understand, but this was ridiculous."

"And then?"

"Then, the management came, the police are called, and I am arrested. It's very satisfactory."

Cherry glanced at Duff, who stolidly kept his eyes lowered.

"It has been done before, Mr Sarinan. Can you explain why it's been done again?"

"Insurance—life insurance. I don't know—how serious is the threat, but when I'm pulling off my biggest deal I can't afford my funeral. What can you do for me?"

Duff looked up briefly.

"I don't quite follow."

"How long can I have?"

". . . how long do you want?"

"Till the 20th, the day after the sale. Once it's clinched—say ten days."

"Or a round fortnight?"

"Yeah—that suits me fine."

"Our system doesn't quite work like that . . . where did you stay last night—the Burlingham?"

Sarinan grinned, something he could do quite charmingly. "So you got my message?"

"No, Mr Sarinan, I got another one, an anonymous call telling us we'd find your body in room 14."

The grin disappeared leaving signs of real anxiety. He recovered a little. "You don't say . . . right—that's what I'm up against. Like I tell everybody. Why else am I here?"

"*What* are you up against?"

Sarinan frowned. "How do I know?" He thrust a hand into his pocket and came up with a scrap of paper. "This, pushed under my door in Frensham Court. I'm watching television. Out of the corner of my eye I see it appear. Read it."

He passed it to Cherry who read it aloud.

"Anyone involved with selling the Treasure is a bad risk." He contemplated Sarinan with some care. "Why not show it to someone here?"

The perennial shrug. "Already they tell me nothing doing. Why should this convince them something is?"

"But you show it to me."

"*After* I show the judge, he says 'why break windows?' I say because I got this piece of paper—and then I explain. He will think I'm nuts so I'm held for medical studies, right?"

Cherry suggested he start at the beginning.

Sarinan, a dedicated solipsist, launched into saga with gusto, was happy to answer Cherry's questions—about castles in Italy, for example.

"Is that when you first suspected you were being followed?"

An emphatic shake of the head. "Not till Zurich."

"Then someone phoned ahead to Zurich?"

"I don't see it. No one knew my affairs. Who should tell?"

"You travelled by road, from where to where?"

"From Rome I go to Turin, I stay overnight at the Cassio Hotel—I meet no one, I talk to no one. From Turin I go to the Castello."

"How—by car?"

"Sure by car—why not?"

"Your own?"

"No, I—" some significance appeared to take him unawares. "When I need to travel I hire one—it's convenient."

"Very . . . and presumably there's evidence on the car that it's hired out?"

"Sure—in large letters—a sticker on the rear screen—Casa Mobile. It's a big outfit in Rome."

"Then what's to stop someone determined to find out where you're heading?"

". . . that's right." He glanced at Cherry briefly and gave an odd, prep school, sneery smile. At which the Inspector flared—inwardly.

"And you saw no one when you left?"

"No. No one."

"The Marchesa was to meet a delegation of churchmen. Did she tell you why?"

"Something crazy about teaching them a lesson."

"By defending her decision to sell a red hot relic?"

"Maybe. That wasn't my concern. I had to collect and deliver—that's all."

"The Treasure *and* the documentation?"

"Sure. There had to be something in writing about that cup."

"To get a better price?"

"My friend, what's in that box doubles the value, no sweat."

"So how much are we talking about?"

Sarinan had no doubts. "Fifteen million dollars plus."

"I see . . . what kind of terms—?"

"My cut was ten per cent gross and out of town expenses."

"I meant, what limitations were on your negotiating position?"

"None. You can read her letter to Peachum's. No matter what happened—the sale was on delegated authority—mine."

"Uncommon."

"The Marchesa is no usual old lady. I dealt for her five years—more. I sold her Bartolommeo pen drawings to the Boston—Siviera nearly went crazy, but it was legal. And del Sarto's *Escobaldo* to Chicago Art Museum—and other things—two, nearly three million dollars' worth."

Cherry thought about this, about the many Conventions approved and signed over the years to regulate the disposal of art treasures. Even Nixon had lobbied the Senate in a worthwhile cause. But it made no difference: and why discuss it with a professional cynic?

"It all suggests an unusual old lady with a purpose."

"What d'you mean?"

"She isn't putting all this money together for her old age."

"That's right. She has plans—good ones. The Deodati Trust. Every cent she makes on her valuables goes to the Trust. When she dies, it creates a big home for orphans and handicapped kids. She knows what she's doing."

"So, if she dies, say tomorrow, there's still no legal impediment to the sale?"

"Like I said."

"And if you die, say, tomorrow—?"

"Don't do it to me! There's no sale. I sign the release, I collect the cheque and I deliver to her or the Trustees. And what about my ten per cent!"

"Mr Sarinan—"

"So they bury me in a fireproof safe deposit—am I better off!"

Cherry calmed him down eventually, but scarcely changed the subject by inquiring who might have an interest in preventing the sale.

"How do I *know*? The Church is crazy, but it's definitely against self-crucifixion."

The Inspector nodded without conviction. He could agree in principle, but who else had as good reason for preventing the sale?

He tried a small point. "This Treasure has importance in its own right, but suppose X is more concerned about the contents— the cup. Would that suggest to you X *knows* it's authentic?"

Decidedly Sarinan shook off the idea. "In this business it's enough for X, Y *and* Z to think a thing's authentic. I don't need move an inch to persuade 'em, one means the other."

"So you want this sale to go through?"

Sarinan's smile was a strange and revealing thing.

"Which means," Cherry continued, "you have nothing to hide."

". . . what's that to mean?"

"The whereabouts of the cup."

"It's locked in the Aumbry."

". . . how?"

"Ask Cellini. It's brilliant you know that—he made it."

"It's not mentioned in his memoirs."

". . . how would you know?"

"My mother taught me how to turn pages, Mr Sarinan."

That was worth a laugh. "You were lucky. Mine taught me how to lift a tourist's bill-fold in the Beirut bazaars . . . maybe

135

you didn't know he wrote a lot more they couldn't publish. Guess what he came up with?"

Cherry shook his head, never taking his eyes from Sarinan.

"Pressure. It's as simple as that. You press the left side, then the right—that activates the mechanism, once more on the right releases a catch, again pressure on the right releases a spring which pushes the drawer forward—that's all."

"Why didn't you tell Peachum's?"

"I had a lot on my mind. I just forgot."

"One left, three right . . . I'll let them know."

"Yeah, do that. It was stupid of me. They don't have all the time in the world to spread the word."

There were formalities to be looked at. With a merest hint of plea bargaining Cherry arranged for Sarinan to be held pending enquiries. He assured the clerkly and pernickety Mr Smith that it wouldn't take more than a couple of days.

They left the court and returned to the car where Duff refused to drive off till he'd had his say. "This is crazy. We hold a man for smashing a window because he literally asks for a bit of custody just to tide him over a bad patch. We also run his errands for him, and just to pass the time we do the Hokey-Cokey."

"By which you mean?" from a genuinely puzzled Cherry.

" 'You press the left side once, you press the right side once'— if that isn't doing the Hokey-Cokey and not a staff Xmas party in sight I don't know what is." Very grieved by it all was Duff.

"I haven't the faintest idea what you're talking about," huffily. "Meantime, I'd be grateful if you'd drive us to Peachum's forthwith."

"Why not shove me into a yellow plush livery and slap a wig on top! You were born to roll over the yokels in a coach and four!"

To tell truth, Cherry secretly relished Duff's rebellious bouts. "I'm not that bad. I'd have flung 'em a handful of Elastoplasts."

"Eh? They weren't invented then were they?"

Cherry curled up and fell asleep.

He awoke with a violent lurch, saved by his seat belt as Duff deliberately braked hard.

"Peachum's, m'lord. Shall I lower the carriage steps or would you prefer to slide down the emergency chute?"

Cherry glowered before taking in the scene ahead of them. One of the firm's flunkeys was holding a large umbrella in one gloved hand over a prosperous-looking old gentleman and helping him into a chauffeured limousine with the other.

"Did you ever see such a nose, Duff? Could be Pierrepont Morgan come to life."

Duff, in spite of himself, was impressed. "He'd need two umbrellas to cover that. Who is he?"

"German industrialist—one of the biggest. Also an art collector . . . let's drive round to the rear. The front of a theatre's not half so fascinating as the stage door."

A fact borne out as soon as they turned into the mews behind Congleton Street. A real St Audrey's fair! Bustle enough to satisfy even Cherry's incurable romanticism. Cars and vans lined most of the mews, somehow parked, somehow inching out, somehow creeping forward, the famed flunkeys came and went, other employees in brown dust-coats were taking in, carrying out, a variety of goods precious enough to bring a gleam to the eyes of Victoria *and* Albert, a huge painting, wrapped in hessian, reverently manoeuvered through one doorway would make a Tate laugh, but not necessarily a National Gallery.

For five minutes Duff had to listen to the Inspector philosophizing extempore on the transience of things. "Which," Duff interrupted, "was all very interesting, but there's a poor philosopher back of us trying to get his lorry in."

In time they strolled at leisure to where a miserable individual supporting a doorway eyed the activity with a jaundiced expression quite matching his yellow knickerbockers.

"Shouldn't you be helping with the removals?" Cherry wondered, pleasantly.

The man, down at mouth, a haunted look in the eye, spat disgustedly at his buckled shoes.

"Not my job, just out for a breather and half a drag."

"That wig's almost back to front I'm afraid."

"Is it? I'm not surprised. Only been here a week. Can't get used to it."

"Not your line."

137

"Compositor. *Sunday Times*."

Cherry nodded his sympathy. "Pays the rent."

"You're living in the past, mate. It's supposed to pay the mortgage."

"None of you do it for love of the job I imagine."

The Peachum's man grimaced. "Spare me! There's two out of a dozen worked more than five years on this caper and they'd be servile tits at any time, past *or* present."

"Big turnover?"

"You can say that twice. Some of the types we have to kow-tow to don't bear thinking about."

"How long will *you* stick it?"

"I dunno. Ask my Building Society."

They continued in to a passage-way badly obstructed by packing cases and tea chests. The floor seemed ankle deep in sawdust and wood shavings. From somewhere distant came shouts and guffaws of laughter. A small, worried looking employee in a grey linen coat came hurrying down the stairs, peering into a red exercise book like a religious at his breviary. "Have you seen Jepson?" Cherry said no, they hadn't, and how did they get to Mr Condamine's office? He frowned petulantly, directed them grudgingly and bustled off calling "Jepson!" as if the fate of the world depended on Jepson, the son of Jep. A foreman, Cherry supposed.

Condamine brightened a little at sight of the two officers, waved them to chairs which they declined.

"I hope you come with good news, Inspector. I have need of it."

Cherry assured him Sarinan was safe and well and had readily passed on the secret which was simplicity itself.

Condamine's delight knew no bounds; there seemed no point in spoiling his day with news of Sarinan's detention.

"Gratified, yes, gratified. I was wrong to doubt the poor fellow."

"Why should you doubt him?"

"In this business, Inspector, everyone is open to doubt."

"Even the bidders?"

"Especially the 'bidders' as you call them. At Peachum's we refer to 'interested clients'."

"Why should they be suspect? It's a straightforward trans-action surely?"

Condamine's smile was pity for ignorance even of police officers floundering in that arcane world where lots are knocked down for lots and lots. "I could tell you many a tale, Inspector, were it not for the sealed lips we directors of Peachum's take with us to the grave."

Cherry cast a powerful glance at Duff, who seemed on the verge of finding that immensely funny.

"I'll take you to Mr Cuthers immediately. Poor fellow, he's quite distraught, what with the Press and TV on our heels for a glimpse of this marvel."

The Chairman and Managing Director, no less, conducted them to Cuthers' hideaway.

"Courage, Cuthers, succour is at hand."

Duff raised his eyes but said nothing. Obviously Condamine knew a sucker when he saw one but why noise it abroad?

"Thank God for that! We have the lab test lined up, TV's breathing down our necks, Fasely's tearing his hair out and—"

"Yes, yes," soothingly, "these gentlemen quite understand. Everything's *comme il faut*." He beamed on all and sundry until he came to Duff's blank wall visage.

"Why couldn't you contact the Marchesa?" Cherry had to ask. "She'd have answered the problem."

"We've tried no end of times," Cuthers said. "The Italian phone system is diabolical. A faulty line can last for days."

Nothing more to be said. The Inspector, anxious to find out for himself, took a step to the "whigmaleery" as Doctor Cherry would have described it, glanced at Condamine and Cuthers briefly, before following Sarinan's instructions to the letter.

The drawer snapped forward and three of those present craned forward to inspect, to observe, to marvel, while the fourth stared, almost unseeingly at the ancient *tour de force*.

"And you'll generate interest in this. For what?"

They stared at one who spoke in riddles or had he simply taken leave of his senses? Only Duff really understood the gleam in his eye.

"If it's capable of proof by dating the—" Cuthers began confidently, but appeared to lose the thread. That gleam . . .

"We have a duty to do our best for a significance," Condamine kindly explained to his other self.

"By knocking it down to the highest bidder?"

Condamine's nose wrinkled into a lump of distaste. Such presumption in a mere . . ."We act under instructions, Inspector."

"Yes . . . I suppose we all do," but *weltschmerz* or its Anglo-Saxon equivalent had struck yet again, leaving Cherry in the mood that makes much tedious. Momentarily he looked distinctly fastidious, grudging his part in most of the company he kept, including the sacred vessel all this farrago was about . . . four grown men taking a doubtful receptacle seriously—TV cameras to focus on a nullity, theological arguments disinterring old and discredited "certitudes"—while the real world plunged and reeled very nearly out of control.

The priority man felt sickened. Too obviously despised what he could not remedy, lacking power and authority to change those priorities.

A cup!

"Would there," he wondered rebelliously, inanely, "have been a saucer to go with this?"

Condamine frowned and said he must return to his office.

Cuthers took the question seriously. "No, they hadn't got around to such refinements till the eighteenth century."

Cherry smiled grimly and said "I see."

He turned abruptly and left the room.

Duff followed, had to move fast to catch up with a man who cannoned into this and crashed into that as if he couldn't wait to get out of the place and, preferably, out of this world.

Climbed into the car, sat silent as a reactor on melt-down. Duff stared ahead, trading silence for silence. Until—

"To be called upon to monitor the doings of these *shysters* playing hunt the dollar—and for what?"

While he maundered on, Duff tried hard, but couldn't call to mind a single job opportunity that might, at this moment, have made of Cherry a tolerably happy man.

He had other things to do that day; luckily they kept him out of Cherry's way.

★

Remote, inaccessible as the Victorian Himalayas, surly to occasional visitors, the Inspector spent a lot of his time preparing a report on the affair as far as he could understand it. At best, it explained much about the man, his disregard for the niceties of communication, evidence of a style so acidulous it might have read better on litmus paper. And there was that underlying question betraying his utter disregard for consequences.

Why am I here? What, after all, do I care?

It began promisingly enough, even percipiently.

"Something is happening in Italy, or has happened, that makes all present investigation futile." And it ended: "All else apart, I don't give a damn whether the 'treasure' is genuine or not. In fact, I wouldn't buy the thing at a jumble sale."

Not surprisingly, he tore up ten pages of anger, frustration and plain cussedness, consigned all to the WPB and went home. Went home by bus, as if time had retreated twenty-five years or more.

What *was* wrong with the man?

Eleven

WHATEVER'S WRONG WITH him, Cherry is such detestably bad company at this moment we can afford to abandon him briefly until he has as much to tell us as he can impart to himself. For an interval, there *is* a gap between his world and the one we all share spite of hell, damnation and the government of the day—*quis separabis?*

In an ideal cutting-room, the film editor ruthlessly disposes of precisely those snippets that mar a grand design. He'll cut twelve hours to Rama down to nine for more reasons than euphony; but snippets are the very items that make our world such a fascinating place. Ask Cherry, the paper millionaire stuck with a houseful. Ask him, for example, when Columbus discovered America. He can spend five minutes explaining why the man from Genoa did *not* make landfall on the 14th July 1472 but the 13th. The date was doctored for superstitious and religious reasons. So, history was manhandled, the Big Lie began, and the rest of history was unlucky whatever the date . . .

More to the point. A day later, Sir John is handed a translated cutting from *Osservatore Romano*. A memo attached by some gumshoe mandarin mildly requested the exercise of discretion on this one.

Officials in Vatican circles are expressing concern that a relic reputed to be the cup set before Our Lord prior to the Passion is to be sold to the highest bidder at the premises of a well-known London-based firm of auctioneers. The Church, as such, has no interest in what appears to be a dubious transaction continuing, as it does, to question the validity of the claim made by the vendor.

Nevertheless it is widely felt that a degree of insensitivity is displayed, remarkable even in today's materialist society, to a proposition however notionally erroneous. Many in the highest places speak of constructive blasphemy rather than wilful sacrilege, and express their conviction that no well-disposed collector or institution would connive with error in the face of overwhelming doubt on the one hand—and cause for suspicion on the other.

A clever pasquinade, killing all manner of birds of ill-omen. Through the ultra *Osservatore* the Church is on record as distancing itself from a rumour anxiously investigated by a long dead pope.

Onus to the Deodatis and their end of the line for daring to profit by such a rumour!

With excelling hair-line logic the Church left ajar the door it hesitated to slam, by distinguishing blasphemy and sacrilege. If, inconceivably, the cup be proved authentic a commercial transaction would be blasphemous; until it *can* be proved, any attempt to pass it as genuine implies sacrilegious intent at the least—thus protecting the virtue of one still to be found in a Genoan chapel.

To do him credit, Sir John thought hard on the wisdom of passing this news from next door to nowhere to the volatile Inspector.

He would learn of it anyway.

But it does lead on to another snippet.

The press showing at Peachum's.

Most people are familiar with auction rooms, so it's enough to say Peachum's is as shabby as the rest, though it's hard to describe the I-don't-know quality of that shabbiness. Whether it's a result of benign neglect or a simple *tour d'artifice* is another question, but unkind competitors tend to sneer that much of the dust is years of residue from what's thrown in the eyes of the bidding public.

Dust-laden it is. And begrimed it always has been, thanks partly to the charming conceit of a fire waxing merrily in old Adam's fireplace summer or winter. Sometimes the chimney is swept.

An air of olde, one might conjecture. Taken with the ubiquitous flunkeys in those adorable knee-breeches and buckles—Woman's Hour—and a plethora of candles to light up the disposal of time-worn remnants, the fostered illusion isn't half bad.

So, journalists and flash cameramen fill this minor palace of varieties and Mr Condamine, on the rostrum above the displayed treasure, is fielding questions with the greatest complacency—and Mr Cuthers in attendance.

Most of the queries were predictable until a ticket-of-leave man from Wapping artlessly leads up to a shrapnel-filled leading question.

With half an eye on the Reynolds (attributed) above the Chairman's head he mildly wonders aloud: "I suppose this 'treasure' is well documented?"

Condamine replies huffily that he supposes correctly and reads aloud the proof chapter and verse.

"So it remains a rumour *because* of the papal letter?"

"If you mean the cup—yes, of course. It obviously hinges on that single mention."

"How was the letter found?"

". . . I've no idea. What matters is, that it exists."

"All kinds of relics were fabricated in those days. How can you be sure this isn't one of them?"

Condamine nodded to Cuthers who seemed, to the lynx-eyed gathering, badly on edge.

"The historical evidence supplied by the Marchesa Deodati is strong, very strong. The cup is of a kind commonly found in that area in a fairly broad time scale. It's an inferior bronze—but quite indestructible—there's certainly no doubt it was brought from the Holy Land. A thermoluminescence test will verify a great deal I'm sure, quite sure."

"As to time or place?"

"Er—both one hopes."

"How can the test identify provenance?"

"It's a technical question concerned with local mineralogy."

"Would your confidence in this artifact be undermined by any authoritative opinion appearing to cast doubt on its holy origins coupled with accusations of blasphemy?"

A clamour of excitement from the journalists gave Condamine time to recover. Plainly, Cuthers was beyond recovery. "I know of no such opinion."

"The *Osservatore Romano* isn't given to sensationalism."

Condamine summoned his best endeavour and, as he was the first to admit, delivered the finest riposte of his career. "Neither is the *Osservatore Romano* infallible."

Clever enough to deflect further pursuit for the time being. After a few more questions concerned with details of construction and artistic merit, the show ended. Condamine, in a state of panic, called a crash board meeting.

By tomorrow, he predicted, the whole world would know doubts had been cast on the cup by some who appeared to speak with authority *and* conviction—and what could that not do to the value of this likely jewel in Peachum's crown?

Fasely, the PR man, was hauled in to advise but, strangely, he seemed cock-a-hoop at this seeming disaster.

"Let it ride," with almost hand-rubbing glee.

"Let it ride?" an echo and a chorus.

"Of course! What's better than doubt? Faction is action. Controversy creates maximized interest. It's the argument that sells, not the article. The world's real axis is pro and contra."

Without taking quite such a global view, the directors felt the force of Fasely's sucker-punch theories. He earned his salary to get results, not necessarily connected with evaluating works of art and other whigmaleeries so it mattered nothing if he insisted Louis the Quinze was gunning for Harry the Horse.

He reminded them that tonight the Treasure was scheduled for TV treatment, as to which he had a big surprise connected with its promotion. All tending to raise drooping spirits, even Condamine's, who improved the fitfully shining hour by firing off a letter to the Marchesa reminding her of the firm's "no liability" policy.

Much of the day went into dull, plodding, routine work that never makes the headlines. Like any nine-to-fivers, Cherry and Duff found themselves free to share the rush hour. More correctly, Duff stopped off to eat at Cherry's place, where they were scheduled to watch the evening "News Current" on a portable TV borrowed from the Duff household. *Some*body had to be there simply to show Cherry how to "stabilize the damned thing".

A meal was ready laid in the kitchen.

"Isn't that nice?" Duff beamed with hypocritical satisfaction. "Soup, salad and fresh fruit salad."

Cherry glared at the tastefully set out table, certain that Mrs C was nowhere in evidence. "That's the second time this week! It's too much! I'm a no-nonsense man when it comes to food. Stodge and two veg, steak pie and—and that sort of thing. Look at it! Grated turnips and desiccated god knows what! Take it from me, Duff, you won't get far on such pallid pabulum . . . you especially. Damnit, it'll be yoghurt on toast next and—"

"I hope that's to your satisfaction, Mr Cherry."

Mr Cherry spun round, quite goggle-eyed, like a consternated Lot wondering what on earth he could do with all that salt. "Mrs Craxton! Good heavens, it can't be—I mean—surely it isn't your—"

"If you remember, you very kindly invited me—yesterday I think—to stay and watch an item on TV."

"Why?"

". . . you said you thought it might interest me."

"Did I?"

"How very nice of you," said a genuinely surprised Duff. "I must say it only goes to show we're *all* human."

If looks could kill *is* a cliché, but it's not the worst of them. Duff retreated behind one of that morning's papers.

"Ah yes, so I did. A duster in your hand—you've been dusting I see."

"Fifteen thousand books. Much like painting the Forth bridge. If it's convenient I'll go back and . . ."

"No, no, stay. Er—have some of this delicious looking—er—salad. I was only saying to Duff—"

"So he was, Mrs C. I've never known a man so gone on desiccated god knows what."

Mrs C smiled and retreated gracefully to dust another hundred or so volumes while the two men ate in somewhat sombre silence.

"It's all beginning to look rather serious," Duff essayed to Cherry moodily forking about with his fruit salad, mind manifestly elsewhere.

"You're absolutely right. I haven't seen apple pie and custard for weeks."

146

"I *meant* the Sarinan affair."

"Oh that. I'd say it's progressing nicely, very nicely indeed . . . I have to admit she makes an extremely good custard—important with pies."

"*Can* I press you to biscuits and cheese?"

"No thanks. Couldn't eat another thing. Very filling all this, but it doesn't last, y'know."

Duff lapsed into puzzled silence, idly resumed the paper. Tried an appeal to the intellect. "I see the editor of the *Daily Strip* has agreed to do something about the page three tarts—he's blacking out their faces to preserve their—"

"Tarts! Apple tarts, raspberry tarts, *jam* tarts—you simply never see them nowadays. People don't cook anymore."

Duff lowered the paper to stare unbelievingly at this sudden gourmet gone berserk. Normally so perceptive he quite failed to recognize Cherry's mind was more on Mrs Craxton than even Cherry could know.

"While we're on the subject would it not be apropos to discuss the virtues of prunes—with or without?"

Cherry flared briefly at Duff's highly effective powers of withering sarcasm, then caught a glimpse of himself in a mirror, as it were, and rancour died.

"I'm sorry, Duff. At odds with myself."

"Not to mention the rest of the world?"

"Doesn't it ever get to you?"

"What can I do about it? You're mourning the death of the individual, but the funeral's been over a long time. Read the *Guardian* or the *Daily Strip* you're a circulation figure, watch TV you're a TAM rating, follow politics, you're a gleam in the pollster's eye, unemployed you figure in the statistics—doesn't matter what—you're just a number. Christ! when will people realize the endangered species is *us*!"

Duff caught off guard, Duff at his bitterest, sounding the despairing note that rightfully belonged to Cherry who, for once, remained silent and a little concerned—which also made a nice change.

Both toyed with coffee; neither saw any advantage in words for their own sake. By degrees they returned to that bit of the world so contrived as to justify their existence. They could no more afford to look back into the darkness or down into the depths than any other ordinary mortal who'd sacrificed his destiny in the race to belong—to anyone or anything other than his very own being.

"Serious?" Back to reality with a bump came Cherry. "Assume it is; what can we do about it? We're not characters out of a hack novelist's repertoire, filled with insight, full of superior logic, everlasting victors in some sort of sadistic contest. As if *their* violence is an exception to the norm—society is violent, full stop, almost one hundred per cent—not in deed so much as in desire—and *then* the deed . . . emulation."

"All in the mind."

"I've just said! It's *not* all in the mind. People act up to the EastEnders. TheEast Enders doesn't play down to their natural pre-TV level of behaviour."

"Meantime?"

"Meantime, Sarinan's in custody—and the Deodati Treasure can't be in two places at once—can it?"

Duff wondered strangely. "What does that mean?"

"We'll have to wait and see." And with an Asquithian injunction the sergeant had to be content. But the lack of professionalism in Cherry's attitude bothered him. Fatalism he knew, created more problems than it solved.

That he under-rated the Inspector on this one was hardly surprising.

They went to the study and complimented the cook. Cherry, with clumsy courtesy, invited her to take a chair while Duff switched on the portable. Cherry sat in stony silence watching the earlier items.

"Mr Condamine, I'd like you to meet Mrs Trumbull."

This invitation from Fasely, the PR man, came half an hour before the recording to be shown later. The ten minute slot "straight from Peachum's auction rooms" could only impress the sated, jaded nation by broad-brushing with the fullest dramatic treatment. Careful lighting, splays of candles, the evidential flunkeys—even the Treasure itself—were insufficient.

Fasely cast about for the megawhat gimmick and, by chance or coincidental inspiration he hit on precisely the same ploy favoured by the Commission of Cardinals. He recalled the renown of a certain Mrs Trumbull who, like Signor "Vanilla" Saachi possessed the sensitive touch. He promptly located and invited her to try her powers on the Treasure.

The TV producer was enthusiastic, the anchor man proved ecstatic, Condamine was mildly cautious but saw no real objection, Cuthers thought it a splendid idea.

The scene was set and rehearsed to the point of Mrs Trumbull's introduction. After a few facts laced with historical superficialities, a brief interview with Cuthers and a dimming of lights leaving the Treasure an island of glitter and gilt in a sea of darkness, the anchor-man made nice noises about Mrs Trumbull and the lady herself was revealed to the viewers—or as many stones of her as could be packed into the 22-inch frame.

It may be remembered that Mrs Trumbull had been instrumental in discovering the murderer of a pop star's mother through the agency of the weapon—a hammer. The pop star was the killer but only Mrs Trumbull tumbled to the fact. A formidable lady, with many such successes to her credit, she'd created a large and lucrative demand for her services. Fasely saw no reason to damage her exquisite sensibilities by refusing a demand for a fee of two thousand plus expenses. Formidable indeed. Sizeable certainly. Middle-aged presently, she could scarcely remember her married life, except her late husband had died on their wedding night, and on that point she was extremely sensitive.

Unlike her practising, mainly sisterly, colleagues, Mrs Trumbull was hearty and downright. She never stuttered, seldom faltered and scorned the pretence of a trance, or even a delicate shade of coma.

"This is the subject is it?" Oblivious to camera, crew, Condamine, Cuthers and the rest she marched like a militant hippopotamus to the Treasure, showing it no more reverence than Billy Sunbeam's hammer. Lightly she ran surprisingly delicate fingers over the whole of the jewelled surface, eyes half-closed, as if to catch emanations unawares; then, in business-like tones:

"There's something odd here . . . I sense I'm in the presence of a mystery—a great mystery. I don't much care for it, quite frankly. This is altogether on another plane . . . yes . . . the thing is incomplete—quite definitely a missing object—something's missing—long associated with it . . . yes, a lot of trouble, but a tangle of knots."

By any reckoning it was an impressive performance because Fasely then led the lady to another table on which reposed the cup—mounted like a Tiffany loss-leader on rich blue velvet that threw its simplicity into poignant relief.

As she approached it under the camera's scrutiny the thickest viewer could remark each facial nuance, from the puzzled frown to slow dawning recognition that here indeed one stood before another kind of mystery fit to be relayed by an intermediary and shared by millions.

"This belongs," authoritatively. "Somehow, this is part of that thing over there . . ." Again she ran fingers rare as sonar over the cup while the camera reflected her feelings, a sense of awe, half-stifled, but undeniable, the softening of none too soft features. No actress could have bettered her wide-eyed surprise as she stared down at what the Arabs would call a *fingan*, carefully embraced by those feathery hands.

Millions won't easily forget her next words.

"Murder . . . attempted murder . . . perhaps—years . . . two thousand years ago—quite positively—someone knew—they refused to drink—this was a deathly chalice . . . and it was refused, no doubt about that . . . I sense nothing more . . ."

And, for a space, there was silence over the land. Everyone knew what the Treasure was supposed to contain and here was Mrs Trumbull more than hinting at attempted murder before the fact.

This was the big one, sensational enough to feed the media for days, intriguing enough to spawn a dozen books of pseudo-analysis, topical enough to keep the lager flowing in every bar from city to village.

Big enough to shake Cherry out of his *laissez-faire*.

As for Condamine and Cuthers, their reaction to this immediate trial and verdict by TV was of some interest. Condamine's business eye watered uncontrollably, the other seemed outstanding with upon-my-soul astonishment. Harder to define what this revelation meant to Cuthers. Contrasted with Condamine's background volubility the few glimpses of him on the screen showed a man bludgeoned into silence, pale and distraught. Plainly the PR man simply couldn't believe his good fortune.

The interviewer they loathed to bother with was so charmingly obnoxious, he almost stuttered into the sequel of a magnificent scoop.

"I should explain to the viewers, Mrs Trumbull remained totally incommunicado while we discussed the Treasure, but I must ask you now, Mrs Trumbull, how much you knew beforehand about this—this work of art?"

"The short answer is, nothing. I am incognisant of such matters."

"In spite of press coverage and advertising?"

"What is that to me? I never read newspapers, and I have *never* observed television."

". . . Never?"

"It's necessary though regrettable to remain in a state of total chastity as to the world's doings. Too much input can ruin one's output."

". . . yes."

"I cannot, you understand, allow my gift to be defiled by knowledge."

"I see."

"You seem mystified. Do you suppose, for example, scientists would allow their so-called knowledge to be defiled by the facts?"

". . . Mrs Trumbull, do you recall anything of what you said just now about these objects?"

"Anything? Everything. Frauds will readily deny remembrance of statements made in trance. Well, we can say all manner of things in a state which is, by and large, incapable of proof—but in a condition of heightened consciousness how can I possibly forget?"

"I see that naturally, but can you admit to visual impressions evoked by—?"

"None. They were too distant in time; the nearer the present, the more I'm likely to see. All the difference between long and short waves."

"What do you make of this—the Deodati Treasure, which you described as a mystery—incomplete."

"Well, I take it to be a piece of religious furniture—overdone,

151

in my opinion. Does it open? Yes—well, you've only to look at those pictures. If the Passion of our Lord isn't religious I don't know what is."

"Quite so. And is that all you—"

"You don't have to be a sensitive to see it belongs to the past, but don't ask me what past because I haven't the faintest idea. The Italians are very good at this sort of thing aren't they?"

"Let's move on to the cup. You remember it seemed to occasion some disquiet . . . Mrs Trumbull?"

". . . don't misunderstand me—I recall my words perfectly—and my feelings too well—they're still with me. It's just that I can't seem to focus my—this object is unlike anything previously experienced . . . I find it incomprehensible."

"And you really have no idea what it is? Of its origins?"

"None. Why should I have?"

"You spoke of murder—"

"I corrected myself I believe—attempted murder."

"Two thousand years ago—"

"I could as well have said 'three'."

"But you didn't, Mrs Trumbull. You specified *two* thousand years . . . doesn't that tell you what I think is clear to all of us?"

"Oh, you're referring to Jesus Christ, I suppose, and what he might have said to Matthew or someone. Well, perhaps he had other reasons not to drink. He was the centre of a power struggle wasn't he? Didn't he say 'my time is not yet'? No, I stand by what I sense when all's said and done. The threat of death was there and still is."

The rest of that memorable scene is unimportant. Enough told to explain why the world would buzz with speculation as Mrs Trumbull's performance was transmitted, translated and spread broadcast.

Let that pass. What matters is the impact it had on Cherry, Duff and, perhaps, Mrs Craxton.

The silence might have got out of control if Duff hadn't ventured a word. "Well?"

Cherry returned from some mystery tour of his mind. "Well what?"

"Sensational?"

The Inspector looked at the adjective first, Mrs Craxton second. "What do you think?"

"I think," reflectively, "Mrs Trumbull is a dangerous woman in her innocence."

"Why?"

"New shibboleths for old. A fresh excuse for controversy. At a stroke she creates a million DIY theologians and artificial zealots who'll pick over a subject they know nothing about because there's nothing to know. That can't be good."

"What about the cup itself?"

She seemed surprised by the question. "I see no reason to be impressed. If I had genuinely Christian beliefs it would mean no more to me than it could to the Bishop of Durham."

"Relics are meant to help sustain belief."

"'Relics, sanctified left-overs, call them what you will, proclaim a poverty of faith, demonstrate panic of belief, which to be total must be of the spirit or it is nothing. Nonconformity carries conviction precisely because it refuses to degrade the purity of its message with a veneration of blood and bits of the dead that has much in common with unhealthy enthusiasm for the exploits of Dracula.'"

"You're quoting."

"Yes—from your copy of Reinecke's *Religion as a Growth Industry.*"

"Further?"

"Nothing. I've watched a number of dots forming and reforming to create an illusion of a lady demonstrating that a little knowledge is a dangerous thing—and not without profit."

Well, I'm jiggered! This extension to a Hoover not only dusts my books—she reads 'em. And, good Lord! the Reinecke's in German!

He tried his damndest not to look—well—jiggered. "How do you read it, Duff?"

"I reckon Mrs C's about got it right. But I'm bothered about what Mrs T had to say. 'The threat of death', among other things."

"Suppose it was the cup. Wouldn't she be right? After all he died."

153

Duff nodded but seemed unconvinced. Cherry caught Mrs C shaking her head. "Yes, Mrs Craxton?"

"Two things occur . . . there isn't, in strict logic, a single artifact in the world that doesn't connect with the death of *some*one. It's self-evident. We just don't dwell on the fact . . . she talked of attempted murder—"

"Go on," he urged.

"It's difficult . . . I think she may be a genuine sensitive but I suspect she can't tell the past from the present *or* the future. The lines get crossed so that she sees correctly but not necessarily aligned with a temporal or historical sense."

"She confuses past evidence with future indications and vice versa."

"Something like that, yes," smiling.

". . . thank you, Mrs Craxton. Very interesting—and not unhelpful. Duff, it may be this charade means we're in business."

Duff couldn't see that far.

"Mrs Trumbull doesn't really know when or what she's talking about. Sarinan doesn't know why he's scared. We don't know what we're looking for. So much ignorance *has* to infer knowledge. Mrs Craxton has a point—this woman may have pointed to the future in her confusion, while trying to indicate the past which may or may not have present importance."

The sergeant's despair was more comic than tragic. "You know, Mrs C, I sometimes suspect that Mr Cherry actually understands what he's talking about."

He insisted on driving his portable *and* Mrs C home which mildly annoyed Cherry, though wild horses wouldn't have dragged from him the reason why.

After all, he genuinely didn't know why—as he repeatedly reminded himself at intervals of turning pages of Reinecke . . .

Twelve

BRIDGES TO CROSS, and one more snippet to come. An important snippet—from the least expected source.

The next morning found Duff at the Inspector's place for coffee and the ritual scanning of the dailies. Plenty to scan with Mrs Trumbull's explosive performance close to being front page news.

"Medium Claims Attempt on Christ's Life" was one of the more restrained headlines.

It was the *Telegraph*'s unusually thoughtful analysis of the event that had Cherry looking more animated than normal for the time of day.

"Listen to this, Duff.

"Last night's appearance on TV of a medium or 'sensitive' highly regarded by those who know about such things must be rated as impressive given a world made hungry by what it feeds on, a craving for the sensational at least every other day.

"Time may be needed for the message to come through. An attempt made on the life of Christ before his on-the-record execution. What effect this 'opinion' may have on Christian faith is not the bone for our contention, but we are entitled to ask where the current fashion for revising and tampering with history will end. Historians we know about. They are paid, in part, to fight the Wars of the Roses all over again, but what of a woman who openly confesses to almost total ignorance of things historical and theological? Is the uncommon touch enough?

"Or are we witness to the common touch running amok? Democracy tampering with the accepted reading of the past? We may be paying too high a price for the right to speak beyond our competence on any and every subject between heaven and earth.

155

"One wonders if private enterprise is to be encouraged at any cost in spite of its present position as a cut glass jewel in the cardboard crown of democracy.

"Those charged with the disposing of this 'Treasure' are rightly concerned to command the highest possible price, but to encourage side-show speculation of such prurience is to degrade too much of potentially spiritual value in the name of profit.

"As an antidote to their euphoria Peachum's might do well to check that they have the right treasure since it appears a duplicate may exist in the very castle from which this one originates."

"Another one . . . how would they know that?"

"They were informed obviously."

"Disinformation?"

Cherry doubted it.

"So the old lady's playing a double game."

"With nothing to gain and too much to lose . . . there might well be a copy. The next best thing to parting with a rarity is to keep its replica—it happens."

"And where does that leave us?"

Cherry sat back and lit his first cigarette of the day. "How many strands? One or two or more? Do they entwine? Is the Treasure in danger? Is Sarinan?" He paused, hopeful that Duff might have something to contribute. He hadn't.

"Exactly. Perhaps you were about to suggest there comes a time when one has to make something happen—to force the issue—before the issue forces us."

"If you know the pattern," Duff cautioned.

"If you suspect the sequence and the sequel," Cherry countered.

"Is one permitted to ask—?"

"Permission granted—that's all. If I choose to take a calculated risk and it fails, you're in the clear because you didn't know about it, yes?"

"You could try a hint," bitterly.

"If there is a case, it depends on Sarinan's flat in Frensham Court."

"Notes under the door?"

"No. The carpet."

"And the calculated risk?"

The Inspector shrugged. "Have it your way." He stubbed the half-smoked cigarette and showed signs of leaving. "Getting Sarinan discharged from custody. Let's do it now."

"Hold *on!*" the sergeant's face resembled a picture painted in a frantic rush. "Discharged from *protective* custody."

"Protection against what?"

"Threats!"

"Empty . . . Duff, as police officers, we're expected to be fooled some of the time. There are limits—this is one of 'em. Let's to Marlborough Street."

Twenty minutes later Duff was still bothered. As he explained. "It's just that I can't help thinking of Mother Shipton's prophesy last night—death in the future if not in the past."

Cherry positively wriggled with irritation.

"Didn't you *hear* Mrs Craxton's little pearl of wisdom? Death is implicit in everything we touch—we're all involved in a symbiotic process of decay—non-stop mutation—it's a universal fact, like it or not. But if Mother Trumbull had prophesied Sarinan's death in a car-park at one o'clock next Monday morning *that* would be impressive—if it happened—she merely stated what everyone should know."

"There has to be more to it than—"

"Of course! Ten million dollars more, *things* men will kill for, authorize murder for, good God, do we really need the Trumbulls of this world to teach us how to suck eggs!"

Special clearance procedures had to be gone through, much signing of documents and arrangements made to compensate the damaged party before they could claim *habeas corpus*.

They found Sarinan in expansive mood, perfectly content with his novel if restricted way of life.

"Ah, Inspector, I'm glad you come. I have many things to discuss. And I must first tell you I change my mind about who is responsible."

"I'm listening, Mr Sarinan."

"The Church would not descend to this kind of thing—but

fringe groups, the real fanatics who stop at nothing to protect the interests of their faith, yes?"

Cherry nodded—once.

"So, in spite of the food, I am better where I am, for these people know that I, Sarinan, hold the destiny of the Deodati Treasure in my hands alone."

"How do they know?"

"It's simple. From them nothing is hidden."

"You stand, do you, between 'these people' and a priceless symbol of spiritual significance?"

"Such poetry! I cannot do better."

"Well, Mr Sarinan, I can tell you our enquiries are now well advanced, and we *know* the Treasure is under threat from another quarter entirely. And they haven't the faintest idea of your part in all this."

A kaleidoscope of reactions played havoc with Sarinan's incredibly mobile features which skidded to a halt at the point of perplexity.

"You *know*? But—but that is—unbelievable. I am dumbfounded so that I can hardly speak for—"

"Dumbness?" Cherry obliged.

"That's right. I don't know what to say, so I don't say much . . . but *who* is responsible and why do they follow me?"

"You can't expect me to tell you that. But I can assure you they're only interested in the Treasure. So you're at liberty to leave—there's a question of reimbursing the authorities for payment of compensation."

"Of course . . . of course. I will do that but—can you be *quite* sure I am in no danger?"

Dramatic, the change in Sarinan. Dramatic. That was the problem. Impressions of one at his ease, impressions of a badly worried man, received by Condamine, Cuthers and now Cherry. Was he, the Inspector wondered, just another brilliant actor, master of the quick change, conditioned by a lifetime of cajolery, of persuading hard-boiled magnates to pay his price for pricelessness? Or was he the natural son of Proteus?

Either way, the freedom being thrust on him seemed to strike Sarinan as a diabolical liberty.

"No danger?" Cherry considered the plea. "That can't be

158

guaranteed to anyone these days. Street accidents—air travel—and so on."

Sarinan snapped finger and thumb as if dismissing a naivety out of hand. "Accidents! I am thinking of accidents on purpose. You don't know this business—the people involved. Ruthlessness? I tell you, drugs don't compare with desire to possess a rarity. Women? cheaper by the dozen. But the Deodati Treasure in a man's eye . . ."

A moment of truth, sticking like a sore thumb out of that pell-mell persona; a moment he could ill afford—even, a badly disguised cry for reprieve. Stuck with his calculated risk, Cherry sympathized, but had to follow through.

They saw him off the premises.

"You'll be at the private viewing—day after tomorrow?"

"Sure. Or maybe not . . . can I afford to go public? What d'you suggest?"

"Use your flat."

Sarinan stared hard at Cherry. Like so many it took time, it appeared, to "see" him for the first time. "For the sake of my health?"

"We'll be watching it." Ambiguously.

Sarinan nodded. "I'm—glad." He hailed a taxi.

"One other thing, Mr Sarinan. Did you know there's a copy of the Treasure in Italy?"

Sarinan drew a deep breath, stared hard at nobody's fool, then that short sneery chuckle. "Who cares? I've got the one that matters."

They watched him duck into the taxi, loudly demanding carriage to Frensham Court. One of them doubted they'd see him again to talk to.

The taxi heads for Regent Street, and yet Cherry shows no inclination to go anywhere, idly watches the passing traffic. Duff, for want of anything better to do, watches it too.

"Hey! That's Robbins!"

Cherry smiled. "I forgot to mention. I called him early this morning—told him where to be."

Duff grinned his relief. "Calculated risk my eye."

Robbins was one of the best tails in the business and a never-far-distant third party in Cherry's small team.

★

159

They called on Condamine to satisfy curiosity. How, Cherry wanted to know, had Peachum's reacted to the press comment in general and the *Telegraph*'s leader in particular?

His complacency surprised them no end. Apparently everything was progressing very satisfactorily indeed. Allegations of a second Deodati Treasure? Quite true. All correct and above board. They'd managed to get through to the Marchesa at last, and she'd confirmed there *was* a replica—gave a very sensible explanation—an old piece, made as a form of protection—insurance. The original had been taken to Switzerland for safe-keeping during the war years.

As for the TV showing, the switchboard had almost broken down under a multitude of enquiries—many of them transatlantic calls. What was more, a very simple laboratory test had given a firm dating, two thousand years plus or minus a few—but all tending to bear out Mrs Trumbull's remarkable powers. Market expectations were climbing very nicely indeed. And how was Mr Sarinan?

Cherry, dead pan, assured him Sarinan was in the best of health and at liberty, hoped they might be permitted to attend the private viewing, was assured he'd be more than welcome—evening dress obligatory—and they left.

There was nothing more to be done for the time being.

Badly aware of fighting a battle on two fronts, one of them a thousand miles away, unsure of the enemy, the why and wherefores of its motives, Cherry pinned his hopes on a single, tiny, irrefutable fact, potential as an acorn newly planted, but downright meaningless until it did something.

Sarinan changed his mind about Frensham Court. The taxi did a U-turn in St James's Park and headed east for High Holborn dropping its fare at the main entrance to Postern House, a mammoth office complex bedizened with towers, walkways, courtyards, piazzas and fountains. Already it was the favourite haunt of loan sharks and DIY companies established 1986 and still going strong. A dozen exits made life difficult if one's interest was in following any suspect one of them.

The essence of shadowing is to avoid signalling the fact, so it's bad practice to enquire at the desk who's heading where, because mere enquiry can alert the wrong people through the wildfire spread of gossip. Covering every point of in and out is out of the question.

Robbins could only watch Postern House swallow Sarinan whole, leave it at that and report back. Obtaining a listing of every company on the site was an easier matter.

Sarinan, in fact, made his way to Block B, Floor 7, and the modest but modish office of Buonaventura Security Holdings, the part-time President of which is a Mr Luigi Morisco, a more or less American citizen with wide interests in casinos, a real estate company, an instrument maker's and a big advertising agency.

Mr Morisco spends a lot of his time in the UK, roughly coinciding with those stressful periods when the going gets rugged "USA wise". Hardly surprising, since Morisco rates as one of NY's most prestigious drug barons. Somehow none of this is laid to his credit in his favourite land of hope and glory, mother of free enterprise. Extradition proceedings would be unthinkable . . . he's not *that* kind of terrorist.

Strange chance! Morisco always knew when to run. Has the best inside information of any crook stateside. There's more than a rumour he donates half his two hundred million dollar income to the Church.

Known affectionately to his friends and enemies as "a cruel fat slug covered with spit" Morisco is crazy about business, money, religion, Reagan, Thatcher and Iain MacGregor in that order. To be on the safe side he's also crazy about the Monarchy.

He's no mobster he'd have you know. "Violin cases is strictly for fiddles." Protects himself naturally. "D'bigger your calibre, d'bigger your ass-hole enemies. And you're bound to have your share of those when you get an audience with d'Pope".

Fond of the arts he ran a singer or two in New York, a string of pop groups around the country. And he saw beyond the competition how legitimate business can fuel the power house where the really big money breeds. But that's a long story taking one into a graffiti-covered world stretching from Wall to the Street of the Lombards which is maybe where Morisco's fore-fathers came in.

Morisco happens to be in Town to pay a debt. When someone

scratches your back—you'd better scratch back, no matter the hazard of catching God knows what. Morisco is not too happy about it but he knew what happened to Calvi, knows why popes have to die, knows Sindona got his with a suicidal dose of murderous cyanide and, at any time they like, they can prove he has no choice so why *should* he be happy about it?

Keeping his nose clean in this country was difficult but essential. Nothing illegitimate except a few kickbacks here and there to keep his business running sweet, but that's normal practice in any democracy. Guns, drugs, armed robbery, organized prostitution and hard porn were definitely not British. He left that kind of stuff to the natives.

A determined Anglophile, he works at it till he breaks out in a sauna-sized sweat. For instance he hated flowers except they play a part in his opponents' funerals; but he swooned over the Chelsea Flower Show. This kind of contradiction revealed the nicer part of his character, that of a shallow-minded ignoramus who'd long overstayed his welcome in this world because the queue was too long for the next.

That "office"—modish, or just full of decadent furniture a department store based in New Zealand couldn't off-load on to Arabs—and that says all. The ante-room was one big three point plug for all kinds of hi-tech gadgetry that didn't work and a page three secretary who couldn't even spell the word.

Morisco usually sat at a really smart desk which converted to a day-bed at the touch of a button. Currently, he's kneeling at a large prie-dieu mumbling to someone on the wall. When page three announces a visitor he heaves himself to a standing position, crosses himself, and waddles to the day bed which he converts to the desk.

Fat featured to his eye-balls, the pupils not much bigger than shreds of black pepper in his favourite Mortadella—a plate of which appears at a flick of his fingers—Morisco in an English lambswool and Gallery 69 slacks is a living example of what's wrong with the country. Why he should be allowed is a question of who does he like—and that we know already . . .

He is not alone. Morisco can't stand being alone. Considering the kind of company that would mean keeping, it's not surprising. So, there's always a thug in the room, sitting quietly in the

162

corner, ready to do his any bidding, from fixing a drink to fixing a trouble maker. Two or three such take turn about on a very demanding job. He treats them as tyranically as he treats his bloodstock back in Westchester. Years ago, they hint, he'd eliminated his youngest for being muscle-mouthed. "He talked to me, *me*, his own father, about ethics and associate crap of like nature. I don't like that. I brought up my kids good. No bad language."

Thus, Luigi Morisco, stuffed behind his convertible "at this moment in time" to use really bad language—looks more than a little surprised to see Sarinan at any time of the day.

"What ya doin' here? I thought we got a commitment."

Sarinan began to doubt, too late, the wisdom of disturbing Morisco at his Mortadella; it's repeatable that he had an abiding passion for the stuff, slicing it off with a razor-keen knife and slipping it deftly into a hold-all maw straight from the blade.

"Can good news wait?"

"What kind of answer is a question? Siddown. When d'ya get back? Will you take tea or coffee?" As a practising Anglophile Morisco took his role seriously, sublimely ignorant of the bizarre effect on his personality.

"A lemon tea maybe?"

"*Lemon*! that's communist crap. Try again."

Nervously Sarinan decided he needed something a little stronger.

"Norman! Kindly fix d'gentleman a slug."

Something black-haired, dead-eyed and mean-mouthed left its corner, opened a door in the prie-dieu and found wherewithal for a Scotch and soda, which it handed in silence to Sarinan before returning to its place.

"So what's new?"

"I come to tell you everything goes smoothly."

"That I know. That I pay for. You wan' applause? Okay, clap, clap, but no *da capo*."

"Believe me, Mr Morisco," Sarinan stumbled from bad to worse, now convinced he'd made a serious error, "it's better than you could have hoped for. I have it from the police themselves, no problem. They look elsewhere."

163

Morisco left off massacring his Mortadella, looked up slowly—so deadly slowly. "You what?" quiet as the grave.

"They made it clear. They don't even look at me—we we have nothing to—"

"Wait a minute, wait a minute, let me think . . . you followed your instructions?"

"All the way from Zurich. I tell everybody I am followed. I do it so well I begin to think I *am* followed."

". . . what about the consignment?"

"I pass it to your diplomatic friend in Rome—he fetches through to London, I collect and take it to my flat when I return. No problem."

"Followed!"

"How could I be? Sarinan was missing for two days."

"So why," slowly, "should the cops tell you," deliberately, "you have nothing to fear?" Chill as a morgue. Well, cold enough to freeze the man from the Lebanon to his chair. From where he sat he could see Norman playing "battleships" with pencil and paper while he served the boss with both ears.

"Because I go a step more—and I get myself arrested. I smash a window and I tell them I *want* to be arrested." It no longer seemed a brilliant idea. A pathetic attempt at laughter simply died.

". . . why?"

"To make it plain, I am genuinely scared. So how can I be involved?"

The Anglophile took a very long time to find words. "What are you doing here?" hardly more than a whisper.

"I—naturally I come to tell you . . . the good news."

". . . drink your drink."

For his size Morisco could move fast. He reached the window at the far end, gazed through the double glazing as if he might just *see* what had happened, what exactly Sarinan was muttering about—and what he should do about it. Sunshine happened to throw his great shadow far enough to lap at the dealer's feet.

Morisco turned with the speed of a handicapped snail. "What you tryin' to do to me?" still in the well-bred tones of a diplomat rehearsing his part for a tramps' ball. It couldn't last. "You crud! In this country I got respect. I support charities. I donate

164

to the new Chelsea private hospital of St Francis with a double bed named after me in gold letters! I got friends in the Sunday Club—in the Westminster House of Representatives *and* the guy on the Sadsack in the Senate—what you tryin' to do to me? There's a sweet old lady in Downing Street SW1—her eyes sparkle at my name. I'm negotiatin' for a *whole floor* in the Tower of London, block C, for my new tabloid. What ya tryin' to do to me? I got connections across the spectrum—time, sweat, blood, money! In five years I maybe get my first garden party invite, the cardinal dines with me à la carte, I got two fuckin' horses lined up for Ascot—I'm just *ten feet* away from the enclosure. What ya tryin' to do t'me! Here! take this genuine Sheffield and cut my throat before they cancel the honorary knighthood I pray for every night on my bended knees to the Holy Mamma—end me while I'm still respected!"

Morisco's gradual approach, the climb to an Italian grand opera climax arrayed with cheap emotions reduced Sarinan to such a state of panic he almost accepted the invitation and the shining steel hovering barely an inch from his nose.

"D'you know what they're screwing outta me to keep *you* respectable? Norman! Ring Geoffrey *now*. Tell him hoist that consignment outta Frensham Court *now*—tell him take care of it till I say so. Tell him don't bring it anywhere near me if he likes wakin' up every morning. And gimme that pencil and pad."

Movement, swift and silent, till the two men are alone, one in hell while-u-wait, the other in a panic-stricken quandary.

"And you—too stupid for others' good—he warned me that black-eyed guy—watch that ratbag—so right! *You* make it crystallized clear *you're* in the clear—smart guy—smart guy. So now they look for *what*!"

"Not for you, Luigi. You're not in the art racket. They look in their National Rogues Gallery for that kind of crook—they don't heed you."

"That's right . . . but they let you go."

"So they look elsewhere—it's simple."

"But what's the point!" bellowed hysterically, then repeated in that raucous whisper many had cause to dread. "What's the point—here, take this and the pad. Now write down three times like a schoolkid, 'What's the point?'. Three times . . . now sign it . . . okay, give me your homework."

Morisco snatched back the pad, lowered the greasy knife and returned to his chair with the air of a man at peace with himself at last.

"Mr Sarinan, you gotta learn, be smart, don't be artistic . . . you made a blunder—for you I don't bother, but I gotta pick up the tab for what I don' want in the first place. So I'm stuck with it—debt of honour—and I got the Brit's stiff upper lip to do it—tha's Luigi Morisco—no imitators. What you got to lose—three million dollars? that's the deal—"

"Believe me, Mr Morisco—"

"I don't believe anyone! I don't even believe my priest anymore—I only just believe myself *after* I double check who's in the mirror, so who are you? . . . get back to your residence and stay there till I say so. Don't move—don't talk to cops, don't talk to anyone—don't even talk to yourself. Just be around at viewing time."

"And—and the sale?"

"What sale?" He leaned heavily across the Italian leather-topped desk. "Just dream about two-timing the old ladies and your slice of a cake costing me millions already."

Sarinan looking whipped as a cur, edged towards the door. It took time to reach it.

"Sarinan!"

Sarinan stopped dead, ready to drop or smile if either was needed.

"The next time you see the cops . . ."

"Yes, Mr Morisco?"

The American borrowed the smile Sarinan had no use for. "Never mind."

The Lebanese left under a cloud no bigger than the bulk of a very unpleasant humanoid.

Which returned to the prie-dieu and knelt in solitary soft-spoken prayer. "Mamma, did you ever meet a guy that stupid? It's no wonder the Kid got zapped with the world so full of them. Too bad he didn't use a glass. They break easy—no more problems . . . no Sarinans . . . do me a favour, Lady, tell me how I handle him . . . yeah, tha's my idea too . . ."

★

One is tempted to ask, with all this happening behind his back, can Cherry possibly know what Cherry is doing? The short answer is yes—and no, because outside of novels, mystery is a pedestrian affair, a toilsome trek through nomadic territory, a dull plodding in circles, memorizing landmarks on the third, fourth or fifth circuits, watching for the acorn to betray its presence.

Meantime, and later that evening, while he broods solitary over a list of almost six hundred companies huddling under the Postern House umbrella some of the world is discovering how unimportant the Deodati Treasure ought to be.

Through one of those hasty puddings thrown together by TV, just fare enough for street-wise intellectuals contriving to salve consciences grown fat with sly helpings of *Crossroads,* or *Dallas* or *Dennis the Menace,* or by watching that quality quiz, "Questions of Moment", thumb supporting chin, index finger to the brow.

What they experience is one of those forays by interested parties into the arcane world of theology *ad captandum* and, very nearly, *ad nauseam.* To kick off the new season two leading churchmen are invited to give their considered views on the validity of Christianity's greatest find since the Donation of Constantine.

The Bishop of Whatchester and Father Norman St Clair, S. J. are locked in spiritual combat under the eye of George Mandeville, a sort of roving religious and correspondent for the *Morning Star.*

"Gentlemen, can I set the ball rolling by asking you severally for your initial reaction on last evening's view of the Cup in particular. Bishop Ridley?"

Ridley: Cautious optimism. Dare one go further? Take an article, set it to words and you have all the ingredients of a controversial soap opera everlastingly promoting the value of a soap we may use, but never worship.

G.M.: Father St Clair?

St Clair: Even if cleanliness is next to godliness I doubt I could see it in quite such blatantly commercial terms. To begin with, there is an "if". Soap advertisements are far more positive.

Last night, we were confronted with a sensational "if". The notion of the Cup as to origins is beguiling and I confess to a slight excess of adrenalin at first sight. Certainly the camera cannot lie, but may it not be guilty of half truths? As the item continued I did find myself questioning—ambience—as it were.

Ridley: I know what you mean. The circumstances do tend to fit a little too snugly. Out of the blue, a member of the Italian nobility reveals possession of a cup steeped in family history. It's to be sold, I understand, for charitable purposes, and that's laudable up to a point. But I must admit to qualms, sale by auction, payment of gross sums of money for an object of small intrinsic value—

G.M.: It *is* of a piece with the aumbry which has a market value of—

Ridley: That somehow compounds the offence. Two objects of veneration for the price of one—and does it follow they'll fall into reverencing hands? Only this morning I read that a powerful American fundamentalist plans to bid for the Treasure—I believe his sect is just three years old.

St Clair: A golden opportunity.

Ridley: Indeed, but antithetical to the purpose. Just as the deployment of a practitioner in haptics for dramatic effect is, in my view, a golden opportunity for tastelessness.

St Clair: Well, my own firm has never recoiled from publicity in matters promotional and devotional. I think I can accept the lady's good faith without altogether trusting to its direction.

Ridley: Your "own firm" I believe questions its authenticity.

St Clair: And rightly so. To question is not to deny, only to require a convincing answer however long it may take to come by.

Ridley: And if we never receive such an answer, isn't everlasting doubt worse than emphatic rejection?

St Clair: Only if one accepts the validity of emphatic denial *or* affirmation.

Ridley: With respect, your "firm" is required to do just that.

St Clair: In matters of faith—not substance.

Ridley: Which therefore leaves the question open now and forever, not only for this cup but for all material things, the Holy Shroud for example?

St Clair: . . . I think the two are not comparable.

Ridley: But a definitive decision has to be made some time surely? I mean, there were *two* Shrouds in competition if my memory serves, just as there are now two cups in conflict.

St Clair: The one pleads my point about the other. Time is needed before correct deductions based on genuine co-operation between scholars and scientists can safely produce a verdict.

Was ever the clash of swords louder than the clangour of words? And what would those words profit a man wrestling with an equally intractable problem concerning the Deodati Treasure?

It's all the difference between *posse* and *esse*.

Sacerdotal dispute centred on what its content might mean. Profane investigation concerned itself with things as they are.

In a few hours' time the private viewing was due to be held at Peachum's. The dilemma belonged to Cherry—what, if anything, was likely to happen? And why should he assume that something would happen?

As the churchmen fumbled towards an inconclusive "maybe" Cherry's eye snagged on the name Buonaventura Security Holdings . . . and it stayed there.

Thirteen

BY MIDDAY FOLLOWING, Cherry had all the information available on Buonaventura and its President, Luigi Pia Morisco. Transatlantic contact with the FBI filled in the background which he duly reported to Sir John who, as usual, took everything with a pinch of anything to hand.

"A long shot, Cherry—six hundred to one?"

The Inspector agreed.

"No Church involvement?"

"I'm not assuming anything at this stage. I've one fact to work on and one fact only. Sarinan is playing a crooked game and someone at Postern House is a part of it."

"But you've no proof."

"Sarinan is playing a *very* crooked game." Obstinately.

"I don't see it—not from what you've said."

". . . you asked me to look at the case of a badly scared dealer and the reason why someone in Rome should take the trouble to warn us this Treasure is a suitable case for the fraud squad."

"Well?"

"What are my instructions?"

The AC ground his teeth audibly. "If you're so sure about Sarinan you must have evidence to—"

"But I haven't."

". . . Cherry, don't try my patience too far."

"I have no way of knowing what he *intends*. He's part of a well concerted plan worked out long ago. The Treasure is genuine—so the call from Rome is a scare story, a smear *and* an attempted delaying tactic. Someone's anxious to prevent the sale—but it's going ahead. Sarinan is *not* a badly scared man—yet."

"Yet?"

"He's overplayed his part—I saw his performance—an actor who doesn't know the stage from the auditorium . . . he's back at Frensham Court and nothing happening."

"A plan presupposes a purpose."

"Of course, but is it to discredit the sale, to prevent it—or simply a matter of possession? Before I know which, something more has to happen."

"But dammit, if Sarinan is so obviously—"

"Sarinan smashed a window—that's his only illegal act so far. He smashed it because subconsciously he wanted to be out of the way when something happens. He didn't exactly thank me for putting him back in circulation . . . I'm sorry, I'm clutching at two substantial straws—they're just not strong enough to bear a theory."

Sir John relented. Common sense and long experience advised him Cherry was near breaking point on an assignment lacking form and content. No point in rushing things.

"Perhaps," he suggested, "we've been persuaded to read too much into this affair. Stick with it till the sale and we'll see how it goes. Hewlett tells me you're late on your leave entitlement."

"The last business took longer than we'd expected."

"Anything in mind?"

"We've booked a craft on the Broads."

"Very nice. We?"

"Sergeant Duff and his wife."

"Anyone else?"

"No, sir." Much safer than his stifled retort: The BBC Women's Chorus.

"Never thought of an ocean cruise? Meet some interesting types. Quite a romantic experience. Never know who you might—"

"Very constricted."

"Ah! But the company—imagine rubbing shoulders in the moonlight with—"

"The BBC Women's Chorus."

". . . the what?"

"Sorry. I was day-dreaming."

Sir John gruffly advised him to go chugging on the Broads. Monotonous adventure was about all he was fit for.

Cherry smiled all the way to the outer office door. Once outside he grew serious and wondrously intrigued by a thought that had gate-crashed quite unbidden.

I can't save Sarinan.

A thought wasted apparently. There at Peachum's, much later in the day, was Sarinan, large as life and twice as capable of dealing with it. Perhaps not so flamboyant as heretofore but charming still, a man who'd palmed his way so elegantly and profitably through the back-alleys of a bazaar existence.

Viewing day at the auction rooms compared favourably in the social calendar with the RA Burlington House's private view. It very nearly surpassed the actual day of sale. Not all of them of course. Just one or two per year were given the full treatment when society, hospitality and publicity came together in one glorious glitzfest to demonstrate the superiority of matter over mind.

Rather Glyndebournish, too. Evening dress *de rigueur* befitting the occasion and time—half-past seven. On the rostrum a string trio sawed Haydn in two in revival of a custom that had lived and died with the first Peachums, one of whom had played patron to Mr Handel no less.

As then, and ever since, a cloud of flunkeys circulated with wine of the finest vintages salvaged from the wrecks of past family disasters: champagne, hock, claret, fine Madeira and Tesco's best sherry to ease the pressure. Delicate sandwiches, cakes, petits fours and heaven knows what else went the rounds for two or more hours as the *beau monde* promenaded in and out of the Peachum's extravaganza.

Cherry in evening dress seemed to the manner born. Not so with Duff, who'd been dragged protesting into the hurly-burly. "To broaden your horizons." Vainly, he complained about sticking out like a sore thumb. "I thought you'd say that" and Mr Know-all produced an Elastoplast to prove it. In sheer cussedness Duff wrapped it round his little finger.

The sergeant, to put it succinctly, agonized. Cherry realized his mistake and mouthed an aside two minutes after they arrived.

"I don't know you—you're cramping my style—keep away from me. You look like a cack-handed conjuror soliciting rabbits. Meet me at the car when it's over."

"Meet you at the—and *I'm* soliciting," bitterly. But Cherry had already disappeared.

Duff had plenty to agonize over. Some of the biggest charlatans in show business paraded against that gorgeous backdrop. Most of them were there for the publicity; some wouldn't be seen dead in a less theatrical soup-kitchen. Mr and Mrs Bore-Hampstead, the famous husband and wife act, were already poised to strike with their doggie-bags.

Ten a penny pop-stars included two despicable has-beens who couldn't, so to speak, leave it alone; and the latest rave in subterranean culture surrounded by a coterie of worshippers. Virgin Mary, no less, otherwise known as the Pout on account of some very fancy lip work performed by a private hospital providing, quote, better treatment and facilities than are currently available on NHS . . . unquote.

What else do we have passing under Cherry's watchful eye? The usual magnates with millions to spare, socialite members of the kakistocracy, the world's leading refuse collectors, Arab princes graduated from tents but barred from Marks and Spencer's, a few Hooray Henrys, but no serious collectors. They'll seldom show their faces to signal in advance what their hands will do on the day that matters.

Of course, he dodges the ubiquitous BBC reporter person, accosting whatever came to hand with an exquisite finished school accent. Delicious was Cherry's pleasure when he saw it bearing down on Duff in the act of reaching for his third champagne.

The Inspector eased himself unobtrusively into a position of eavesdrop.

"Tell me, do *yew* expect to bid for the Deodati Treasure?"

"Me? Er—I suppose so—or I wouldn't be here."

"People are talking of ten millions—perhaps more. Would *yew* be prepared to go that far?"

"Oh yes. I'm a devil when I'm roused."

"Yew must be an industrialist."

"That's right. Buttons."

". . . buttons?"

"I make 'em. Started with button-holes and worked my way up."

". . . really? Er—what are your feelings about the cup of Christ? Could you bear to possess all that charisma?"

"Not really. I prefer a glass of lager."

Nose in the air moved away while Duff scowled blacker than his tie at a highly amused, apparently detached bystander who passed him with the lightest of side-mouthed comments. "Not too much of that stuff, Sir Armstrong-Vickers, you're supposed to be on duty."

But who was Cherry to ration Duff's genuine need for alcoholic oblivion as he sweated in a hot-house atmosphere made to cultivate orchids tipped with curare?

There, before Peachum's jewel-encrusted showpiece stood Broadway's golden boy, Johann Sebastian Fürdasgeld, million-aire composer of one religious *durchfall* after another. He too has his spellbound devotees.

"Sure, I'll bid for it, no matter what. I can see this baby laser-beamed twenty feet up in the second act. Man, when I heard what that box contained I ordered Concorde. Believe it, ten minutes before we hit Heathrow I had the scenario *and* the theme song stitched. This is gonna beat *Singing Solomon* and *Jesus Christ You're Late*."

"'Momentous Mary' is the loveliest song in the Anglo-Sexual language," a nearby zombie in a blue and white striped evening ensemble with maquillage to match, came in right on cue.

"You've heard strictly nothing yet, Frederick"—which was truer than he'd meant—"I can see the high spot now—he raises the mug—*this* one—to his lips and sings: Sometimes a Man's Gotta Drink and Let Tomorrow Take Care of the Sorrow."

Murmurs of incredulity and admiration.

Which was worse, J. S. Fürdasgeld cash-calling his divine Mealticket or another of today's screaming half-breeds fingering the sacred vessel and lisping through lips soft and bloodless as marshmallow, "I feel Jeesie is so near". "Jeesie" being this thing's nickname for God's own son.

One day soon that quote would end as another number in the charts . . .

Pointless to go on: financiers, moghuls of the mouth, of oil, of airlines, of rackets without number, they were genuine supernu-maries in a truly Rocky Horror Show, easy, greasy riders on a gravy train going nowhere.

Take one more example.

Gumbo was there, courtesy of Corporate International America studios—the weirdo who conquered Redland single-handed then personally gave it back to Gorbachov so he could do it all over again with next generation weaponry.

"You gotta be there, Gumbo," said his controller. "There's no way you can spit in the public eye unless you're in it—all the time." So there was the insignificant draped in a gold-lamé-trimmed evening dress and black string tie trying hard to look couth before a Flemish tapestry depicting the death of Hercules.

Like any bored spectator, Cherry went elsewhere, wandered at will through every part of Peachum's. Noted the position of offices, departments, appraisal rooms, library and research, the workshops, the accounts department, the lower back regions, vast cellars filled with flawed rejects, the packing and transit area under a great roofed space stretching from house to mews where chaos reigned in working hours. He noted the small makeshift canteen supplying coffee and tea breaks for seventy or more employees.

All these signs of prosperous hey-day, smelling of centuries, led Cherry into endless speculation. He felt at peace awhile, enjoyed respite in that sprawling world filled with Time's left-overs, returned unwillingly to the mainstream, passing through the main entrance on either side of which flunkeys stared superciliously then grinned at his broad mischievous wink. He was in time to catch a stab of repartee between two young sprigs left over from the last aristocratic shake-out.

"What's *wrong* with an élite?" one vacuous, fatuous, chinless, gormless, Polo-mouthed twit was demanding of his jaw-thrusting, bow-legged, supercilious counterpart, thumb protruding belligerently from hand in pocket.

"*You!*" barked the jaw with a thrust that could so easily have decapitated.

Taking a view of the scene, all hands shaped to one kind of glass or another, lips of those fat, flushed, fed-to-the-teeth faces, moving soundlessly in a general hubbub accompanied by Haydn, it struck Cherry that not a single plutocrap apart from J. S. F. was actually giving the ineffable treasure the least modicum of attention. Not one blasé, bleary eye so much as wandered to dwell, however briefly, upon the sacred utensil.

175

It might have been just one more of countless drinking vessels abandoned on chiffoniers, occasional tables, even under chairs. Just one more excuse for an elegant booze-up.

The curl of his lip said all.

Nothing was going to happen. And there's Sarinan to prove it . . . what an unmitigated waste of time. A quick glance confirmed Duff degenerating nicely, very nicely indeed, a glass in each hand and a benign smile for all and sundry including an eighteenth-century bronze blackamoor supporting a clump of regimented blooms in its turban.

He was about to rescue his friend and colleague from dereliction when a sudden prospect of Cuthers gave him pause; long enough to study this immediate impression of a man left out of things. He could marvel a little at the meek and mild enthusiast who might raise his eyes in ecstasy but never a fist in anger; a doubtfully acknowledged expert in his field, but ignored otherwise, he currently betrayed the other side of a personality badly caught, as it seemed, in the act—scowling out of character at everything within eyeshot. This alter ego, Cherry noticed, not so much drank as snapped at his glass, taking short medicinal sips, grimacing after each to complete the illusion of a resentful invalid.

The Inspector recalled his very first sight of the man and compared then and now . . .

Made his way through a dozen knots of flaneurs and parvenus, too preoccupied with preening their egos to allow him an easy passage, but he got near enough at last to acknowledge Cuthers' citric smile of recognition and, for a space, both men shared a survey of the crowded perspective.

"I can't think why you're here. Took you for a sensible man, Inspector."

"Line of duty. Just checking everything's in order and likely to remain so."

"We all have our reasons. I'm here for the money."

Cherry took that in his stride. "You stand to gain, eh? Very nice."

A wry smile and another sharp sip. The man was far gone—the likely loser in a breathalyser test.

"I mean, my salary depends in part on being present to answer any stupid questions a prospective bidder cares to ask. So far I've had two enquiries for the toilets."

"Contempt?"

"Does it show? I'd have sworn I had my feelings under control."

Cherry smiled and supposed Cuthers had strayed a little too near the madding crowd.

"Had it but one head!" viciously.

"Yes?"

Cuthers shrugged, tugged at his glass and made an effort to recollect himself. "I mean, one would do for all of them."

Cherry let his eye stray to the reason for at least one man's bile. After all, perhaps it hadn't been a waste of time. He cast his line, behind the fish's back, as it were. "Security seems lax. I see nothing to stop anyone purloining that cup at least and slipping away unobserved."

Cuthers shook away the idea, head side to side in a gesture of moody intoxication. "Doesn't work like that. No one's going to risk his reputation for a dubious article. And certainly not the criminal fraternity."

"Why not?"

"Precisely because they don't know the value—or even what the Treasure itself is worth. Perfectly simple. Nobody's ready to steal a damned thing till it has a price tag attached—that depends on the highest bidder QED and not before."

The Inspector saw no reason to disagree with a reasonable inference however slurred the delivery. "And then?"

"Cupidity takes over. For the moment, that thing's in limbo, in purgatory, *in vacuo*—whatever you care to call a transitional state. But once it belongs—then watch out."

". . . for what, Mr Cuthers?"

"Nothing!" Violently enough to prompt a languid glance or two in his direction. Again, he made an effort. "I'm sorry. This business is altogether too nerve-racking—the last few days . . . I used to work at the V and A—research assessment and conservation. All highly civilized—this!" he gestured a noose of disdain for the rabble, "is a world of artificial pearls and genuine swine."

"And the cup?" nudgingly.

Cuthers frowned as if he suspected a veil over the question.

"It isn't artificial, I can promise you that. The British Museum has one almost identical, brought up from a trireme wrecked off Sidon."

"It poses a deeper problem, surely?"

"Of *course*! The dilemma's already on the front burner. The cup must *not* fail don't y'see? It's the last tangible chance Christianity has in a totally materialistic and therefore incipiently terminal society."

"Why 'therefore'?"

"Materialism is about desire, which precedes acquisition which is about possession, which in turn generates fear; of loss, of theft, of illness, unemployment, war. Anything that endangers cupidity ensures a living death for the affluent society. Christianity can only compete by offering tangible benefits—Catholicism always recognized the imperative need to reach the materialist through the material . . ."

Sombre, by all the Furies! Cherry was bound to wonder, purely as a matter of human interest, why the expert should be so—

"Concerned? I'm not concerned. I just hate those specimens wriggling about on a pound of fat bacon left in the sun. Art was never a dirty word till they soiled it with their brand of degeneracy—beggars in Midas' clothing turning gold into pigswill."

Truly, the iron had gone too deep to leave much worth saying. But the Inspector watched that restless gaze come to rest on the neglected Treasure.

"I hope someone gets it!" a deeply felt imprecation, almost lost in the babeldom accompanied by Haydn, lending its share to the unreality of this "real world".

"Buys it?" Cherry half corrected.

An odd sulphurous smile. "Let the best man win . . . and I hope you fail, Inspector."

Too cryptic to take seriously, too memorable to be forgotten. Cherry moved on, still mindful of Cuthers but more anxious to waylay Sarinan, arm's length from the crowd, irresolute, uncertain of his part . . . black suited him, enhanced his carefully preserved looks and upright carriage, reminded Cherry of a Campari ad.

178

He noted the ill-at-ease glances of one who waits and watches for another. Separated to the furthest point from the Deodati Treasure, he stood by the flickering fire, purposely shadowed by ambivalent light from so many clutches of candleflame.

Cherry's approach seemed not to disconcert. In fact, he appeared relieved to be singled out for police attention.

"So, Inspector, you see I am not dead."

Cherry congratulated him. And waited.

"After all, I am talking to a policeman in black—for some people that's a sign of bad luck, right?" His smile displayed well-manicured teeth, an equally cared-for hand whipped a glass of flat champagne from a passing flunkey with the ease of an artful dodger born to the souk.

"I see you talk to Cuthers—what has he done this time?"

Cherry's attention strayed from the fire. "This time?"

"Cuthers is a fool. He doesn't like Sarinan because Sarinan has done business with him so take it for granted I know what I'm talking about."

". . . why is he a fool?"

"He's an enthusiast—that's no good in this racket. You want to believe a fake is genuine—so, it's genuine. This he does at the V and A and they purchase on his say-so. A real expert comes along and says you're crazy—that twelfth-century ivory was mass produced in Hildersheim five hundred years later—so he's out, like you say, on a cloud."

"Under."

"Okay, under, but is it my fault?"

"You sold it to them?"

"I sell nothing. I just act for a piece. I say, what d'you think? They rub their chins to the bone and say 'it looks genuine'. I admit maybe, but did they notice this and that? The mediaevals never learned how to go with the grain—they don't polish and the colour's too white. I *tell* them why. I tell them how I steal sweets from kids—can they wait to prove me wrong? I get the deal because they cut the cards so bad they need stitches. Believe me, for every Mr Cuthers in this world there's a hundred more."

"And they still trust you," traced with irony.

"Do they have a choice? Nine out of ten say I'm right. Sure, everybody looks, but I find, because every bit of me looks. Sixth sense? I've got six more. With so many I can afford a couple at the laundry."

"The Deodati Treasure—it wasn't arranged overnight?"

". . . I knew what was coming. It's genuine."

Cherry took a metaphoric look over his shoulder to check who'd questioned it. His eye veered from Sarinan to Cuthers propping his despondency against the elaborate moulding of a doorway, the worse for drink, but glass forgotten, clouded eyes fixed *à la* Mesmer on the tiny glittering ark of the Deodati covenant.

The cup . . . was it so difficult to envisage a ragged Sarinan disposing of his wares to some idiot crusader flushed with conquest? . . . I cannot tell for sure, O Martial One, but I have a friend, whose friend is of the Chosen, who swears by Abraham this is the veritable *bikos* that Jesus son of God and Joseph's spouse, which I don't understand but who am I to argue if you know best, maybe drank from just before he had problems. Miracles? How should I know about miracles? I got a living to make and that's a miracle for the marasmus these hard times. To you, one thousand . . . okay, eight hundred, but I don't promise nothing. Only tell you what I hear. Tell 'em it came from Jerusalem—who can argue?

Cherry came back to earth, compared his ten second vision with the immaculate deception before him. He no longer had doubts—not because of what Sarinan had so glibly volunteered, but because of what he hadn't even hinted at. And yet they both knew it had happened. To make assurance double sure he decided on a small gambit.

"Talking of doors, I don't see Mr Morisco here tonight."

Worth it, the draining of colour, the sudden whites of eyes white as immaculate dress shirt. Worth it, to be in at the death of debonair. The years almost visibly fell upon Sarinan scattering what remained of a painstakingly nurtured image.

"What did you tell him?"

And what more did Cherry need to know after a pathetically unguarded question?

With some deliberation he placed his scarcely touched glass on a nearby English kettlestand—possibly eighteenth-century.

"Strong wine, Mr Sarinan. I was beginning to see two of you."

Nothing, he assured himself, would happen that evening. He could safely depart with Duff in tow, let Sarinan stew in his own juice, leave Cuthers to reflect on the perfect marriage of grotesque with Dantesque; withdraw, simply to breathe the relatively unpolluted night air trapped in Congleton Mews.

Sarinan, he conjectured, dearly wants to live a little longer but, like the Las Vegas loser, can't see a way not to die. He glanced at Duff, smiling benignly still, glass in hand. No good asking *him*.

To the sergeant's everlasting horror Cherry drove them both home. By no means intoxicated, he was, in fact, stone cold sober before they reached the first set of traffic lights.

When you *know* a man's driving licence isn't worth the paper it's written on . . .

Fourteen

On a last cup of coffee next morning Cherry floated over the night's events while Duff scanned the papers. Almost all carried news of "the Cup" in one form or another. An eminent bishop dispensed gravitas in a quality paper, an editorial elsewhere speculated on national prestige bestowed by its presence and thought it shouldn't be allowed out of the country. There were reports of "last night's stunning celebrity-packed début of our lord's (sic) cup." One rag devoted to the prematurely senile wandered pathetically round a confused parallel with the World Cup.

"So let this holy mug be played for on the first division fields of England's green and pleasant land. Holier than the Milk Cup it could promote a spirit of peace and goodwill on the terraces that would be an example to terrorists in the rest of the world."

Duff read it aloud. It hardly dented Cherry's reflections. He'd gone through all the papers by seven. By degrees he condescended to return to the here and now of things.

"Questions," he informed his coffee-mate, "are to be asked in the House."

"Whatever for?" the politely surprised response.

"A certain MP is to ask that sick and tired woman if the Cup should not be purchased on the nation's behalf."

Duff wondered how she'd reply.

"'Not while discussions are under way to privatise the Church of England', I imagine."

"Meantime, what did last night's jamboree do for us?"

Cherry lit a cigarette and contemplated the fire in the ash. "We saw a bit of scene-setting, a dress rehearsal for the real thing on Tuesday. What struck me erstwhiles was Peachum's security—lax to the point of incitement. Twice or thrice I went in and out of a back door while an old watchman resembling an eighteenth-century Charlie dozed over his nineteenth-century

182

cocoa with a twentieth-century TV portable on top volume—
drugged into insensibility by zombies libelling the Cockneys of
yesteryear."

"And then?"

"While somebody on the screen was taking an overdose *I* took
a catalogue from his cubicle, located the thirty items for auction
in various crates and boxes dotted about the rooms and passages.
Incredible, eh? I could've walked out of that place with a
thirteenth-century aquamanile and no one the wiser."

"That's the point," sagaciously. "You'd have to know what
you're looking for—need for expertise. It narrows the field
dangerously."

"To what? Someone off the street lifting the old boy's
portable?"

Duff restrained himself admirably. "If anyone meant to nobble
the Treasure, last night was a golden opportunity."

"Who said anything about stealing it? And last night was not
the golden opportunity."

"Which one of us," deliberately, "is forgetting Sarinan?"

"I'm not. Our continuity man was there on cue, on edge and
playing his part nervously in that age old drama: The Lull before
the Storm."

Duff shook his head. "Maybe we're being unfair to him."

"Did you, by any chance," Cherry enquired, "notice the
straw coloured wall-to-wall carpet in his flat?"

Duff confessed he had.

"That's how he went too far. D'you remember: 'I am watching
TV when, from my eye's corner, I see this piece of paper come
under the door'."

"He showed it to us."

"I know what he showed us . . . but why not the letter-box?
When I tried slipping a piece of paper under, the carpet got in
the way."

". . . I see."

"One lie is indicative."

"And the second?"

"There is *no* Italian car-hire firm called Casa Mobile."
Duff nodded.

"Two lies create a strong inference. Sarinan was *not* followed, only created an impression of a badly frightened man. Very convincing until he goes too far—the artistry of vanity—misapplied like an aging woman fumbling with lipstick—flaunts his cleverness to our faces."

"But—"

"He was *not* followed till he hailed a taxi loud enough for us to hear 'Frensham Court'. We know he got to Postern House but poor old Robbins was bound to lose him in that warren . . . I told you to keep Buonaventura Security Holdings in mind."

"The Italian connection—'a very long shot' you said."

Cherry nodded. "BSH is interesting to the Fraud Squad, but nothing proven. It has a front man of impeccable assisted-place minor public school origins but the real boss is a Luigi Pia Morisco who spends time here when America gets too hot. He has a country house in Kent, races a couple of thoroughbreds, cultivates a few right thinking politicians—and others—the kind of transatlantic thug who thinks a Burberry can button over a bad smell."

Duff supposed he had a reputation in the States.

"A god-fearing mobster with interests ranging from credit-card games to off-shore finance. He does business with names who shall be nameless, says the FBI, because those names are written in nitro-glycerine."

"I see."

"Then your eyesight's better than mine." Cherry stubbed his cigarette, glanced at the kitchen clock and reluctantly got to his feet. "What does an Italo-American with much to lose have to do with Sarinan and the Deodati Treasure? He's about as likely to collect that kind of thing as a troglodyte."

"Even supposing he's your man."

"Oh, but well, yesternight I barely mentioned his name and Sarinan almost passed out."

". . . any verbal reaction?"

"Yes. He asked: 'what did you tell him?'."

"There you are then!"

Cherry shook his head in a perverse mood of dubiety. "I'm not sure at all. You see, he was looking at Cuthers as he spoke— and I'd just been chatting to the self-same fellow."

★

If there were lingering doubts in Cherry's mind about the verities hazily emerging from the Deodati affair, one was dispelled that day by Robbins' cryptic report.

"Two sets were ordered. By a Mr Smith."

"Who else? Did they query it?"

"He gave a convincing explanation—and paid cash."

"Good. You won't get much further on that one. Don't even bother to look for an address."

He replaced the receiver with enough satisfaction to tide him over the weekend. Until three o'clock on Monday morning, as it happened.

"I can't save Sarinan" came to mind as he stood with Duff on the third level of a multi-storey car stack not far from Battersea Park.

Mildly regretful he stared down at what remained of a fatal suspension, mildly surprised by stones found in the pockets of a raincoat, although the weather had been unusually fine for the last thirty-six hours, then, after a last cursory glance at a man, frightened to the very death, he wondered of the local sergeant standing nearby. "Anything found?"

"Usual personal papers, passport and effects—and this."

Cherry glanced at the passport and nodded over its final page. "That's it." Decisively.

"This" proved to be a strangely repetitive note, signed by the deceased.

"What's the point?" Cherry repeated aloud—three times.

"A suicide note," Duff ventured.

Cherry's gaze faltered on its way up, and he could wonder why Duff should regard him so—oddly.

"What's the point?" but, query or quote, it was hard to say.

"All the signs—"

"Point to murder. Any medical opinion?"

"An hour or two, not more, the doc reckons."

"That's right . . . murder," Cherry insisted.

"No signs of a struggle. Not a hair out of place." But the voice came from a great distance, almost beyond the Inspector's hearing. Almost.

"And the eyes tightly closed." Derisively. "And orange baling twine easily come by in the centre of London by a Lebanese who'd know exactly where to find it!" He turned to the District Inspector who knew his temper and reputation well enough. "This is a murder enquiry. Yours. Seal off the place, usual routine. Question everybody with a car if you like, but it won't help. Ten to one on a stolen vehicle and it's an automated entrance—much more automation and we'll all be out of work— if you find witnesses *and* a stolen car you're a lucky man."

"But no signs of a struggle," doggedly from his counterpart.

"I believe it. Arrange an autopsy as soon as maybe. Suggest they look for minute punctures back of either hand and if they don't find thiopentone sodium or something like in the liver I'll dine off a dictionary."

Cherry, in this vein, both feet on the ground, only superficially resembled Cherry in the clouds. Some equivalent thought occurred to Duff as he watched a routine investigation build into a thirty-second spectacular. He suspected a more significant, even sensational notion floating about somewhere in his early morning head if only he could pin it down.

"Press?" the local man was a detective of few words.

"Preliminary enquiries point to suicide—name unknown. *Definitely* unknown."

In due time Cherry and Duff wandered out into the street of a great city that still slept, fitfully, as if it knew the worst was over and life must wake and go on, managing as best it could without Sarinan . . .

Pensive and mildly dejected they returned to the car and sat gazing ahead at nothing very much, simply winding down, taking the dead weight of a man off their minds. Murder on time, or any time, isn't the most edifying experience.

Murder on time! Duff's elusive thought struck him hard amidships—so affected him he hardly dared a glance at the enigma beside him.

A few days ago enigma had dashed off a supposition. "If Mrs Trumbull had prophesied Sarinan's death in a car park at one o'clock next Monday morning *that* would be impressive."

And—there they were.

For the good of his nervous system Duff wisely left well-I-never alone. Suggested instead it might be time to point the finger.

Cherry lit a cigarette and immediately stubbed it out before considering the necessity. "At me for a start."

"We couldn't hold him forever."

"No . . . and I suppose he couldn't live forever . . . it's utterly damnable. They'll argue forevermore about who drank out of that thing and even whether it's *the* one, but, as of now, you and I are stuck with a killing cup . . . and somebody with a small blue plastic gun . . ."

Duff frowned his disquiet; not for the first time he furtively considered Cherry's mental equilibrium. Decided to ignore what had to be a flippancy in strange if not bad taste.

"Morisco?"

"Perhaps."

"You said yourself—"

"We question. He answers. We accuse! He denies. Calls on his high-powered pals to protect his reputation—that's the end of ours. Besides, it's all happening, Sarinan helped make sure of that—so why stop it? We'll just follow where it leads—then we'll question him."

The dead split. He doesn't care about Sarinan dead or alive but feels responsible. Once more it's got to him. Tread carefully, Duff, or you'll go over the top on the back saddle of his tandem.

". . . meantime?"

"Frensham Court, Flat 178."

"Now?"

"Now."

Five minutes fast driving through streets filled with dead traffic brought them to the riverside block and face to face with a drowsy night porter who handed them the key.

Signs of recent occupation: an electric shaver and the usual toiletry in the tiny bathroom. A few clothes in the sitting room, including a hired evening dress thrown over a chair—a half empty bottle of Gian D'Oro and a glass on the table. Nothing in the kitchen.

Cherry examined what little there was with excruciating care. Like a human geiger counter he even appeared to scrutinize nothing with interest. Or so it seemed to Duff when, at the end of half an hour, he came to a prolonged standstill behind the single low armchair facing the TV.

Duff's patience almost died of boredom.

"Come and look at this."

Duff gladly accepted the invitation.

"No, don't come too near—that's far enough."

"What am I looking at?"

"The pile of the carpet . . . two indentations—about nine inches long. Faint but just visible."

Duff had to admit the strong possibility.

"Covering an area about two feet six by a foot or so?"

The sergeant nodded, cautiously.

"Something heavy. It wasn't here when we first visited . . . it isn't here now."

Duff waited.

"Probably moved it around as a precaution . . . or panicked."

"Moved what, sir?"

Cherry seemed surprised by the question. "I was thinking of the Deodati Treasure."

Askance is a way of describing Duff's reaction. "We have to be a bit careful don't we? Both of us saw it three days ago at Peachum's, and if it went missing later I'm sure we'd be the first to know."

"I only said I was thinking about it." But the Inspector seemed more fascinated by a near invisibility than by Duff's appeal to common sense.

"Take another look at that patch of carpet . . . what d'you see?"

"Two marks and . . ." he bent closer, seeking hard to find, then stared up at Cherry who simply smiled.

"Handle with care," he invited.

With care it had to be. Duff straightened up with the merest spiral of wood no more than an inch or so of length, well defined away from that yellowish carpet, held tweezer-like between finger and thumb.

"Easily missed in that pile," Cherry admitted.

"But you didn't miss it."

Cherry shrugged, sighed heavily, as if tension must out. "The fall of the sparrow. Is anything known till it's at our feet?"

"And now?" gently.

"It's becoming less—opaque." He sat in the only armchair, a

man suddenly overcome by the mischievous weight of a splinter. "We have to follow where it leads."

"Peachum's."

Cherry nodded. "As far as tomorrow—Tuesday. We'll see an end, grave, comical—even farcical. I don't know."

"But Sarinan's dead."

"He's only the beginning of the end. A part of the perfected plan—"

"Involving?"

"Others, Duff. Morisco almost certainly, and . . . somewhere in Italy, a diabolically shadowy figure probably—one far beyond our reach."

Duff thought hard about this, anxious not to let Cherry drift into those regions eternally capped with clouds. "I'm not raising objections so much as asking a few questions."

Cherry smiled wryly, world wearily. "Both if you like. I'm probably up a small creek somewhere."

"What exactly am I holding?"

"A woodshaving, packing material fallen from a crate."

"Which isn't here."

"As you say."

"What's in the crate?"

"A copy of the Deodati Treasure."

"From?"

"The Castello Deodati."

"And what's it doing here?"

"Stolen."

"That's what I thought you might be—what *I'm* getting at is this. You put through a call to this Italian woman to confirm there *was* a copy."

"Right."

"Then why didn't she mention it was pinched?"

"She doesn't necessarily know. It's even more probable she doesn't want the fact publicized. Suppose it's stolen and makes news—would that do the sale of the genuine Treasure any good?"

"Why not ring and ask her?"

"To be told what I'm already sure of?"

Duff shook his head almost pityingly. "It's not for me to

remind you of the Copper's Lament: but 'we do all need a little something to sustain our beleaguered belief'."

"Oh, that." Cherry fished in his pocket and produced a greenish-looking passport. "I should've mentioned it." He handed it to Duff. "Just glance at the last entries."

Duff did so. And saw the point at once. "Rome—the 15th. London—the 17th."

"The two days he went missing between his first arrival on the 13th and window bashing on the 18th." Cherry enlarged to be on the safe side.

"So he died because he knew too much."

"I don't think he was meant to die at all. But I'm damned sure he made a shocking bad mistake by getting himself arrested— can't you imagine him telling a really practised crook like Morisco, say, and Morisco's answer?"

". . . 'what's the point?' "

"Guesswork, or maybe even *some*one saw him talking to me the other night."

"Someone would have to know who 'me' is."

Cherry was amused. "That's right."

Duff passed over that, being too full of another instant notion. "Without Sarinan, there's no sale. Maybe it's a drastic form of sabotage."

"Sarinan was about as vainglorious as anyone I've ever known. The world only moved because he was at the very centre— solipsism can go no further. But he wasn't essential . . . no, it's more likely he was sabotaged because he threatened to sabotage, by a stupid ploy, the sabotage of the sale."

Duff said he was feeling tired. Cherry tucked his wood shaving into a small plastic sachet and reckoned aloud no advantage could come of remaining there longer.

They went all the way home in silence except for Cherry's idle brevity. "The Copper's Lament. Are you sure the word is 'beleaguered'?"

Fifteen

HE WOKE TO the day of sale, prey to mixed feelings; the likelihood of failure, the chances of success, slim to the point of emaciation. Dressed and breakfasting done he pondered as he sifted through the day's Press on those two parts of one world and saw nothing in the new day that could promote him from one to the other. Yet, right or wrong, he knew he was right.

A redundant clown might have approached his cornflakes with fewer misgivings.

The schedule would be tight. The "Yard" by eight, two hours of briefing an expanded team, countless phone calls, a few harrowing moments with Sir John and, after a quick change, an interesting careers interview with Condamine . . . it was all, he assured himself and Duff as they drove to work, still happening.

The officers were assembled in Cherry's office, suffered his meticulousness to the screaming point—every contingency covered, no detail neglected. They left in search of strong coffee leaving Duff to reconsider a flounderer who'd been planning even as he appeared to flounder.

"You're not really going to—?"

"Why not? What was good enough for Sherlock is good enough for me."

"Thank God you don't play the fiddle."

"Have a care, Watson. I once took lessons."

He drummed his fingers till eleven when the pathologist, Cherry's favourite inveterate enemy, rang with what he was wanting.

"Clever Dick. There *is* evidence of sodium pentathione in the liver and who told *you* I can't imagine."

"Anything more?"

"'More' he says! There's such a thing as breakfast which I haven't had and sleep which I haven't had. Yes, there're tiny punctures in the left hand back, which are puzzling because—"

"Much obliged to you. I'll explain those later."

"Ex—!"

Cherry downed the receiver on a spluttering doyen of his grisly profession, more than half persuaded that what was happening very nearly equalled what he'd expected to happen.

Dynamic? Nobody had ever accused Cherry of that kind of behaviour; not even Sir John.

"I can give you five minutes, Cherry."

"I'm afraid I can't spare more."

"You—?" a convulsive clutching of that ill-conceived briar—a quick glance over his shoulder as if haunted by a mirror image of personified insolence. He swallowed something unpalatable and privately hoped the swine still had toothache.

"Sarinan's dead!"

"Yes I know."

"What else do you know!"

"I've a fair idea who's responsible."

"Then what are you waiting for?"

"Proof."

"Have you seen the day's *Telegraph*?"

"Yes. I finished the crossword over breakfa—"

"Damn the crossword! I draw your wandering attention to yet another pasquinade by a high churchman claiming the Dotiarti Treasure is a fraud."

"Yes, I saw it . . . I wonder which Dotiarti Treasure he meant?"

A long, smouldering regard. "You have my ear, Inspector—I didn't invite you to chew on it and spit out the pips."

Fastidious Cherry couldn't repress a grimace. "I thought I'd mentioned there's a copy."

"Oh . . . I see."

"Then again, he may be confusing it with another one."

". . . what other one?"

"I can't positively claim it exists—just a possibility—so I doubt he means that one."

"Cherry! I can't recall a time when I didn't need a corkscrew to get a straight answer from you. Sometimes I suspect you're laughing at me."

Resentment was immediate and obvious. "Life's getting too

painful to laugh at anyone . . . and I do a serious job because any man can make a mistake beyond the possibility of correcting it." And obvious was the bitterness.

". . . I'm sorry, but you do have a habit of complicating issues."

"If things were that simple I wouldn't be here now. If the Church of Somewhere wasn't remotely involved I'd not be here at all!"

"That's unfair and untrue! You've every latitude to find out who or what and no holds barred, and let me remind you, Cherry, the sectarian game doesn't apply in *this* part of the UK."

For moments both men waited till red needles on personal pressure gauges flickered to zero.

"I just don't see what anyone has to gain by stealing this thing."

"It's not a classic snatch." To Sir John's infinite surprise Cherry kept him enthralled for a minute or two with pure historically based theory. He explained that, though money was involved, the motive went beyond the mercenary. Two possibilities: the desire to destroy an embarrassing anomaly—or the theory of telesmata—the concealment of present anomalies to be revealed at future critical moments in history. A kind of instant miracle. He described how the pagan Temple of Mars in Florence had been re-dedicated as the Baptistery. The Church had removed the equestrian statue but dared not destroy it because it was written in the stars that the temple—and its contents—would stand forever. Cherry traced the history of that statue, its disappearance and reappearance, to become, at last, the nub of the grand feud between Guelph and Ghibelline.

"And where is it now?"

"It vanished in 1333—a flood I think."

To do him credit the AC, a never less than busy man, showed great interest—even asked for more examples which Cherry gave.

"Yes, feasible . . . I *think* I see what you're—and you'll know by tonight?"

"I'm sure of it."

"How?"

Cherry told him.

"Is that strictly necessary?"

"It's vital." He almost added, "because that's the way things are destined to happen," and thought better of it.

Sir John nodded fumbling abstractedly with the infamous chained ball-point as he considered new, unfamiliar premises not noticeably connected with smash and grab.

"When you *do* know, contact me here or home, whatever the hour. Call it curiosity."

"Yes, I'll do that, sir."

"Don't let me keep you."

Cherry saluted the irony with a bleak smile, took to his heels and got as far as the door. To be arrested by the Assistant Commissioner no less!

"You claim to have polished off the *Telegraph* crossword— what's the solution to 14 across? The clue is—"

"Green jumper kicking its heels. Twelve letters. Stridulating. Grasshoppers. He must mean the short-horned species."

And he'd gone before Sir John had quite finished nodding. Less than ten minutes later it struck him unawares that Cherry actually *had* completed the damned thing at some unearthly hour when sane men were still going through the day's first motions. He could have wept.

"All set, Duff. Cut along and take up your position. Check your back-up for reception and don't miss a thing ingoing and outcoming till—things happen." Could Cherry resist that last touch of whimsy?

"Shall I give you a lift?"

"From now on I wouldn't be seen dead with a copper."

"Charming. Transport's fixed us a souped-up Porsche. Robbins wants to know where to park it."

"I *told* him. Congleton Street, round the corner on the left outside the Pâtisserie. You'll be in it at seven-thirty ready for off—head on a platter if not."

Cherry, as such, disappears from this narrative for a few hours.

What emerged miraculously from the underground car park at about mid-day was a character so hang-dog, so down-at-heel, so lacklustre that a short-sighted faith healer couldn't have believed in him. Soiled jeans, a none too clean sweat-shirt printed with a never-to-be-forgotten legend: "I'm a boy, George", and a pair of clapped-out trainers did nothing to rectify an over-drawn sketch. Ye gods! he was the very parody and splitting image of much that's wrong with today—so many playing a part—and playing it badly.

The very bundle he carried looked grotesque and out of character.

It was Cherry's way. The first stage of his theory on the perfectibility, not of disguise—that's a mere papier-mâché device easily stripped—but of mutating personality and evolutionary character, performed, so to speak, at 78 and slowed to 33⅓ rpm.

Thus, en route for Peachum's, he transformed from Cherry, the ham actor, to Jimmy Boyson, the guy with a grudge, the effluent under the affluent. He takes a bus to the West End, modifies his sour expression, takes the excess hunch out of his shoulders, smokes a butt hand-cupped prison-style, buys a *Sun*, stuffs it in flak-jacket pocket, gawps at a video window display, waylays a WPC and queries in Londonese, "I'm lookin' for Peachum's. Gotn'y ideas?" Police person tries not to look disgusted and curtly directs him. Man says "Ta" with a leer before slouching off under her suspicious gaze.

He turns into the mews and sizes up the to and fro of traffic, hammering from somewhere, crates everywhere, must be the packing department. Takes in the familiar bustle with a newcomer's eye. A florist's assistant carries in great sheaves of hothouse gladioli to bedeck the auction room.

Three back entrances and a custodian for one. Asking for trouble. He ambles in looking vaguely about him till the timekeeper or whatever catches his eye.

"Want something?" For nothing, the censorious eye suggests.

"Yeah—I got an appointment—Mr Condamine."

The door-keeper softens reluctantly. "What's it for?"

"He promised me a job—in-house staff."

"Another one! Christ! we've got more than needed already."

"Temp'rary, he says."

"Have to be wouldn't it! And what's it got to do with Mr Condamine? Joe Dodds does the hiring and firing for you lot."

"He told me to get the gear and ask for him—that's all I know."

Cerberus raised his eyes to heaven and, being economy minded, kept them there. "Up those stairs back of you—three flights and along the passage, turn left down where the carpet starts, knock at the door opposite the walnut console table on which is a Nankeen vase full of bloody futures—and wait."

It was, in good sooth, a sort of Bedlam, people on the move, the clatter on bare floors and stairs, beautiful eighteenth-century panelling scarred for life, tattered paintings, long withdrawn from old sales, disfigured the stairwell walls like bad advertising on a dead escalator.

He easily found the Bleeding fuschias, knocked at the opposing door and waited.

"Come in." The remembered voice made its important announcement.

Jimmy Boyson entered.

Startling Condamine no end; he wiped the natural unction from his vocal chords and swallowed it. "Isn't my man out there?"

"No."

"Who are you?"

"Inspector Cherry—mostly."

Stunned disbelief, forcing the auctioneer to peer closer at this little lot and decide its value. "You don't look terribly like him."

Cherry showed his ID.

". . . well I'm bound to say, I'm amazed, Inspector. And somewhat at a loss. What—what can I do for you?"

Cherry explained briefly.

"You mean, a definite threat to the Deodati Treasure?"

"Exactly that."

"But—but that's impossible!"

"Why?"

"Because nothing of the kind has happened in our long and unblemished history."

"History has a way of defeating itself . . . if I'm not within ten yards of that item tonight there'll be no sale."

Condamine considered the unthinkable with very specific gravity. "Perhaps it would be wiser to postpone?"

"Certainly, if you're prepared to go through the business of re-stimulating interest while more doubts are cast on its authenticity."

Remembering some of the recent press comments, Condamine easily saw the point. "It isn't our fault, you know. We take instructions much like counsel from solicitors. We, as it were, present the case for judgment by the bidding public. So we don't, you see, enquire into guilt or innocence; nor do we depend entirely on *bona fides*. For example, a second test has confirmed the date of the cup *and* revealed traces of antimony on the rim . . . you seriously feel it's necessary to take on yourself the guise of a—a Peachum's employee?"

"With a free hand and a pledge of silence as to identity—this is between you and me."

"Of course, and I give it freely, but our general foreman is most pernickety—an invaluable fellow—but everything has to be just so."

"Just tell him you've hired extra help for the day."

Condamine rubbed his ample chin reflectively. "Better if you tell him, Inspector."

"Boyson."

"Ah! A *nom de guerre*. Quite right," Condamine entered by degrees into the spirit of things. "Well, er—Boyson, tell Dodds I hired you personally because of the inevitable crush. With him my word is law. We expect three hundred distinguished persons and Thames Television. Our doyen, Sir Norman Stoppit is tonight's master of the gavel. There will be no violence I trust, Boyson?"

Cherry, badly in a mood to giggle, said he didn't think so, but in an uncertain world . . . at which Condamine nodded sagely, one with large experience of uncertainty—mainly as to whether a lot would reach its reserve price.

"That will be all, Boyson. Find Dodds. He'll tell you what to do."

"Very good, sir."

Condamine alone, marvelled at such elegant deference from one accustomed to wield authority. He sighed, devoutly wishing all his staff could play their parts with the old *comme il faut* touch of servility—even if they didn't mean it.

197

Back along passages, jostling with a motley of valuation assistants, office staff, experts, cabinet makers skilled in restoring every possible wooden conceit and there, on the lower stairs, someone carries an enormous mahogany bird-cage probably pre-Revolution, French.

Where, he wondered, did it all come from, as he searched for the fussy little man in a grey linen coat, a long-serving employee who'd come to the firm in a demob suit and was there yet: trusted, dependable, rare. And very probably still looking for Jepson . . .

"I really can't imagine what Mr Condamine is thinking of. I've more staff than I know what to do with. You say you have a livery?" Dodds peered doubtfully.

"No," said Boyson, "I got this uniform."

"Well, I suppose I can find space for you. Go down the passage, cross the mews and the changing room's by the canteen. Report back to me when you're ready. If I'm not about make yourself useful. Sale day's always hectic."

Cherry thanked him and went.

"What's your name by the way?"

"Boyson, James."

"Boyson. Nobody said anything to me about it." Soulful as a dying swan, early Meissen, slightly chipped.

Cherry took his time, looked around, noted the makeshift canteen and the few employees hunched over coffee, cigarettes, newspapers. One, a "servant" in livery, sat with his back to the wall, legs outstretched, wig cocked at a rakish angle, surveying the scene with total detachment as if to deny his part in it.

Upstairs, in an abandoned store-room, Duff, he knew, would be in place, noting every movement in and out.

The changing room was sadly unOlympic, a few metal cabinets, a set of hooks, two or three forms and a cracked mirror over a cracked wash-basin summed it up.

Cherry, its sole occupant, changed at leisure, tumbling his own rags into a locker with no lock and a single hinge. He needed leisure to fit himself into the unfamiliar—white stockings, knee breeches with side buttons, a shirt with jabot attached, the swallow-tailed cutaway and, last of all, the peruke with its black bow like a midnight butterfly feeding on hair.

In the dusty, fly-specked mirror Cherry saw enough to give him pause, to force the sardonic grin of recognition. There you are, Cherry, at it again, when you might have been doing something useful for your living—or words to that effect.

He wriggled his hands into spotless white kid gloves, ignorant of an old Peachum's diktat: servants must never touch persons or property with bared members. Glanced at the total effect— and almost changed his mind.

Come on, idiot. Let's get it over with or you'll die laughing and that'll set up a fatal chain reaction when Duff finds the corpse.

Having time on his gloved hands he wandered into the makeshift canteen where an equally makeshift girl was vigorously blowing down the spout of a large pewter teapot.

"Wastin' your time, Effie," someone in a carpenter's apron advised in passing. "You need a bloody flue brush up that and the tea'd still be sooty blocked."

"Have to manage with what I'm given don't I?"

"Nothing personal. I meant the tea-pot."

He'd gone before she could pelt him with language worse than rotten fruit. "Bloody liberties they take. Spend too much time in Coronation Street if you ask me. Tea or coffee?"

Cherry took his cup of whatever it was to where the lazy servant still supported the wall. With cigarette hanging from his lips he suggested an interesting variation on domestic bliss.

"You're new a'n't you?" As Cherry slumped at the table.

"Yer. Started today."

"Give up. There's nothing in it."

Cherry noted the cigarette was out—the man was too damned idle even to relight it. "A job's a job."

The long lean face crumpled into a cartoon of surprise. "You don't call *this* a job? I mean, you don't honestly—? Listen, this is a carry-on. A chimps' tea-party's got more dignity. Know what we are?"

"No."

"Gilded fringes on the panoply of the filthy rich."

". . . we all end up somewhere."

"Christ! A philosopher in drag. *I* can't afford it, mate."

"Yer. That's why you're 'ere."

The long face contracted an inch or two. "Smart-arse. I'm just explaining, right? I've read the lot, from Marx to Spencer. And what is it—words! Words is a way of explaining why words don't solve my problems or yours. When there's factories I'm a necessity—now there ain't I'm not, see what I mean?"

"No."

"You're thick. Either that or wigs don't agree with you. Take it off and ask y'self what are we? No don't bother—I can tell there's nothing under it worth the answerin'. I'll tell *you*."

"Suit yourself."

"*We* are the indispensable cogs in the service industry that old cow's always going on about. She should know, dragged up behind a counter with one finger on the scales, St Francis standing behind her when she promised poverty eight years ago. Now she's done it all over us, right? Don't bother, you're as likely to carry 'er 'andbag for 'er as swipe it. Well, where's that leave you and me?"

"Employed, I s'pose."

"Jesus Christ! No wonder this country's goin' to the dogs— the lackey mentality, kow-tow, touch your fore-lock and what's a tongue for if it don't lick boots? My granny was in service— loved the gentry—always voted Tory—true Briton, never never shall be slaves but can't wait to be butlers, maidservants upstairs downstairs and a quick bint in the pantry when no one's stabbin' the bell-push."

"So?"

"So I'm not 'aving it, stupid! I wasn't born to look like a bunch of bloody daffodils!"

Sullen silence reigned awhile.

"Start a revolution then, pick up where Marx left off."

"In *this*? And ninety-five quid a week *before* deductions? You need finance for that kind of caper."

"Yer . . . Social Security'd give y'more time to work it out."

". . . I never thought o'that."

"Or start a small business. The government'd finance yer."

". . . like what?"

"I dunno. Y'could make riot shields and work y'way up."

The long, lean, lazy servant eyed the new man suspiciously.

200

"You got a mouth on you. Should 'a' tried the law—they need some good defence counsels."

"Wha's the difference? I'd still end up with a wig on me nut wouldn't I?"

Enlightenment flooded that cadaverous countenance, a "face" being too tame a description for what Cherry was looking at.

"Yer, tha's right. I never thoughta that. I been 'ere six days and it never once occurred. I mean it comes back to what Marx said dunnit: 'All the world's a stage'."

"Yer," said Boyson—Cherry was too screwed up to say much else. "What's the form then?"

"The big one's tonight. We're all on overtime. Talk about Ayatollah Baba and the forty thieves. There's stuff in there worth millions."

"No security?"

"Security? Who'd wanna pinch crap like that? Persian carpets! Worn-out rest-homes for geriatric moths. I got better stuff in my bathroom."

Cherry stood up. "I'd better go and look willin'."

"Why bother? Dodds is prancin' round like a ballerina six months' gone and nothin's done till an hour before the sale."

Nevertheless, Cherry left the canteen and plunged into the bustle of back-stage Peachum's, keeping his eyes well open to all the activity around him, but more and more, he hovered about the area connected with the sale.

The mechanics were simple. Thirty large and small lots were deployed in a room separated from the main auction room by a short passage. The more important items remained in crates until minutes before they were needed. Everything was plainly numbered.

Once, he saw Cuthers fussing over a particular crate, giving tediously detailed instructions to the "bearers" whose job it was to fetch and carry the lots at the rise and final fall of the hammer.

Later, Cuthers asked him to fetch Mr Dodds but recognition went one way only. Cherry set off to look for the foreman and conveniently lost himself elsewhere. Occasionally he'd pick up nothing much and carry it from A to B and back again, creating an illusion of being gainfully employed. But he seldom strayed far from a room in which someone had guestimated "an eighteen million pound haul".

He discovered there *was* security. All two of them, liveried like himself, patrolled the front show-rooms as if honesty had taken refuge in the back regions. Amusing but convenient.

Three hours after he'd arrived, Cherry had the room to himself just long enough to note the apple-pie order, every object placed conveniently to hand and the Deodati crate in evidence, a printed 14 identifying the contents. It took less than ten seconds to sign the back of the crate with an indelible marker. Signed, that is, with a stylized Cherry.

There were two passages through which goods would be transported. One was kept reasonably clear for the staff's convenience; the other, a fire prevention officer's nightmare, proved to be chock-a-block with cartons, tea chests, broken furniture and discarded piles of packing materials. Beyond the debris was a cross passage which led to the setting-out room.

To avoid attracting attention he made short dashes upstairs or down to the basement area, much of it filled with detritus, lumber that had once been carved, fashioned, bought, sold, damaged and finally dismembered when a piece of rosewood, mahogany or whatever was needed for restoration. The wine cellars were securely locked.

Later he discovered a small cul-de-sac to one side of the passage, almost filled by a magnificent wardrobe gutted sufficiently to hold brooms and cleaning materials. By opening one of its massive doors he'd found he could stand unobserved, sensing rather than seeing what was happening only feet away in the passage.

He posted himself there and waited. At about five-thirty, patience got its reward.

Just when he thought he could stand there no longer, listening to the in-growing silence as the place slowly emptied of homegoing staff, a small rush of activity brought him to razor sharp attention.

Footsteps and a voice in a hurry. "Where to drop it?"

"Here—anywhere in the passage he said. Don't let's hang about."

Something mumbled indistinctly by the first voice, the thump of a heavy object hitting bare floor-boards and a rapid retreat of footsteps.

Cherry eased himself out of his hiding place, noting the crate that hadn't been there before, quickly reached the open door and the long passage end, and just glimpsed two men disappearing under the arch of the mews. The main gates were still open.

Duff and his contacts would watch the situation from thereon.

Returning he examined the crate with some care. If his theory held, then all was as it should be. If not, he could change out of fancy dress and go home.

He easily prised up the lightly tacked lid, glanced in, breathed a little more freely and replaced the cover. Could afford the faintest smile of satisfaction as he regained his hiding place.

Once more he played the waiting game, savouring a silence so rare as to be therapeutic in today's world of indiscriminate decibels. Had time to reflect, like the blind cobbler of Mannheim, on aspects of age and character revealed by unseen footsteps before the theory was put to the test.

Hesitant steps, introverted, lacking the free gait of insolence or innocence. Out of phase enough to suggest more than one person in the darkened passage. They came, he judged, from the front premises rather than somewhere at the back. A pause, then a few more hurried steps, followed by others, slower, more reluctant.

"It's not here."

"Five-thirty he promised . . . over there next to those tea chests." A recognizable voice?

"The size matters."

"That must be it."

"We'd better take a look."

A pause before the faintest sound of retching wood.

"That's it. Quick, you grab an end."

"Are you sure Dodds—?"

"He's gone for a snack before the show."

Heavier, shuffling footfalls as the two unknowns passed the cul-de-sac in which a strange, bewigged figure listened to sounds as if life depended on them. After an interval, more noises, a repetition of gravid steps, returning to end with the sharper impression of wood striking wood.

"Okay, let's flush out."

"You're sure we've—?"

Cherry heard no more than a flood of undertoned abuse from the other as both made rapidly for the door.

As it slammed shut on two more or less unknowns he very nearly sighed for the relief of it. Days of tension evaporated now he could say with conviction: it *was* happening . . . it still is.

The idiotic fredaine had been worth it after all.

He left the cul-de-sac feeling an irrational touch of homesickness. One gets attached to the stupidest things—cupboards—cosiness—hide and seek—childhood . . . but *his* step was buoyant enough. It helps to be proved right once in a while.

Along the dim corridor, down three steps, right, up another three, to where gilded, polished, burnished trash was set out in neat array, a queue of pedigree derelict inanimates waited for hammerfall to reduce their circumstances further.

Limited, Cherry's opportunity for some such reflections as he hurriedly returned the Deodati Treasure Mark II to its crate and forced the nails into place. It took him less than five minutes to reverse the process, carrying the crate to the passage, before replacing the original with its genuine contents in the preparation room, set out as before.

He had time to realize how nerve-racking a double switch can be, before a clattering on the stairs warned him seconds too late. He'd reached the door as a figure appeared, seeming not best pleased to find company, disconcerted by a flunkey who should know his place, and that elsewhere.

"What are you doing here?"

"Mr Dodds sent me to check everything's in horder, sir. 'E's a bit dicky about that there gilt piece."

Suspiciousness changed down to a worried frown. "He should be. It's a matter of millions—a small question of how many."

"Really as valuable as that, eh?"

"Men would kill for less."

"Ah."

Ah indeed. Familiar words, familiar as Cuthers' anxious face peering obsessively at the Deodati Treasure.

"I'll be off, sir. Let Mr Dodds know it's all right."

"Yes . . . yes, do that. His heart's none too strong, you know. Can't have him worried to death over trifles."

Boyson went, accompanied by Cherry in a small quandary. Could Cuthers, unobserved, have seen him manoeuvering the true and the false? And if he had?

Halfway along the passage he stopped to wrench off the buckle of his shoe—both were killing him, purely as a side issue—and loitered to fiddle with it until Cuthers reappeared.

"Oh, trouble with your shoe?"

"Buckle's come adrift."

"When you see Dodds tell him I'll be back at seven."

"I'll do that, sir."

Cherry clattered along the passage like a man on an errand, but carefully aware of Cuthers' footfall receding up the stairs. Opening the far door he stood for a moment breathing the fine tuned air of a late Spring evening. One more act to go. He knew the predictable end because logic is like that. Only the details were any man's guess.

Hunger broke in on the idle thoughts of an idle fellow. Nothing since breakfast. He thought briefly of Mrs Craxton and the meal that would be ready to—unless, of course, it wasn't her day. He smiled sadly, reminiscently but for why or what he couldn't rightly have said.

A small knot of lackeys from the canteen began to drift through the mews gate in time to set out three hundred chairs for the evening performance. Cherry, personally, had never seen such a bunch of hang-dog actors approach a stage door.

Boyson, master of the skive, made himself scarce for the time being.

Sixteen

THE TIME BEING ripe for a return to the real world of unreality.

Later, Cherry would look for a reason why his contempt for the evening's gathering would be another animal entirely, unlike that of the viewing time. He hadn't so far to look. On the first occasion he'd played a part, albeit reluctantly, in the total charade. Later, he saw roughly the same situation from beneath, as it were, the worm's eye view of a domestic creature, an employee dressed as Servility, and he could understand the unsmiling defensive posture of anomalous lackeys briefly disarmed by a conspiratorial wink making a nonsense of evening dress as a symbol of station, of superiority.

The setting was familiar, of course, but even on a second showing—and perhaps because of his change of costume, he was more impressed, unwillingly compelled to admit just why a Peachum's sale so easily aroused delusions of grandeur.

Spacious enough to hold three hundred silver-grey upholstered chairs, the salon blazoned with a contrast of colours. Those crimson gladioli, like fans of sanguined swords: delphiniums, tall as stands of pikes; delicate palms that would live and die a day, exiled from tropical forests. At intervals, about the umbered walls, more pedestals supported huge candelabra. Beside each a liveried employee stood, with no other function but to grasp the elaborate and becandled monstrosity as if he held it effortlessly. Careful lighting conspired to foist the illusion. Fellow menials conducted the children of Tyche to their seats for all the world as if t'were a play.

The gallery accommodated reporters, salesroom correspondents and a TV camera crew poised to screen highlights of the sale for that evening's viewing public.

Opposite, and far away, the senior auctioneer and his assistants will occupy a podium worthy of a tribunal. Below them, a simple deal table, baize-covered, would support each item—spotlighted for effect.

Into this Barmecidal scene a succession of the wealthiest individuals, museum curators and eminent others from all parts of the world drifted for an hour or more.

As time passed and the rows filled, the scattered snatches of conversation and chatter merged into a substantial murmur undertoned by excited speculation. Media hype and PR man Fasely had worked the oracle, bringing a new dimension of elegant vulgarity to the scene.

After all, the Cup of Christ was to be sold by public auction. No one could recall such a thing happening before . . .

Small knots of dealers stand in the aisles deep in consultation. Unless they're acting for a principal, they're wasting their time and they know it. Most of the other items are beyond their resources and the Deodati Treasure is merely a question of curiosity and occasion.

The name Sarinan crops up again and again.

The real Khans are the silent, tight-featured curators of the megamuseums who can touch gold and not burn their fingers. Moghuls are many and polyglot: the industrialist Herren, Japanese bankers, Italian car tsars, oilmen from Araby and American everything.

Not to mention our very own pop and bingo parasites, the natural children of a woman who taught them how to make money at any price. They'll bid till the stakes go out of sight and be satisfied to know they were *seen* to be bidding. They learned from her, image building is as tatty as that.

Make your own list. There are plenty of them. And not one worth the paper a writ for libel is printed on.

Disneyland is bidding, would you believe it?

The eye ranges over collective charlatanry and retires hurt.

Made of stronger stuff, the TV camera pries busily, zooming in on this or that celebrity while a velveteen voice describes, identifies and, between times, condescends a lecture on the virtues and delights of being rich. The majority of viewing mugs, conscious of their fifty BT shares—up 2p today—nod sagely, forgetting the mortgage and over-heated credit cards.

Does the bankroll call end there, or should the drug barons be forgotten? Pity them their fortunes built on death and degradation. Those fugitive millions have to go somewhere now the authorities are chasing certain numbered accounts.

The superb Peachum clock above the doubtful Reynolds takes a lordly step towards the half and tension begins to mount. In the preparation room Dodds harangues, agonizes, checks and rechecks his share of the proceedings while, out there, in the auditorium, catalogues are scrutinized, waves of recognition exchange, and the last, usually the most distinguished members of the caste settle in their places. At the rear stand several members of the establishment, including Cuthers.

All noted by one sharp-eyed flunkey who contrived to be where it best suited him; not far from the passage . . .

Theatrical! What else when an electrician at the lighting console plays *diminuendo* till the glow from the chandeliers is drowned in candelabra light and one almost succumbs to an illusion *à la* Cocteau. An island of light splays over the dominating podium and a single spotlight makes a doily for each exhibited item.

Peachum's had learned much. Peachum's had been in the game a long time.

Theatre! Stars! Enter Sir Norman Stoppit, past master of ceremonies, groomed to the hilt, immaculate in Moss Bros, hair *distingué* grey, oiling his way about the room, a word here, an exchange of pleasantries there, ignoring some and knowing them all, down to the most intimate details—of their bank accounts and security holdings. He smiles icily at Lloyds, nods sympathy to a Name, looks through Count Patrick Michael O'Shea, beams warmly for Getty, flutters his eye-lids at the Metropolitan, raises eyebrows at the Yankee fundamentalist Robertson, smirks at Baby Doc, simpers at Mrs Marcos, winks at the Fayeds but barely acknowledges the fellaheen hot from Harrods, oil prices being what they are.

"Our Norm" as he is villified below stairs strides on to the rostrum with the assurance of a von Karajan, a maestro *ma non molto,* cynosure of all eyes, knighted for his services to the lot.

An eye to the Peachum clock, he waits teasingly till it shows the half, though cognoscenti know it's always five minutes slow.

"Good evening, ladies and gentlemen." Tones mellifluous as

208

those of an actor reciting a new contract to his bathroom mirror. "You'll doubtless be aware we are, tonight, present on a momentous occasion. It is, I'm sure you'll appreciate, seldom my privilege to preside at the sale of an article transcending so much that, however fine and rare, has gone before. I refer, of course, to the Deodati Treasure, details of which you will have found on page fourteen of our catalogue. That it partakes of the nature of a reliquary may be gathered from reference to St Foy's tooth contained therein.

"But I feel bound to take the unusual step of emphasizing the significance of its other content about which there has been and doubtless always will be, some controversy. What is reputed to be Our Lord's Cup has been scientifically confirmed as to dating—the rest must depend on faith and its bearing on the historical details which again are printed at length in the catalogue.

"I propose to say no more than that I now invite your esteemed offers, Ladies and Gentlemen, for Lot One."

Which appeared on cue, borne by a dignified lackey who'd played the part for many years. With a becoming flourish he placed two silver fourteenth-century pricket candlesticks on the pool of light: rare examples by an Augsburg master, said the catalogue.

"Shall we begin at five?"

Silence, and the merest flutter of a white vellum catalogue.

"I'm obliged to you. I have five on my left. Six? Thank you . . . shall we close at six? Seven? Eight on my left. Most obliged, Madam. Eight—do we close at—nine I'm offered—to you Madam, ten on my left. Ten . . . no further bid? Do I hear from you, sir? Twelve—we have twelve, at your service, sir. Thirt-fourteen—no advance on—fifteen! obliged to you—sixteen? Going at sixteen thousand to—seventeen—seventeen I'm bid, eighteen on my right . . . eighteen—I close at—nineteen! obliged to you . . . nineteen thousand—do I hear twenty? Going at ninety—twenty from Laneshill—going at twenty, closing at twenty . . . thousand . . . pounds . . ."

Gavel rises and falls, sharp and decisive as a pistol shot.

Twenty thousand wheedled from idiots by the king of beggars, and all for a pair of prickets worth five at the most and damn all at the least.

So it continued: thirty-five for a fragment of threadbare late fifteenth-century Aubusson, seventy for an early dole cupboard, fourteen for six sucket spoons and what not else, till a mediaeval prie dieu, Lot 13, is knocked down to Maidenhead Mary, persuaded to it by those with an interest in keeping old images fresh. Her smile at losing forty-five thousand was as nothing compared with her glare as an anonymous voice to the rear announced too loudly: "With her reputation she'll need extra knees to keep up with it."

Sure enough, within a month, she would be seen on TV's "Top of the Morning" show singing "What Do I have to Do to Be Like Her?" on bended knees at Lot 13. Justice is not dead. On the third sickmaking verse the woodworm, shattered by her massive vibrations, evacuated their holes *en masse* leaving Mary and six pieces of powdered wood on the studio floor. But that's another story.

This last hors d'oeuvre heralded the main course. Upthrust of tension resumed as the fabulous "treasure" of the Deodatis was borne stately to its place, and one apart from the unsuspecting hundreds prepared for the last phase of now or never.

It began innocuously enough, with an exquisite degree of underplay from Sir Norman. "Lot 14, the Deodati Treasure, a late twelfth-century portable altar with a later triptych by Giotto, and further additions, the whole refurbished by Cellini to incorporate a pressure-lock drawer, reputed to contain the Cup of the Last Supper. The St Foy tooth is inset at the base of the altar."

Intolerable, the heat generated by myriad candles, the open fire, that carolific press of toxically perfumed humanity, and another, more subtly generated warmth when three hundred hearts pant after whatever's going.

Faint alarm bells troubled Cherry's hearing and he moved nearer to the door leading to the passage. Another door beyond the rostrum was opening very slightly, but he could do nothing about it.

Sir Norman prepared the way for bombshells. "I open the bidding at the reserve price of six million pounds . . ."

Silence on earth for a space. Then, an almost breathless

"seven". Most people were mannered enough not to turn round. Cherry's attention remained on the door across the room.

"Mr Nakamura, seven, thank you . . . seven . . . eight, Mrs Marcos. Eight millions?"

Thickening, sickening, the atmosphere, casino-like, all eyes on the turn of the wheel; bingo-similar, the straining of ears to catch the winning number. Acme for gamblers where fortune wagers against fortune.

And all the time suspense building—who would get it, who could dispense with that kind of money? A subject more important than the object.

"Fifteen . . . fifteen . . . sixteen Metropolitan . . . seventeen, Mr Getty, thank you . . . seventeen—shall I close at—eighteen, Smithsonian—Mr Ripley . . ." for the first time Sir Norman betrayed inner excitement by the faintest vocal tremor . . ."Do I have nineteen? Nineteen, thank you . . . Norton Simon . . . nineteen I'm bid . . . twenty, do I hear twenty?"

Sir Norman did. He also heard Mr Cuthers who appeared, as it seemed, from nowhere at the auctioneer's shoulder. Sir Norman, obviously annoyed, bent an unwilling ear to some frantic whispering, but his expression changed dramatically and an exclamatory "Oh!" could be heard in the nearer rows.

Ordering his assistants to move into the main body of the salon he turned to the gathering. "Ladies and gentlemen, we have received an anonymous call warning of a bomb placed somewhere in—in the building. I must ask you to leave quickly but without undue haste through the—" he raised his voice against the mounting hubbub, "please go through the rear two doors, through the showrooms and into the street. I must apologize for—" he checked, realizing apologies were hardly in order as a dull thud and a dense pall of acrid grey smoke began to fill the area immediately about the rostrum. The orderly withdrawal turned to a *sauve qui peut* rout in which Sir Norman, the Peachum's employees and most of the press joined in.

TV coverage continued and would be awarded the Golden Scoop of the Year for its total disregard of the danger . . .

Cherry stayed, trying hard not to be overcome by the spreading fumes. Watched for a moment as two lackeys entered and carried out the Deodati Treasure under Mr Dodds heroic direction. The man looked in a bad way.

"The hall is rapidly emptying, but two liveried servants and another man have actually returned to—they're just visible through the smoke—it's a quite incredible climax to this sale of the century, they're bearing one of the world's most precious bequests—already valued at twenty million pounds out into—one of the employees has collapsed—overcome by—"

Nothing Cherry could do for Dodds. He was out and away, just leaving enough time for the real villains to carry off the crate in the overcrowded passage, carry it unopposed and unquestioned out into what remained of the day.

A walk-over—exactly the word the red-eyed, rumpled wigged fellow decided as he watched them slip through the mews gate. Their plan, his theory. Both parties had cause for satisfaction so far.

As he approached Duff's car out in crowded Congleton Street, Cherry heard the distant two-toning blare of sirens, the blah-blah of ambulances and maybe the fire service. Patrol cars had orders not to follow. Whatever was happening must be unimpeded—even at this late stage.

Duff had the car moving before Cherry was quite in place.

"What are they driving?"

"A Peugeot '26 B70526, I've sent out a general."

"The crate?"

"On the back seat. That's the one—heading for the bridge."

"Drop back a bit—a lot."

"Might lose them."

"I know where they're going."

"To the end of the story . . ."

"What end? Every story has consequences, repercussions."

"Meantime, we'd better set an example to the public."

"With?"

"Seat belts."

Cherry grinned and dutifully restrained himself.

They had time to compare notes on a fast drive into the hop-house atmosphere of Kent.

"One was tall, lean faced?"

Duff nodded. "A jaw like a bull's-eye lantern."

212

"Yes . . . turn off at the next junction."

They were travelling at speed along the M2. Duff squinted into the distance. "If we get that far . . . something's happened."

Something had indeed happened and that not more than a minute earlier, judging by the glare and a plume of smoke rising a rapidly closing mile away.

Seventeen

IT ALL APPEARED, Cherry concluded, as they gazed at the charred wreckage of the Peugeot and two distorted things coiled into the shape of sudden agony, to have been an utter waste of time.

Nothing to be done.

They stood alone on the verge, staring at disaster and its offspring, debris. Occasional traffic sped by in both directions, slowed, then went its way. Nothing to be done. Duff, tense and puzzled, glanced at his superior—a pillar of melancholy, incongruously fancy-dressed.

"All that? From what? No collision—even a blow-out couldn't spread rubbish that far."

Cherry came out of apathy, sighed and addressed himself to the question.

"I didn't think of it," he confessed.

"Of what?"

"A bomb. There really *was* a bomb in that thing. In the drawer I suppose. Which means I killed those two."

"Inspector." Duff forced Cherry's notice by the unfamiliar. "*They* might have killed more than two."

Cherry nodded and said he supposed so. Said they might as well go back.

A patrol car's bleeper grew louder, the headlights brighter as it slowed to a nearby halt.

"Morisco," Duff reminded.

"What Morisco!" bitterly. "They were heading there. They didn't reach him . . . there's no other evidence to prove Morisco's involvement in anything."

He listened without interest to some alien voice accusing and incredulous.

"Just had word from a motorist up the road—a flash and a ball of fire, he said. You gentlemen saw it?" Another suspicious glance at the strangely attired figure brooding like a guest on Elba, incongruously lit by motorway lights and a few flickering tongues of flame.

Duff did the talking. "And you'd better troll up and down a bit—some of this could even be on the other side. I can only count three wheels."

"Somebody was lucky not to be behind. I'll alert the fire people."

"I've done it. We'll send in a report for your gaffer."

And one for theirs. Late as it was, they returned to the Yard to make out a preliminary before Cherry contacted Sir John with a personal report.

Unmercifully, they were treated to the last surprise of the day. At about the eleventh hour, almost before Cherry could change into something more fetching and less Mary Quantish, as Duff would have it, he got word that the AC was still in the building waiting to appreciate the pleasure of his company, "*if* he could spare a few moments".

"You'd better come too, Duff."

"No frightful fear! I wasn't invited—you were."

"Wait for me, then. It shouldn't take long."

Nor did it.

Sir John would admit later Cherry's ten minute account of a devilishly complicated plot was masterly, not least because it started beyond the end and finished somewhere near the beginning.

Two men died, he was informed because they thought they were snatching the original Treasure containing the cup. Only two possibilities existed as to what would have become of the original.

Either it was to be destroyed, which Cherry doubted, or, more likely smuggled back for cold storage in Rome—a trump card with potential. He reminded Sir John of the telesma factor—nursing a sop to the future, miraculous reappearance of the Cup that Cheers, the importance of material, tangible objects to a sect that takes the longer view while today's generation passes away, taking with it a memory of the short term.

The bomb characterized the intent. A phosphorous compound

timed to blow up the copy—no doubt containing a clumsy replica of the cup—reducing it by fire to a nullity. Nothing to identify for the simple reason that *it wasn't there*. However many people died, the illusion of a masterpiece obliterated must be total.

Cuthers gave the warning, yet Cuthers never moved from the rear door for at least an hour until he hurried to the rostrum . . . before dashing past Cherry into the passage.

What remained of Cuthers in a smouldering Peugeot was not a pretty sight, but it strongly suggested criminal intent, and the end of an accomplice. Cuthers' diatribe aimed at the world, suggested an easily suborned failure, soured enough to destroy pricelessness for more money than he'd ever made not always successfully evaluating such things.

Cherry's impression of Cuthers and Sarinan at the viewing was of two antagonists separated by an unwitting crowd; watchful of each other as if one might give away something too much to a police officer in black, or why did Sarinan regard Cuthers so fixedly as he demanded "What did you tell him?".

It all tied in with Cuthers' part in switching the Treasure in the passage—only six or seven hours ago—helped by the lazy servant.

Cuthers all the way, back to Sarinan who'd threatened the whole plan by overplaying his part *and* disastrously leading the decoy duck chase to Postern House to Buonaventura Security Holdings to Luigi Pia Morisco.

Who panicked. Saw his part-time expatriate life-style under a demolition order because of a stupid blunder. Plausible, that a volatile Italo-American thug would scream, "you come telling me how clever you trick the cops—what's the point?" Maybe he made him write out exactly that three times—forced him to sign his death warrant.

Highly circumstantial evidence against Morisco unless one ignores news from the States linking him with a little blue plastic gun allegedly used by his hit men to eliminate the competition.

Latest and vilest of transatlantic toys it seems some states favour its use for crowd control and knocking out dangerous criminals. Basically, a kind of stun gun, cheap, humane—and virtually undetectable by any scanning device—its propellant, a

216

cartridge of compressed air could, on discharge, project either bullets or a cloud of tiny needles tipped with an anaesthetizing agent.

God's gift to the Mob, according to the FBI. They improved on the original by using a powerful magnet to extract the needles after a hit . . . the point being, it makes suicide easy to fake unless one looked harder at the doctrine of final causes. Futile, searching for the murder weapon. They had the orange baling twine . . .

The bogus Treasure had to be removed as soon as possible from Sarinan's flat before his death. Morisco's aides saw to that. Possibly it was taken to Cuthers' bachelor quarters for safe-keeping. Cherry strongly suspected the possibility of substitution from evidence found in the flat. Certainty came from a glance at Sarinan's passport.

A thirty-six hour journey in and out of the country—Gatwick-Rome-Heathrow—seemed to confirm the disappearance of a frightened man while covering his role as a courier, taking delivery of the stolen copy and arranging transit with specialists in contraband contracts using dubiously diplomatic channels.

Cherry was first alerted, as he admitted, by Sarinan's gratuitous lie—the note that could *not* be slipped under the door.

Finally—or to begin with, the Marchesa put too much faith in a rogue well-versed in playing a double game. Possibly he was content originally to collect his percentage as a middleman but, at some stage, he *must* have been approached by someone, possibly in Rome, with a proposition glittering enough to face him both ways. All he had to do was act for the Marchesa while appearing to fear for his life, lightly sketching the impression of being followed just enough to convince the authorities he had nothing to worry about.

A subtle ploy, a clever artifice, Cherry conceded, but Sarinan wasn't the only gilder of lilies. Unknown to the dealer, Morisco and Cuthers, some unknown in Rome made the call that gave *a* game away for no practical purpose. The 999 calls from Sarinan were neutralized by the long distance call which, taken together, said Cherry, is where I came in.

A long approving silence, then a brief nod of appreciation. "Very good, Inspector. But why explain it all backwards?"

"Because it's less boring," was the surprising response. "And there are times when a straight account from A to Z is more confusing than the reversal. I'm sure Alice Through the Looking Glass makes more sense seen in a mirror."

"Yes . . . just one thing. Who threw the smoke bomb?"

"I couldn't cover that. Probably a bogus employee put in place by Cuthers—I suspect he escaped in the confusion."

"Did you know one of Peachum's employees died in that confusion? Heart attack, I believe."

"No. No, I didn't."

Mr Dodds . . . poor conscientious devil in a grey linen coat. A good man, as good as murdered by the malign antics of freaks, misanthropes, frauds and homicidal scum of this world; murdered, no matter how he died, no matter what coroners might say about misadventure, natural causes or the thousand heartaches coffins are heir to. He felt utterly dispirited, weighed down by a sense of failure if "success" meant the death of innocence and decency.

"—and you saved the Treasure," Sir John was saying.

Perhaps—perhaps he could follow through, continue the investigation, sift the wreckage, track down a henchman or two, find a way to that despicable son of Sicily at last.

"Cherry!"

"Sir?"

"I said, go home—take a rest. Start packing for a well deserved holiday."

Cherry made an unawares exit pondering, dream-like, the one thing he could not explain to Sir John, to Duff, even to himself. The pain of it went deep into his defeated understanding: that uncanny sense of fighting an unknown, way above the common run of malefaction, a militant with power, influence and arrogance enough to act under no man's law but his own. He could visualize such a phenomenon not half so clearly as its shadow; a shadow, he divined, that had crossed more than one fresh grave.

But the worst was surely over, Duff tried to convey by a look. Cherry understood and nodded. They left the office, quite forgetting to switch off the lights.

Both were too tired or sick of it all to talk shop or commonplace on the drive home.

Duff wished him goodnight.

At which Cherry smiled a canny smile. "Perhaps. *Sed nec scire fas est omnia.*"

The sergeant watched a lone and lonely figure traverse its path to the dark and silent house possessed of all that was still worthwhile in a rapidly shrinking world. Sadness accompanied him back to Marjorie and the family.

The Broads, he decided, would do them all good, even if they fell overboard one by one.

Maybe Horace Cherry is right, maybe it *isn't* permitted to know all things; but the night passed and did no evil. True, he slept badly, but woke early, bathed, shaved, dressed and pottered about the house, at odds with himself and much else. The coffee he made was worth a grimace, the papers when they came, failed to enthuse.

"Jackpot Sale Bomb Scare." "20 Millions, But Only Just."

Throwing aside hyperbole, he made his way to the study, half-inclined to browse an hour before day threatened to begin all over again. But, as he turned into aisle D-E, his eye snagged on a spasmodically familiar object just projecting from under the lowest shelf. Bending, he drew out an old violin case, well-remembered from youthful and half-rebellious days. He grinned reminiscently and recalled his threat to Duff. Snapped open the stiffened catches, resavoured a filleted sensual thrill at sight of highly polished wood, the colour of treasured conkers, curiously shaped, against the tranquil green of the baize.

After all that, the boy would lose interest. How, he'd illogically demanded, could one possibly spoil the image by scraping the top off the scale of G?

Interest rekindled for once. In a shockingly aimless mood it served as well as else to take up the instrument, unlatch the bow, straighten up and settle the poor inoffensive article under his chin. Clumsily, he positioned his fingers, drew a bloodthirsty bow across the unsuspecting throat of low G and was instantly promoted, in his temporarily diseased imagination, to the level of a Paganini.

Peace to a slandered genius! He climbed painstakingly through

219

the octave with the grim determination of a mountaineer short of rope but long on string.

It was desperate. Only Paganini's notorious diabolism survived the deathly illusion. Fascinated, like any amateur, by his rapidly maturing powers of wreaking musical mayhem he ascended and descended the scale with a flourish.

"Mr Cherry—are you there? Are you all right?"

He froze, round about C, give or take a quarter tone. "Ah! Mrs Craxton. I had no idea it was so late. It *is* your day? Yes, of course, Wednesday—er—I was playing the violin."

"I—thought you were unwell." Her expression suggested a three-cornered scrap between gravity, concern and downright amusement.

"No, no. I was playing the violin. Surprising how quickly one picks it up again . . . I'm er—I'm fond of music."

"Really?" Her surprise equalled his conviction.

"In that case I'll get your breakfast. Unless you mean to polish off the Sibelius concerto first."

He smiled and lowered the violin to a cease-firing position. "*Recherche à la temps perdu*, I suppose . . . it could just as well have been a rediscovered train set."

"We hanker more than we think," gently.

He studied that, or her pleasant countenance, or both, with his customary care.

"You're right. Yes—especially after the unpleasantness of things, tastes in the mouth toothpaste can't touch . . . most times I'll pick up *Treasure Island* or *Huckleberry Finn*—yes, you're right."

"I'll see to breakfast."

"Mrs Craxton."

She turned, regarded him gravely.

"I meant to tell you—I won't be holidaying with the Duffs after all. Not really green enough to play the gooseberry. Quite happy pottering . . . take a few day trips—museums, concerts and things . . . I was wondering—a day on the river at Marlow— picnic you know—there's a hamper in the attic, I think . . . well, if you'd care to join me—on the river, that is—I'd esteem it a pleasure."

Ragged as the scale of G perpetrated on an old, long-forgotten violin.

". . . it's a lovely idea, Mr Cherry. I'd be happy to join you."

And that day was sunny and cloudless in Clapham though they say it rained, apparently, in torrents, in the mountains of Northern Italy.